The Passions & Perils of the Prodigy

The New England Boy Prodigy Becomes the World Renowned Memory Genius

GJ Neumann

WestBow
PRESS
A DIVISION OF THOMAS NELSON
& ZONDERVAN

Copyright © 2016 GJ Neumann.

Other books by GJ Neumann:

Almighty God Said Remember
Xulon Press 2014

Trouble in the Temple
WestBow Press 2015

All rights reserved. No part of this book may be used or reproduced by any means, graphic, electronic, or mechanical, including photocopying, recording, taping or by any information storage retrieval system without the written permission of the author except in the case of brief quotations embodied in critical articles and reviews.

Scripture taken from the King James Version of the Bible.

Certain characters in this work are historical figures, and certain events portrayed did take place. However, this is a work of fiction. All of the other characters, names, and events as well as all places, incidents, organizations, and dialogue in this novel are either the products of the author's imagination or are used fictionally.

WestBow Press books may be ordered through booksellers or by contacting:

WestBow Press
A Division of Thomas Nelson & Zondervan
1663 Liberty Drive
Bloomington, IN 47403
www.westbowpress.com
1 (866) 928-1240

Because of the dynamic nature of the Internet, any web addresses or links contained in this book may have changed since publication and may no longer be valid. The views expressed in this work are solely those of the author and do not necessarily reflect the views of the publisher, and the publisher hereby disclaims any responsibility for them.

Any people depicted in stock imagery provided by Thinkstock are models, and such images are being used for illustrative purposes only.
Certain stock imagery © Thinkstock.

ISBN: 978-1-5127-4630-3 (sc)
ISBN: 978-1-5127-4629-7 (hc)
ISBN: 978-1-5127-4628-0 (e)

Library of Congress Control Number: 2016911025

Print information available on the last page.

WestBow Press rev. date: 7/26/2016

To

My Grandchildren,

Jason and Amber Christopher
Jonathan, Ellen, Aaron (AJ), Jonah, Clara, and Benjamin Neumann.

I hope you leave no Life Stone unturned,
In gathering Wisdom and Truth.

I love you,
Grandpa.

Sirs, why do ye these things? We also are men of like passions with you, and preach unto you that ye should turn from these vanities unto the living God, which made heaven, and earth, and the sea, and all things that are therein (Acts 14:15).

PROLOG

The repulsive condition of the two young Cambodian girls, rescued Friday, August 15, 1980, weigh heavily on Chris. Lt. Schroeder's crew, nicknamed 'Champions', located the children, aged thirteen, and fifteen, at the home of a Cambodian Government official, outside of Phnom Penh.

Tinos, a subordinate of the official, is one of several employees invited to enjoy the slave girls. The man purchased the girls from traffickers for the entertainment of his guests. Tinos is an eyewitness to the abuse of these children. Lt. Schroeder is grateful to him, for the tipoff. His testimony will be critical for the outcome of the jury's verdict.

How can the Champions develop their rescue missions, when local government participates in these horrendous crimes?

Undernourished and frail, the girls were raped and beaten repeatedly. The eyes of these abused children disclose unspeakable sadness, which burns a permanent image on Chris' perceptive mind,

"Oh Lord; the evil of these people is so painful to me. How can I conquer my repulsion against these abusers of innocent children?"

Tonight, the day after the rescue, while the rest of the house is sound asleep, Chris cannot get any rest. Hercules, Wilbur's dog, barking furiously, interrupts his thoughts. Chris is able to distinguish between the dog's casual bark and the ferocious bark at an intruder. It is obvious that the dog has spotted intruders.

The shot that silences the dog carries the threat of serious trouble. Wilbur had given him a revolver, but Chris never shot it and actually has an aversion to guns. He is not sure he could take another man's life. Nevertheless, he takes the loaded weapon to the window, and peers into the darkness. The yard light casts the shadow of two men standing by the dead dog at Wilbur's front door. He freezes. What will they do next? To his horror, Wilbur appears at the front door. Without hesitation, the men shoot him several times. Then they step over his body, and enter the house. Annie will be next. Chris darts to the house...

Chapter

I

The uncommonly pleasant spring weekend in the New England hamlet of North Billirica, Massachusetts, transforms its winter-tired citizens into cheerful, helpful and friendly neighbors. All are frolicking in the great outdoors. Young people are swinging baseball bats. Kids are building lop-sided castles in the sand, and mothers are gently propelling baby swings occupied by tots born during the winter months.

Water sports enthusiasts, their canoes and kayaks released from winter storage, head for the thrills offered by their beloved Concord River.

Martin and Glorya Storm's living room window faces the river. They enjoy watching the entertaining activity. Typical for their Saturday evenings, after a light supper, they watch mystery movies on TV. Martin, a civilian employee at Hanscom Air Force Base, relishes these leisurely weekends at home. He glances at the wall calendar,

"Today is the last day of March," he announces. "Tomorrow is April Fool's Day."

Glorya grins. "So what?" she teases, "You never could pull a good April Fool's joke. Are you going to try again tomorrow?"

Martin twists his face into the most mysterious smirk he can muster. "Just wait 'til tomorrow. I'll catch you this year."

Glorya's smile suddenly fades into a serious, concerned look. "You know, Martin, the baby is due any time now. The doctor estimated the fourth or fifth of April."

Martin, set back by Glorya's concern, takes her hand. "Isn't that okay, Glory? We are ready, are we not? As always, you planned everything perfectly. You bought all the needed baby clothes and stuff. You got the room ready. Yesterday you called the midwife again to make sure she could be here at a moment's notice. Isn't everything okay?"

Glorya fixes a long look at Martin before speaking again. "Martin, you remember that I have a heart murmur, right?"

"Well, yes, of course, but we have not discussed your heart murmur for over three years. I thought your doctor said that you have nothing to worry about." Glorya sighs,

"Yes, that was Dr. Drummer, our family doctor, but the obstetrician, Dr. Krueger, said there is some risk, if the birth is difficult. Anyway, Martin, if something happens, please promise that you will take care of our child, and start going to church. I want our child to be raised in a Christian home."

Martin stares at his wife, mentally recycling what she said. Purposely ignoring the part about church, his face stern, he bellows, "I can't believe you kept this from me, Glorya. We should have discussed this together. Forget any plans to have the baby at home. I'm calling Dr. Krueger right now to alert him." He snatches the phone off the hook. "This baby will be born in the hospital."

Martin always calls her *Glory*; *Glorya* is his angry name for her. Careful not to sound overly argumentative, Glorya says,

"But Martin, it's Saturday night. You don't want to bother him at home now." With the phone in his hand, Martin pauses for a moment and studies his wife's face. Glorya, grabbing her belly with both hands, moans in pain.

"Oh no," Martin shrieks. "Your face is snow white. What is the matter, Glory?" Martin throws the phone back on the hook and rushes

Chapter: 1

to Glorya's side. Glorya, seated on the sofa, meets his eyes with a blank stare. She does not speak and slumps backward into the sofa cushions.

"Glory, talk to me. Can you hear me?" She does not reply. There are drops of sweat on her forehead. Touching her hand, Martin finds it cold and clammy. He reaches the phone in a few leaps and dials the emergency number. The operator assures him that the ambulance will get there quickly, but will come from Concord or Lowell because Billerica does not have ambulance services.

Hanging up the phone, Martin breaks down in tears. "Oh Lord, please don't let her die." He has not prayed in years, but with all his heart, he means this prayer. Then he recalls a discussion about the midwife, Mrs. Wolf. Glorya mentioned a pad with her phone number, fastened to the refrigerator. He panics when he cannot locate the pad. A couple of curses later, he spots it on the floor. A young boy answers the phone. Martin yells, "Let me talk to Mrs. Wolf right away. It's urgent."

"You want to talk to my mother?"

"Is Mrs. Wolf your mother?"

"Yes and my aunt is also Mrs. Wolf."

"I want the one who helps with babies."

"Why? Are you having a baby?"

"Kid, get Mrs. Wolf right now!" he screams.

"She's not home."

"Let me talk to an adult right now."

"Okay, okay, I'll get my uncle."

Curt Wolf takes Martin's information and explains that his wife is at the theater, but carries an emergency beeper. He will contact her immediately. "Please turn on an outside light," he reminds Martin.

Martin gazes at his motionless wife. He feels lightheaded. How could everything go so wrong when minutes ago all seemed so right? Glorya maintains the same position on the sofa. Grabbing a moist cloth, Martin hurries to Glorya's side and gently wipes her forehead and neck.

"Glory, can you hear me?" Repeatedly he pleads with her to answer him. Glorya moves her head ever so slightly and opens her eyes halfway, then closes them again.

Finally, he hears the welcome sound of the ambulance siren. He runs to the door, flicking on the front light on his way out. A woman in nurse attire and a man, the ambulance driver, leap from the vehicle and rush a gurney into the foyer. Martin points the way and then dashes ahead of them into the living room. Martin, feverishly filling them in on details, watches as they gently transfer Glorya from the sofa to the lowered gurney. Opening black cases, they attach test equipment and insert an IV in her arm.

"What is wrong with her?" Martin blurts out.

"Give us a moment." The nurse's voice, kind and soothing, has a calming effect on Martin.

"Will she be alright?"

"Mr. Storm," the nurse says, this time firmly, "You did not tell the emergency operator that your wife is pregnant. We have two serious problems. The fainting is heart related, probably brought on by sudden pain. The baby has fallen into delivery position. There is no time to transport her to the hospital. Does your wife have a heart condition?"
Martin drops into the nearby armchair. "She was diagnosed with a heart murmur several years ago." The ambulance employees exchange a concerned look.

"Your wife's breathing is shallow, and her pulse and blood pressure are extremely low. This injection should help. Unfortunately, it is a temporary solution. After we deliver her baby, she must go to the hospital."

The doorbell rings. Martin had forgotten about the midwife. Entering the foyer, Mrs. Wolf, who has delivered dozens of babies, immediately takes over.

"I am Ellie Wolf. Call me Ellie. Who are you?"

"My name is Angela, and this is Donald," replies the nurse.

Chapter: 1

"Okay, remove the gurney belts," she orders. "And Mr. Storm, you leave the room and don't come back until the baby is born." By the tone of her voice, Martin considers it futile to argue and quickly retreats to the bedroom. He drops onto the bed. For the first time this evening, he realizes the extent of his exhaustion.

Mrs. Wolf folds back Glorya's robe. She glances at the nurse.

"How long has the baby's head been visible?"

"It was visible when we arrived, about ten minutes ago." As Ellie begins working, Glorya groans in pain. Her groaning continues until at last she lets out a scream.

"I think our injection is starting to work," remarks the nurse. "She should be stronger now."

"Glorya, can you push?" Mrs. Wolf demands.

There is no answer and no attempt to push. The nurse places her fingers on Glorya's wrist,

"There is no pulse!" she cries. Both ambulance attendants immediately work to revive her. After several minutes of resuscitation attempts, the nurse exhales noisily and announces. "It's no use, she's gone." Everyone stands motionless for a few seconds.

"We must deliver the baby right now, or lose it," Mrs. Wolf shouts. After making a couple of incisions, she begins moving the baby through the birth canal.

"Angela, come here and help me," she orders.

At exactly 12:03 a.m. Sunday, April 1, 1951, the midwife lifts the skinny, twenty-two-inch frame of a baby boy from his mother's lifeless body.

"The boy is weak, but he will be fine," she says.

"Who will tell Mr. Storm about his wife?" the nurse wonders aloud.

"I'll do it," Mrs. Wolf volunteers. Had to do it once before with another couple."

The ambulance, with Glorya Storm's body, leaves for the hospital, where the doctor on duty officially pronounces her DOA.

Mrs. Wolf prepares the baby and goes to the bedroom to present him to Martin. Martin hears the knock on the door, springs to his feet and flies to the door. Ignoring the bundle in Mrs. Wolfe's arms, he demands,

"How is she? How is Glorya?" Mrs. Wolf lifts the baby. "It's a fine boy," she urges. "You should hold him." Martin explodes in anger. Pushing the woman with the baby aside, he runs to the living room, where the ambulance employees had placed Glorya on the gurney.

"Where is she?" he pressures.

"Mr. Storm, did the ambulance people not tell you that they would take her to Emerson Hospital in Concord after the baby's birth?"

Martin calms down a bit. "Okay, so I can go see her in the hospital," he mumbles more to himself than to Mrs. Wolf.

"I will take the baby with me," volunteers Mrs. Wolf. "We can make arrangements tomorrow." Mrs. Wolf is not sure that Martin heard her, or even cares about the baby. She decides to let the hospital staff deal with Martin about Glorya's death. Within moments, Martin sets a heavy foot on the accelerator and speeds toward Emerson hospital where Dr. Krueger cared for Glorya during her pregnancy.

Chapter

2

Rebecca Goodall, Glorya's widowed sister, is returning home late from a visit with church friends. They had been especially supportive when her husband died suddenly, about eighteen months ago. Steering her blue VW into the driveway of her Lowell home, she glances at the dashboard clock. It is almost midnight.

Once inside, she showers and gets ready for bed. Reclining in the comfortable chair next to her bed, Rebecca takes the Bible and the daily devotional by Oswald Chambers entitled *'My Utmost for His Highest'* from the nightstand. She admires Chambers' direct literary style. He always urges Christians to surrender totally to Christ, who will then guide them by His Spirit through all of life's decisions.

Her devotions finished, she picks up the alarm clock to set it for the Sunday Morning Service. With a sleepy yawn, she crawls into bed. Even though it has been a mild day, the down cover feels good. She arranges the three pillows the way she fancies them and snuggles up. When they were teenagers, Glorya teased her about needing three pillows. Rebecca always knows what she wants and usually gets it, even if it means hard work.

Growing up a contended and happy young woman, teasing, and criticism did not bother her much. She taught her teenage Sunday school students that constructive criticism is their friend.

"If you resent it, you have too much pride. Pride will turn you into a miserable, unhappy person and cause trouble all of your life. If you don't believe me, ask Pastor Rudy." She respects Pastor Rudy and knows he will agree.

Reaching to switch off the light, the shrill ring of the phone startles her. It is 1:15 a.m. "Who in the world...," she mumbles as she retrieves the handset. "Hello."

"Mrs. Goodall?"

"Yes, this is Rebecca Goodall."

"I am sorry to call so late. This is Dr. Spencer at Emerson Hospital."

"Oh no," Rebecca interrupts, "Is something wrong with Glorya or her baby?"

"Mrs. Goodall, I am calling about your brother-in law, Martin Storm. He had a nervous breakdown brought on by his wife's death during childbirth." Rebecca, convinced that she misunderstood, springs out of the bed like a Jack-in-the-Box.

"What do you mean his wife's death?" she screams into the phone, her voice trembling. "I talked to her Friday evening and she was fine."

"I am so sorry, Mrs. Goodall. Your sister died at home during childbirth. The midwife did deliver the baby. I assumed that someone had contacted you." Rebecca begins sobbing uncontrollably into the phone. At last, with a deep breath, she pulls herself together.

"I am sorry, Doctor...?"

"Spencer ...I am the night doctor on duty. Martin should not be home alone in his condition. We will keep him here overnight, but tomorrow someone should be with him. He gave us your name."

"Of course," Rebecca manages. Abruptly she hollers. "What about the baby? Is the baby okay? Where is the baby? Is the baby in the hospital too?" Dr. Spencer speaks slowly, carefully weighing each word.

"Actually, what I've told you so far is all we could get out of Mr. Storm. Martin does not seem to know or care where the baby is. I am sorry to put it that way, but he acts despondent concerning anything about the baby. Mrs. Goodall, we do not need to contact you again tonight. I recommend that you take something to help you sleep. Tomorrow could be a busy day for you."

Wiping tears from her eyes, Rebecca thanks Dr. Spencer and hangs up the phone. Aimlessly she wanders into the kitchen. Leaning on the kitchen table, she lowers herself into a chair. With her head resting on her arms, she sobs until no more tears would come.

The sleeping pills accomplished their task. In the morning, a bit light-headed, Rebecca rises carefully. The conversation with Dr. Spencer last night lingers as a foggy nightmare. Could her only sibling, Glorya, really be dead? Was it possible that she had only dreamed the whole thing? The note on the kitchen table clears the fog; last night, before going back to bed, she had scribbled the name of the doctor and the hospital on that piece of paper.

"Oh Lord," she whispers with her eyes closed. "I am not prepared for this." Bewildered thoughts bombard her troubled mind. What will she say to Martin? What will happen with the child? Did anybody tell Mom and Dad? Am I expected to handle everything? Did he call his mom? Bernice Storm always weeps audibly with every bit of bad news. If only Martin's dad were still alive to take over. Richard Storm was the pillar of the family, the strong one, always ready with encouraging words for those who needed it.

"Oh Lord," she wishes aloud, "If Martin only had more of his dad's qualities."

Since her husband's death, Rebecca has lived alone and acquired the helpful habit of self-talk.

"Pull yourself together, Rebecca," she mumbles. With a bit of new strength, Rebecca goes to the bedroom and runs her hand along her dresses and suits in the closet. Choosing a dark dress, she examines it, and then returns it to the closet.

"That one will do for the funeral," she decides, amazed that she would think ahead to the funeral. Then she realizes that this presents another dilemma. Does Martin's breakdown mean that all the responsibilities for the funeral arrangements will fall on her shoulders? Rebecca slumps onto the bed.

"Lord, all my life I've been calm and collected, helping people in awkward circumstances. I always knew what to do. Now I am a helpless wreck. Lord, help me." Rebecca makes her way to the bathroom. Catching her face in the mirror, she shakes her head. "Who are you, girl?" She demands of the image. "Are you the Rebecca of yesterday, a child of the living God, or are you a coward of the wicked one?" One of her favorite verses comes to mind, *For God hath not given us the spirit of fear; but of power, and of love, and of a sound mind (2 Tim 1:7).*

Rebecca dresses, and then picks up the phone to call her parents. She pauses. Her parents do not like Martin very much because he never attended church with Glorya after she became a Christian. Every week Glorya begged Martin to go with her, but he would smile and say. "You can tell me all about it when you get back."

Rebecca knows that Mom prays for Martin, but Dad stays somewhat angry with him all the time. Suddenly, Rebecca has one of her 'wisdom flashes.' She invented that term a few months ago when Martin had said something offensive about Christians. In an instant, before she opened her mouth, with ugly words already on her tongue, she instead issued a mild plea not to speak that way about Glorya and other Christians. Silently she had thanked God for that flash of wisdom and restraint. After that, whenever she sensed a mental warning to avoid a mistake, Rebecca called it a 'wisdom flash'.

"You must deliver this news in person. Amen," she whispers. Forcing herself to sound calm, she rings her parents and states that she will be there in about an hour to talk to them.

In minutes, she is on I-495 driving toward Salem, NH. Her parents live in the same home they purchased thirty-two years ago, when they were married. Both she and Glorya were born in that house. Back then, doctors made house calls. Rifling her brain for the perfect introduction to the bad news, she can only think of the grossly overused preface to such events. "Mom and Dad, you better sit down." Shaking her head, she dismisses the idea of practicing an introduction.

"The words will come," she assures her racing heart. "Have faith. God will provide the atmosphere and the words and the best possible outcome in this situation." Deep in thought, she almost misses the exit to Hwy 93.ABefteen minutes later, she rings the noisiest doorbell in all of Salem.

Mom answers the door; arms wide open for the expected hug,

"Hi Becky, come in and have a cup of tea with us." Her dad, prying himself out of his easy chair, gives her his famous bear hug and kisses her forehead. Following his custom of coming right to the point, he asks, "So, what's up?" Rebecca looks at her dad, then at her mom; and then without warning, she breaks down and cries. Her mother cradles her in her arms,

"Now, now, Becky, what is it?"

"Just spit it out, Honey," her dad encourages. "Is it Mrs. Finch, that dear lady with cancer you have been telling us about? Did she pass away?" Rebecca shakes her head,

"No, it's Glorya," she blurts out.

"What's the matter with Glorya?" her dad shouts.

"Mom, Dad, Glorya died last night." Her dad stands speechless. Her mother begins to weep.

"What happened?" she finally asks.

"She died last night during childbirth." Her dad has been staring at her with a look she cannot read. Finally he speaks,

"So why did you or Martin not call us last night when they took her to the hospital?"

"Dad, Glorya died at home. I have no other details. Martin had a nervous breakdown and they kept him overnight at Emerson Hospital in Concord. I do not even know where the baby is. The night doctor called at one in the morning about Martin. He wants me to pick him up from the hospital today. I am heading there from here. I will call you when I have more information." Her parents exchange a quick glance.

"We're coming with you," her dad says decidedly. Uneasy feelings about that decision gnarl in Rebecca's stomach. Her parents, Roger and Doris Coulter, are an old-fashioned farming couple. Dad and Martin quite often had words. Martin always calls her dad by his first name and refuses to call him 'Dad'. Roger Coulter considers it rude when young people call their elders by their first name. Would Dad make a scene at the hospital? Nevertheless, how could she stop him from going to the hospital where his daughter lies dead and his son-in-law needs help?

"Okay," she agrees. They pile into her parent's spacious Ford, where their conversation about Glorya, the baby, and Martin continues until they reach Emerson Hospital in Concord.

Chapter

3

The front desk at the hospital directs Rebecca and her parents to room 404. The slow elevator ride provides the only silence since they left the Coulter's residence. Those few seconds prove refreshing. Living alone, Rebecca has learned to appreciate silence, one of the few benefits of solitude. Recalling a verse from the Psalms, she repeats it in her mind. *"Be still, and know that I am God"(Psalm 46:10).*

They find Martin on his bed, fully dressed and his eyes closed. His face is pale. Rebecca touches his hand. "Martin, Mom, and Dad are here. How are you?" Martin does not answer. Finally, he swings his legs over the side of the bed and sits up.

"I just want to die. There's nothing to live for now." Nobody says anything for several minutes. Then Rebecca breaks the silence. Ignoring his statement about wanting to die, she asks. "Where is the baby, Martin? Was it a boy or a girl?" Martin turns his face toward the wall, away from them, and remains silent. Doris has not said a word, but she is eager to learn about the baby. "Martin, come on, talk to us. You are not the only one who lost somebody. You lost your wife, Becky lost her sister, and we lost our daughter." Breaking down in tears, she adds, we all have to get through this somehow."

"Yeah; how?" Martin explodes.

"God will provide the strength," Doris answers. Martin jumps to his feet.

"Do not talk to me about God," he yells. "I am not stupid. It makes no sense that God would take Glorya so he can provide the strength to handle it. I had plenty of strength when Glorya was alive. We were looking forward to having a family and now she's dead, because of the wretched kid." Roger sees this remark as his clue to speak.

"Now Martin, calm down. That baby is your flesh and blood. Do not say things you will regret. By the way, you never answered Becky about the baby. Did Glorya have a boy or a girl?"

Gruffly Martin answers. "The midwife said she had a boy, but I have not seen him, nor do I care to see him, I will blame him the rest of my life for Glorya's death."

Roger, his voice gaining a couple of decibels, demands. "Who got her pregnant, Martin? How is Glorya's death the baby's fault? You are being ridiculous."

"Here we go," Rebecca chimes in before Martin can raise the decibel scale. "We are in the hospital, folks. Let's be civil, please?" Everyone calms down.

"Where is the baby, Martin?" Rebecca proceeds gently. Her soothing voice does the job. Martin turns to look at her and replies much more pleasantly.

"I believe Mrs. Wolf took him home with her. I think that is what she said before I left for the hospital last night. It's all one big blur, but some things are starting to come back."

"We should call her and make arrangements," Doris suggests.

"What kind of arrangements?" Martin demands. "I can't take care of a baby."

"I don't know, but she's not responsible to keep the baby. We have to figure something out."

"I could take a few days off work," Rebecca offers. Doris adds, "I am home all day." Her tone leaves no doubt that she is offering to care for the baby full time.

"Not so fast," cautions Roger. We are not really equipped to care for an infant at our age. Let us consider some other avenues. What about a foster home, or an adoption agency?"

Martin, listening to the conversation, recalls Glorya's words before she lost consciousness. He shakes his head. To everyone's surprise, he calmly announces. "I will take care of the baby. I will hire a nanny and have the boy in our home. That's what Glorya would want, and that's what will happen."

"Are you sure, Martin?" Rebecca probes. "Of course I will help on my days off and on weekends, if you want." For the first time since Saturday night, Martin smiles, and thanks everyone for offering help.

"Now I want the doctor to sign the discharge papers so I can go home." He rings the bell attached to the side of the bed. A nurse appears and assures him that the doctor will come as soon as possible.

Dr. Krueger, who had met Martin during a couple of Glorya's appointments, shakes Martin's hand and turns to the others.

"Family I presume?" Martin rises to the occasion. "Becky Goodall, my sister-in-law, and her parents, Roger and Doris Coulter." Dr. Krueger shakes everyone's hand and politely expresses his sympathy. "I am so sorry for your loss. Could we all have a seat for a moment?" Rebecca joins Martin on the side of the bed, while Roger and Doris move a couple of chairs closer. Dr. Krueger continues,

"Martin, you look much better than Dr. Spencer described you. You had the staff a bit worried last night. So how are you today?"

"I am fine," Martin hastily replies. "I want to go home and get my boy." Dr. Krueger looks around at the faces the room.

"I hope you are not over simplifying the care of a newborn baby. Glorya had planned to breast feed, so there is probably no baby formula at home. We can provide some helpful brochures, but you will need assistance with basic child rearing and shopping for needed items."

"I can help there," Doris offers.

"Me too," Becky insists. Doris gives Becky a strange look, but says nothing. Rebecca had no children and never did any baby-sitting. She is probably less qualified than Martin who had watched his mother with his younger siblings. Becky, younger than her sister Glorya, did not have that advantage.

Dr. Krueger, looking straight at Martin, places the thumb of his right hand on his cheek and begins tapping his temple with the index finger. Glorya had told Martin about that habit. She said it means that Dr. Krueger has a concern.

"Are you worried about something, Dr. Krueger?" Martin inquires.

"Well…where is the baby now, Martin?"

"He is with the midwife, Mrs. Wolf." Dr. Krueger seems relieved. "I know Ellie Wolf and her husband, Curt. They are fine people and quite capable. May I suggest that you ask Mrs. Wolf to keep the baby for about a week? You could visit your boy and learn how Ellie cares for him. You can trust that couple and expect much good advice."

Roger sounds off before Martin can say a word. "That's a great idea," he reasons. What do you say, Martin?" Martin hesitates as though he hates to agree with Roger, but with a relieved sigh, he relinquishes. "I will call Mrs. Wolf as soon as I get home."

Dr. Krueger gives Martin a long look. "About your plan to go home today; if Mrs. Wolf keeps the baby, couldn't you enjoy our hospitality one more day?" Roger is bound to get his opinion on record. He nods and repeats his earlier approval,

"That's a great idea."

"Will you zip it for once, Roger," Martin yells. "This is my life and my decision." Doris pokes Roger's arm, a sign that she agrees with Martin. Dr. Krueger winks at Becky. He has seen many family feuds develop during moments of stress. His experience tells him that Becky is the peacemaker in this family. He sends her a second wink and continues. "That allows time for necessary arrangements; especially if Becky helps." Martin studies Becky's face,

"Will you help, Becky?"

"Martin, you know I will help with everything that needs to be done. You stay and relax another day." Martin rubs his forehead. He finds decision making stressful at this point. He wants to go home, but he also agrees that another day of relaxation would be good.

"If the baby is taken care of, and Becky is available to help, I'll stay," he says simply.

Chapter

4

Martin's conversation with Mrs. Wolf, short and to the point, is a great relief for him, "I'm so glad you called," she says and continues before Martin can even make a request. "I think you will be busy for a few days, with the funeral and all. Why don't I keep the baby until you are settled and make arrangements for assistance with the child?"

"Thank you so much, Mrs. Wolf; for everything. May I stop by in a couple of days and introduce myself to my son?"

"Oh, that would be great; stop in any time."

Martin pulls the phone directory from the nightstand; his head swimming with pending decisions. Nanny, funeral, baby names, diaper changes...it is all too much without Glorya.

"I can't do it," he sobs, heaving the phone book, and almost striking the nurse.

"Danger zone," the nurse quips. "I have medicine for you, Martin. It will help you relax."

"Good," he bellows. "Give me a handful."

"It's only one little pill, but it will make you feel better." Martin thanks her and says, "It's not so bad here. I'm glad I did not insist on going home."

Chapter: 4

Martin cannot imagine going back to that empty house. Glorya's touch made the house cozy and comfortable. Who would prepare the food? He does not even know how to use the coffee maker, or fry an egg. Glorya did it all. She did all the shopping and decorating. Thinking about all these duties, Martin reclines on the bed and closes his eyes.

A minute later, he sits up, grabs the phone, and dials Becky's number. There is no answer. Forgetting that she would be stopping at her parent's house first, he curses, wondering why she does not answer the phone. Finally, he remembers and calls the Coulter's home. Doris answers. Thanks for that small favor, he thinks to himself. He hates talking to Roger.

"Is Becky still there?"

"Yes, she's getting ready to leave."

"I want to talk to her." Rebecca takes the phone from her mom,

"Yes Martin?" Rebecca has a clear, soothing voice. Martin enjoys talking with her.

"Becky, I can't handle it. I need somebody to talk to. Can you come back for a while? And please do not drag your folks along."

"Of course, Martin; actually, I need some company too. See you as soon as possible. Together we'll manage okay." Martin relishes the 'together' part. Becky always reminds him of Glorya. They were not twins, but often acted that way.

Rebecca arrives at the hospital about an hour later. To her surprise, she can hear Martin snoring through the open door before she reaches his room. The nurse catches up with her.

"He will be out for a few hours," she announces. "He needed to relax, so the doctor ordered some medication."

"A few hours," Rebecca retorts. "He asked me to visit."

"I'm sorry. Martin did not consider the power of the little blue pill."

Rebecca considers her options. She decides that she might as well head home. As she turns to leave, Martin's phone rings. She grabs it quickly, but Martin does not even stir, suggesting a deep sleep.

"Martin Storm's room; this is Rebecca Goodall."

"Becky, I can't believe what your parents were trying to tell me. Is Glorya really dead?" Rebecca recognizes the voice, Martin's mother. Bernice Storm is a sweet woman, but she is slow and sometimes tough to dismiss from a phone conversation. Rebecca prepares for a lengthy chat.

"I'm so sorry, Bernice. So much has transpired here that I never got around to calling you. I'm glad that my folks finally took care of that."

"Becky, this must be really hard for Martin. What is he going to do now? I feel so bad for him. Can I talk to him, please?" As expected, Bernice begins weeping and lamenting bitterly. For a few moments, nobody says a word. Finally, Becky answers her question.

"Bernice, Martin took some medication and is fast asleep. I can have him call you when he wakes up."

"Is that his snoring I hear? He always kept the whole house awake when he lived here. I don't know how Glorya can put up with him." Another wisdom flash stops Rebecca from reminding Bernice that Glorya can no longer hear his snoring. She says nothing.

"Okay then, dear. I hope he is alright."

"Martin is ok now; he had a bad night and needed rest. Things will be better when he wakes up. He will call you."

"Okay, bye, Becky."

Rebecca decides to stay until Martin wakes up. She can make some needed calls. She grabs the phone book and begins making lists of funeral homes and florists. Martin will need help with that. He has two sisters, but they are married and live miles away; Betty is in California and Robin in Arizona. She will call them. Realizing that she does not have their phone numbers, she wonders whether Martin had brought the small address book he often carries in his back pocket. Rebecca opens the drawer of the nightstand; great, there it is.

The address book is in alphabetic order, first names first. Rebecca calls Betty, and then turns the pages to locate Robin. Becky recognizes names of friends and relatives; but who is Rosie Nelson? Moreover, why is there a small red heart behind her name? She quickly dismisses her suspicions. Would Martin ever be unfaithful to Glorya? Then again, so many cheating men insist that they love their wives and their affairs mean nothing. Becky shakes her head. She wonders why a man would have an affair that means nothing. Becky locates Robin and calls her, promising to follow up with funeral details.

Rosie Nelson! Rebecca cannot get that name out of her mind. A wicked thought tempts her to copy Rosie's number. She could find out who this woman is. Her mind races back and forth. No, it is none of my business; but I am Glorya's sister; if Martin cheated on Glorya, I want to know.

Martin's snoring suddenly subsides. Quickly copying Rosie's number, she returns Martin's address book to the desk drawer. False alarm; Martin continues his eardrum piercing snoring.

Rebecca studies the face of the man who has always been a good husband to her sister. She feels ashamed. Why would he be involved in an affair when the two seemed happy together? However, why the little 'love heart' behind Rosie's name? For some reason, she does not want to face Martin now. She grabs her purse and leaves for home.

Chapter

5

"Where are you, Becky? I thought you were stopping at the hospital. Anyway, I changed my mind about staying overnight. I am checking out of this place; cannot stand it here anymore; have not had a beer all weekend. Can I crash at your place tonight? I do not want to be alone in that empty house. I will see you about six."

Clearly, Martin was desperate when he left that message on Rebecca's phone recorder. Rebecca glances at the clock. Five-thirty; Martin has probably checked out by now. If he expects beer or any other kind of alcohol at her place, he will be disappointed. She and Christopher never had alcohol in their home.

Rebecca is not looking forward to Martin's arrival, but has no choice. She must help him. Hospital visits are okay, but the thought of being alone with him here, in her home, makes her uncomfortable. A tear makes its way across her cheek. Grabbing a tissue from her purse, she sees the note with Rosie's phone number. She picks up the phone, and then puts it down again. Why does she feel so guilty about calling this woman? Hastily she crumples the note and flushes it down the toilet.

Deep in thought, she goes through the motions of making coffee. A million unpleasant memories come to mind. Right from the start Martin has been flirting with her. Everyone dismissed it as innocent.

"Typical Martin-play stuff" they said.

"He has always been this way with girls," his mother had insisted, smiling at her son in motherly approval. Innocent or not, will Martin be different now that Glorya is gone?

"Cut it out, Rebecca," she demands of herself. "You're a big girl. You can take care of yourself. Besides, Martin is in mourning, he would certainly behave now; wouldn't he?"

Rebecca, expecting the doorbell to ring, lets out a shriek when Martin walks into the foyer.

"How did you…" Martin reads her mind.

"Don't you remember, you gave us a key about two years ago when you went on vacation?" Rebecca gawks at him with her mouth agape.

"You wanted us to water your flowers and look after the place, remember?" Rebecca, recovering from the shock, finally speaks,

"Yes, now I remember. I gave the key to Glorya."

"Well, Honey, you gave it to Glorya, Glorya gave it to me and it has been on this key ring ever since. You don't mind, do you?"

"Please come to the kitchen and sit down, Martin. I've got some coffee on."

"Got anything to go with that coffee, Hon?" Martin takes the chair at the head of the table and Rebecca chooses the other end.

"What are you doing way over there?" Martin demands. "I took a shower at the hospital before I left," he jests. Rebecca does not crack a smile.

"Martin, can we talk about some ground rules if we are going to be in the same house?"

"Of course, Honey; shoot"

"Number one, what's up with you calling me Honey now? You always called me Becky." To Rebecca's horror, Martin breaks down, places his head on the table, and cries audibly. Is this a genuine emotion or one of Martin's tricks? For several minutes, neither says a word; but when Martin cries harder and begins to shake, Rebecca feels awkward. She gets up, walks over, and puts her hand on his shoulder. Martin whips around, pulls her close, and buries his face in her bosom. Rebecca gently pushes his head away.

"Martin, can we discuss rule number two?" Martin wipes his face with the back of his hand.

"Rule number two? What was rule number one?" He sounds so pitiful and defeated; Rebecca cannot help but give him a twisted smile.

"Rule number one, don't call me Honey. Rule number two, don't hug me inappropriately."

"Okay, Sweetie, come here. Let me hug you appropriately."

"Oh…you…you are impossible." Rebecca pours them each a cup of coffee and fetches a few donuts from the counter.

The rest of the evening is pleasant for both of them. They reminisce about friends and family, and make plans for the funeral. Martin suggests that they call the same funeral home that provided services for his dad and Christopher, Rebecca's husband. It feels good to have that settled. Around midnight Rebecca gets some fresh sheets and readies the guest room for Martin.

The next day, Tuesday, April 3, much work lies ahead. Rebecca took the whole week off and together, Martin and Rebecca settle all the questions about the funeral, scheduled for Thursday. They notify family and friends, and arrange details with the funeral home and flower shop. A minor issue arises during the discussion about the pastor to handle the service. Martin never attended church. However, Rebecca has no trouble convincing him that the pastor of Glorya's church should officiate. By the end of the day, they are confident and ready for the funeral on Thursday.

Over supper at a nearby restaurant, one more responsibility surfaces, the child's name and birth certificate. Martin does not particularly care for his own name, but will endorse it as a middle name. Rebecca gratefully agrees when he suggests the name Christopher, the name of her late husband.

Chapter

6

Martin keeps his promise. Two weeks after the funeral, he calls Becky to inform her that little Christopher is home and that he hired a live-in nanny. This is great news. The welfare of the baby is continuously on Becky's mind. She promises Martin a visit Friday after work, to meet the nanny and see the baby.

Becky rings Martin's doorbell. An attractive woman in her early thirties answers the door. Rebecca introduces herself,

"Hi, I am Rebecca Goodall, Mr. Storm's sister-in-law. You must be the nanny Martin mentioned on the phone?"

"Yes I am. It is so nice to meet you; Martin told me so much about you. You were a great help to him after his wife passed away. My name is Rosie Nelson." If there is such a thing as a pregnant pause, this one is overdue for delivery. Rebecca recognizes the name immediately. She recalls the little red heart after Rosie's name in Martin's address book. Only another one of her 'wisdom flashes' stops her from exploding all over this pretentious live-in home wrecker.

Rebecca manages an awkward smile and makes her way toward the baby's room. Before she reaches the door, Martin appears on the scene. With his arms open wide, he approaches Rebecca. She avoids the hug by extending her hand to greet him.

"You met Miss Nelson?" He inquires with confusion written all over his guilty face. He wonders why Becky would not hug him.

"Yes, we met, Martin. Aren't you fortunate to find a live-in nanny so quickly?" She remarks quite sarcastically.

Rebecca passes the time, holding the baby and coping with trivial conversation. Everyone avoids the subject of the live-in nanny. Becky prepares to leave and Martin attempts a goodbye hug at the door. He receives a look that he recognizes as the damaging *'Coulter stare.'* Glorya, Rebecca and Roger Coulter, perfected that weapon and deliver it with devastating consequences on their targets. Without a word to Martin, Rebecca reaches her car and speeds away.

Martin's face is sad, a mix of hurt and disbelief. Rosie moves toward Martin to comfort him. "Not now," he yells and slams the bedroom door behind him. Upset, Rosie bolts off to the family room and flips on the TV. Barely cognizant of the program, she nevertheless takes refuge in the sound of human voices. She hates trouble between her and Martin and misses his closeness. It seems longer to both of them, but ten minutes later, Martin escapes the loneliness of the bedroom, and they are back in each other's arms.

"I think I hear the kid bawling." Martin says, surprising Rosie and himself with his attitude toward his newborn son. Without a word, Rosie slithers gently out of his embrace, kisses him on the cheek and leaves to fetch the baby.

In the car, heading home from Martin's house, Becky, the gentle woman, engages in a serious argument with Rebecca, the angry sister-in-law. Back and forth, she argues that this innocent baby deserves better than to live in the home of this despicable couple.

"But is it my business?"

"Oh yes it is! I am Glorya's sister and I must protect her baby son."

"But Martin is the father. I have no right to interfere." Not coming to any firm conclusion, she concentrates on getting her tired body home and to bed.

Saturday morning Becky is more relaxed. She decides to take it easy all day and does not bother to dress. In her nightclothes, she fixes a sumptuous breakfast, and listens to her favorite religious music station. She has met the DJ in person and has a bit of a crush on him. Doug Carson is an intelligent, kind, and gentle man, a devout Christian. His comments between songs have often lifted her out of the blues. Usually playing three songs consecutively and then naming the song titles, he always concludes with some fitting Scripture verse or comment. The last song is one of Rebecca's favorite. Now Doug's smooth radio voice demands her attention. Repeating the lyrics of the song, Doug comments,

"Have thine own way, Lord, have thine own way; thou art the potter, I am the clay. How many times have I played that song on this station? Why do we tend to reclaim out of the Lord's hands the things we had trusted to Him earlier? Do we doubt His abilities? This morning, if you struggle with anything, will you place it in God's hand in full trust and leave it there? Have a blessed Saturday. This is Doug Carson, signing off."

Rebecca sighs. Ashamed, she realizes that she has not even prayed for that innocent baby in this shameless situation with Martin and his live-in girlfriend.

"Thank you, Doug Carson; you did it again; you steered me back to the right path." Her silent pledge and a promise of total trust go to God. She vows not to interfere with Martin unless there is a clear need. It seems miraculous to Rebecca that this commitment to trust God with the welfare of the baby eases the tension and provides an inner peace. Nestling on the sofa, soft music in the background, and a new Christian novel in her lap, she glances through the window; it is a fine day out there; should I get dressed and stroll to the park? In typical Rebecca style, she reasons aloud, finally deciding that this will be a stay-at-home day.

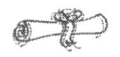

Chapter

7

A week passes. Rebecca experiences no anxiety about Martin and the baby, but Friday evening, after work, she gets the impulse to visit Martin again. An hour later, she reaches Martin's driveway. To her surprise, the front door is ajar. She hears little Christopher's painful cry, almost a scream. Without hesitation, Rebecca rushes into the house and into the baby's room.

Little Christopher, his cute face blood red, enduring obvious pain, needs immediate help. The smell of the full diaper and the crusted secretions on the baby's thigh are clearly the source of his discomfort. Where is Martin? Where is the nanny? What keeps them from caring for the baby? When Rebecca finds them in the living room, watching TV, she loses it. Grabbing the baby, a few diapers, and a blanket, she rushes to her car, places the baby in the passenger seat, and speeds off. Her mind is racing. She wonders. "What have I done? I kidnapped a baby! I don't care," she protests her own statements.

Not wanting Martin to catch up with her, Rebecca takes the road leading to a park. She washes the baby's legs and changes his diaper. With the baby clutched to her chest, she walks in circles trying to clear her head. Now what? She cannot go home. Martin would certainly show up there. Should she go to the police station and report everything that happened? Would they put her in jail for kidnapping? Tears roll down her cheeks; one of the tears falls on the baby's face. The boy opens his mouth and moves his head back and forth with a sucking action.

"Oh no," Rebecca panics, "The baby is hungry!" During her first visit, a week ago, Rosie had fed the baby with a bottle of formula; but what brand? Does it matter?

Rebecca decides to stop at a drug store to buy needed supplies and then spend the night in a motel. The pharmacist is puzzled.

"How old is the baby?"

"He will be four weeks old this Sunday, Rebecca answers."

"Then why don't you know what formula he needs?"

"It's complicated. I don't have time to explain."

"Are you alright, Ma'am?"

"I am fine."

Rebecca adds a can of formula to the pile of purchases on the counter, pays with her credit card, and rushes out of the store.

"That went well," Rebecca mumbles cynically. The pharmacist shakes his head. "There is something strange here," he mutters to himself and watches as Rebecca backs her VW out of the parking spot. He scribbles her license plate number on a note pad and immediately calls his nephew, Ray, who is a police sergeant, currently on duty.

"This may be nothing, Ray, but a woman customer just left my store. She had a baby with her, but did not seem to know much about the boy. She acted suspiciously. The name on her credit card is Rebecca Goodall. If you are in the neighborhood, maybe you should look into this." Ray is a few blocks from the store and when his uncle provides details of the car and license plate, he is amazed to see the vehicle cross in front of him. The car makes a left turn and stops at the Sunrise Motel.

The motel room is warm and cozy. Rebecca bolsters little Christopher between two pillows. He is a bundle of joy that cheers her heart. Thinking aloud, she catches herself murmuring, "Lord, You know, I would have loved a baby of my own."

The pounding on the door, and the officer's firm demand, "Police, open the door," startles Rebecca. The boy begins to cry. Rebecca tries to appear unruffled when she opens the door.

"Rebecca Goodall?"

"Yes, I'm Rebecca Goodall," she concedes cautiously. Flashing his police badge, the officer introduces himself as Sargent Ray Gordon and continues,

"Ma'am, I hear a baby crying; are you his mother?" Wondering how the officer knew that the baby is a boy, Rebecca responds with a question of her own. "Did Martin call you?" The officer seems surprised.

"Who is Martin?"

"Martin Storm is my brother-in-law and the father of the baby in the room."

"No Ma'am, the call came from the concerned pharmacist where you bought some baby supplies. While he was describing your car, you passed by my vehicle...," Rebecca interrupts,

"It's chilly out there, please come in so we can close the door."

"Yes, it is chilly," the officer echoes, rubbing his hands together. He steps into the small room, closing the door behind him.

"Please have a seat," Rebecca offers, pointing to the only chair in the room. The officer nods, but walks over to Christopher, who has stopped crying, his big blue-green eyes wide open. After answering the customary questions about the baby's age and name, Rebecca begins to explain why the baby ended up with her.

"My sister, the baby's mother, died in childbirth," she begins, fighting back tears. "My brother-in-law cannot take care of the child by himself, so I am helping him with the baby."

Ray Gordon gives her a strange look, "But Miss Goodall,"

"It's Mrs. Goodall," Rebecca interjects.

"Okay, Mrs. Goodall, why are you out and about in the middle of the night, in a motel room with the baby?" Her voice trembling, Rebecca assures the friendly cop that she will tell him the whole story.

"Ma'am, I only need to know whether you have a legal right to have possession of this child. Because if you do not, someone is likely to press charges and I need to take you to the station for your formal statement." Backed by her decision to protect little Christopher with all her might, Rebecca's answer rings firm and determined,

"The only one with a legal right to this baby is his father, Martin Storm. I have reason to believe that he is not a fit father and if this boy is returned to his house, he is in danger of neglect or even abuse."

The officer once again walks over to the baby, now peacefully asleep. Rebecca studies the man's handsome face and thinks she can spot a sympathetic smile as he turns to her and explains his decision.

"Mrs. Goodall, may I call you Rebecca?" Rebecca, pleased with this friendly gesture, answers,

"No, but you may call me Becky."

"Becky, I'm sure that you will agree that neither you nor I can make any legal decisions concerning the welfare of this child." Rebecca nods and cautiously encourages him to go on.

"Standard procedures require that I take you and the baby to the station, where your statement will be recorded and a decision will be made by my superiors. However, I can see that you are tired, so I want to suggest another option. I could call the baby's father to let him know that you and the baby are safe and that we should all meet at the police station tomorrow morning at 9:00 a.m. What do you think?"

Rebecca had thought about calling Martin from the drug store, but her uncontrolled anger would have multiplied troubles for her, the baby, and everyone concerned. She directs a grateful smile to the police officer and nods her head in agreement, handing him a note with Martin's full name, address, and phone number.

Hearing only one side of the conversation, Rebecca gathers that Martin is asking a number of questions, but eventually agrees to come to the police station in the morning. As the officer moves toward the door to leave, Rebecca offers her hand and thanks him for his kindness. With a grin he remarks,

"Becky, next time you plan a baby rescue kidnapping, do not stop at my uncle's drug store." Rebecca laughs. From the doorway, she watches the squad car disappear into the night. "I wonder if he's married," she ponders.

Chapter

8

Melanie Marcus, the reporter who earned the nickname 'Melanie Mouth' for her brazen investigation and interview habits, is hanging around the police station Saturday morning when Rebecca arrives with the baby in her arms. A shark can smell blood a mile away, but Melanie can smell a story long before it has the scent of blood, as long as there is a hint of malice.

"What a cute baby," she chirps. "I am Melanie."

Rebecca is fine with letting onlookers speculate that she is the mother of this darling bundle in her arms.

"Hi, Melanie, I'm Becky, and this is little Christopher."

"Are we going to visit Daddy in jail?" Melanie continues. Rebecca does not recognize the reporter and sees no reason to avoid this friendly woman's questions when she answers,

"No, Daddy is not in jail…..at least not yet."

"What is going to get him incarcerated?" Melanie probes. "Is he a wife beater?"

That moment Sargent Gordon arrives on the scene. Sounding official, he addresses Rebecca as Mrs. Goodall and asks her to follow him into the conference room, adding that Martin has already arrived.

Melanie wastes no time and calls her office,

"I need a background check on one Rebecca Goodall, marriage status, relatives, jobs, children, the whole scoop; call me back at the police station." The phone rings minutes later.

"It's for you, Melanie." Melanie thanks the receptionist, whips out her pen and notepad, and repeats the information.

"Married, husband Christopher Goodall, died November 16, 1949, no children, works at Simon & Simon Law office, one sister, Glorya Storm married to Martin Storm, died April 1, 1951, giving birth to a boy child."

Melanie's reporter brain massages the data, trying to develop a newsworthy story. Baby Christopher must be the son of Glorya Storm who passed away during childbirth; but what is the sister doing with the baby at the police station. Moreover, this Martin, mentioned by the Sargent, is he Martin Storm, the baby's father. Melanie is confused. There may not be any story here after all, it makes sense that the sister would help with the baby after the mother died, but then again, nobody goes to the police station on a Saturday morning unless something is awry. Okay, I think I got it. The father messed up somehow. That is why Rebecca made that casual comment about the Father possibly ending up in jail. Melanie decides to catch Martin as he leaves the police station. Martin's wide and swift steps, tell Melanie that things did not go well for him at the station. She calls out,

"Excuse me, sir. Could we talk a minute?" Martin turns around,

"Do I know you?"

"Are you Martin Storm?" Martin's face betrays his astonishment. Nobody knows him in this neighborhood.

"Yes, I am Martin Storm, who are you?'

"I am Melanie Marcus. I work for"...Martin recognizes the name.

"I know you. You are a reporter. I have nothing to say to you. There is no story here. I am sorry, Miss Marcus. Better luck next time." If Martin thought that would be the end of it, he did not really know Melanie.

"Can you tell me why your sister-in-law has your son?"

Chapter: 8

"She has my son because she kidnapped him from my home.....that's why. Now please leave me alone; I am not in a good mood." Martin turns to leave, but Melanie is right on his heels.

"Mr. Storm, is she fighting for legal custody?"

"She's fighting alright, but I can't imagine what is legal about it. She has no husband and no experience with babies. The whole thing is ridiculous."

"Do you have other children, Mr. Storm?"

"No, I don't, but you are getting too nosy. I do not want this in the papers. It is a family thing. Nobody needs to know about this."

"I understand why you are reluctant to have this published, sir, after all, you left the station without your child. It seems that for now the law has sided with your sister-in-law. Why is that?" Angry with himself for feeding the news-hungry reporter, Martin whips around, rushes to his car, and speeds off, his rear wheels spitting gravel.

Melanie spots Rebecca as she leaves the station. Not wanting to seem over anxious, she waits for Rebecca to reach her on the way to the parking lot.

"How did it go, Becky?"

"Sargent Gordon warned me not to talk to you, Miss Marcus. I have nothing to say." Nevertheless, Melanie's next unexpected question tricks Becky.

"Do you think you'll win the custody suit?"

"I sure hope so. This child does not belong with a man who moves his girlfriend into the house a few days after he buries his wife. I am sorry, I said too much."

Melanie wants to learn more about Martin's girlfriend, but Rebecca walks away. Besides, this will do nicely for an eye-catching headline, promising more news to follow. Hoping to make the Sunday paper, Melanie calls in her headline.

'Sister-in-law kidnaps widower's baby boy.'

The article reveals all the details the reporter has learned and promises an update when the courts have made the custody decision. Friday, April 27, 1951, at the police station, Rebecca is granted temporary custody of little Christopher with the stipulation that she hire a nanny to care for the child during working hours.

Brenda Sorley, highly recommended by the agency, proves to be wonderful with the child. Soon Rebecca, a quick learner, plays the mother role proficiently. Visiting officials, assessing the qualifications of the potential guardian and the suitability of the home, are satisfied. At the hearing on May 15, 1951, Rebecca wins permanent custody. Martin has not put up much of a fight. He seems fine with weekly visitation rights.

Melanie Marcus does not disappoint her readership. After her report of the Father's questionable behavior, the people of Massachusetts have taken a deep interest in the child's welfare. As promised, she reports the results of the hearing, engraving this toddler's name on the minds of New Englanders forever.

'Baby Christopher Storm's Aunt, Rebecca Goodall, Gains Custody.'

It would not be the last time the name of Christopher Storm makes the news. In fact, before Chris is seven years old, he will dominate the Local, National and International media.

Chapter

9

Her friends are amused when Rebecca shares how much time she spends every day impressing the title 'Mommy' on her four-month old lodger without success. They offer friendly reminders that babies may utter single syllable words by the age of six months, and that more patience is advisable. To Rebecca's disillusionment, there are no witnesses when Chris, now six months old, unexpectedly looks up at her and clearly pronounces her name,

"Becky, Becky." She picks him up and hugs him while the baby repeats her name several times. "Becky, Becky, Becky, Becky." She is delighted and disillusioned at the same time,

"The name is Mommy, you little genius." She insists. Rebecca reasons that the child repeats her name because he hears it frequently from visitors. I can fix that, she thinks. With the toddler on her lap and pronouncing the word slowly and clearly, she coaches him, "Mommy, Mommy, Mommy." Staring at her lips, Christopher draws his mouth into hilarious shapes, but nothing comes out. He seems bored with this game and twists himself off her lap. He crawls away to the storybooks spread out on the floor. Rebecca shakes her head, thinking that she should give up and admit that her friends understand the stages of child development better than she does.

She will never forget what happens moments later. Focused on the storybook, pretending to be reading, the toddler mumbles,

"Mommy, Mommy, Mommy." Baffled, Rebecca ponders why he would not say the word when she coached him, but then repeats it moments later. Of course, the same had been true when he said 'Becky.' He never said her name around company; but somehow by memory he recalled it today. Is this some sort of latent memory gift?

One Friday, when Rebecca hosts a Bible study for several members of her church, including her parents and Martin's mother; Christopher, then eight months old, astonishes everyone by grabbing hold of a table leg, pulling himself up and wobbling quite steadily to Rebecca seated on the sofa about twelve feet away. This forever replaces his cute hands-butt-and-knee maneuver to transport himself across the floor. Everyone applauds the toddler, producing a pleased grin on little Christopher's face. Walking more steadily every day, strangers presume his age to be one year to a year and a half.

In December, Rebecca dismisses the nanny and begins taking Chris to a childcare facility. One of the childcare attendants reports that Christopher seems to show little interest in baby toys, but often picks up storybooks, making noises pretending to be reading. Rebecca is familiar with the same behavior at home, and figures that he is mimicking her nightly readings at bedtime.

Rebecca decides to test the infant's interest in toys. He has not visited the toy box all morning. She dumps all the toys on the carpeted floor. Chris studies the various toys: Little trucks and cars, some stuffed animals, including the cutest teddy bear, tinker toys, and some blocks with letters and numbers.

As Rebecca watches, Chris picks up and studies several toys, then discards them until he spots the wooden blocks with letters and numbers. He picks up a block at a time, rotating it and then placing it back on the floor. Next, he begins placing the blocks in a single line, occasionally discarding one.

Rebecca has no clue why the child added some blocks to the row while discarding others. Joining Chris on the floor, she discovers that the discarded blocks were all of the same color, yellow. Somewhere Rebecca read that color recognition would be typical of two to three year olds, but Chris' first birthday is still three weeks away. Then Rebecca notices that all the yellow blocks have numbers on them while the red, blue, and green blocks have letters. She shakes her head. Did he discard them by color, or because they have numbers?

"It is all some kind of coincidence," she tells herself. Chris shows advanced behavior in some areas, but recognizing colors, letters, and numbers is out of the question at his age; yet his selection skills definitely point to some special gift.

His father, Martin, has reasonable intelligence, but nothing about him suggests genius levels. The boy's grandfather, David Storm, though greatly admired and respected for his accomplishments in music, as a pianist, had never earned major recognition.

Then she recalls that David Storm made a public claim that his father, Johann Storm, Christopher's great grandfather, was a Child Prodigy in England. Based on his accomplishments in the field of music, he had been nicknamed 'Little Mozart.' Would Prodigy genes skip several generations? Rebecca knows little about him and even less about Prodigy gifts and dismisses this complete line of thought. She reasons that all mothers and grandmothers by nature exaggerate the gifts of their little family members.

Weekends were always special, but now Rebecca passionately embraces them. She loves little Christopher with all her heart. Everything about him brings her joy. While the early progress in his walking skills and overall mobility present some challenges, she is up to the task and vows that she will always watch him closely and keep him safe.

A week ago, Rebecca discovered that Christopher has developed a new habit. He gives her a probing look before getting into something new and unknown. Last night, he gave her that look standing by the bookshelf. Rebecca nodded her head in approval and Christopher took a book off the shelf, sat down and paged through it, mumbling words.

"I must be imagining things," she tells herself at first. "He is much too young for that kind of reasoning." Nevertheless, when the same thing happens an hour later, in front of the supply cabinet, and Rebecca shakes her head in disapproval, the child walks away.

"Come here, Chris, how about a hug?" Rebecca requests, and then gets him ready for his nap. This gives her a chance to work on the guest list for Chris' upcoming first birthday party. To get started, she calls Martin, who declines.

"I am the black sheep of the family. Those self-righteous family members and church attendees will criticize me and cause tension." Without saying so, Rebecca agrees. She has witnessed too many family feuds when her dad and Martin occupied the same space.

She invites Christopher's grandparents and members of her Bible study group who have young children. Rebecca cannot trace the origin of this brainwave, but the name of the friendly Sargent Ray Gordon pops into her mind. She never learned his marital status, but thinks that inviting him and his family will force the issue. Rebecca digs through her desk drawer and finds his business card.

"May I speak to Sargent Gordon please?"

"Sorry Ma'am, he is in the field right now. Is it urgent?"

"No, but I will soon need his decision on a matter."

"Okay, I will radio him; may I have your name and number?"

Ray Gordon's call, restrained by a hint of caution in his voice, comes a few minutes later.

"Rebecca Goodall?"

"Yes, this is Rebecca."

"This is Ray Gordon. You called?"

"Do you remember me, Sargent Gordon?"

"Maybe I will if you give me a hint where we met."

"You met me and my baby at your station back in April."

"O yes. The baby kidnapper," he jests. "How are things going for you, Becky?" Encouraged by his use of her first name, Rebecca continues, "Things are going great. We will be celebrating Chris' first birthday on Tuesday, April 1, and would really love to have you and your family attend. Can we count on you?" Rebecca catches the humor in his voice when he replies,

"I am not sure whether my parents or the siblings would be interested, but I can ask them. Does your invitation also apply to single guys?"

"The singler the better," she quips, coining a new word. After Sargent Gordon encourages her to call him "Ray," they discuss details and an excited Rebecca continues the compilation of her guest list.

The birthday party is a marvelous success. Chris learns new words from the guests and is the center of attention, but the skeptical looks on the faces of her guests, stop Becky from bragging about the toddler's achievements. Nonetheless, Chris supplies his own proof of abilities by opening the large family Bible on the coffee table, paying no attention to the people seated behind that table, and declaring with a firm voice,

"Jesus loves you, Chris." Silence follows. The pastor's wife, Hilda, is the first to speak.

"Becky, you must get this child tested at the University. Dr. Pullman, in Child Development, has experience with gifted children. This boy's brain is developed significantly beyond his age." Everybody agrees; but somehow the positive remark by the pastor's wife breaks up the party. People express various excuses and soon everyone leaves. Only Ray Gordon stays behind.

"I suppose I should go too." He says timidly.

"No, Ray. It is still early. Please stay a while. With all these people here, we did not have a chance to get to know one another." In his humorous way, Becky has come to appreciate, Ray laments,

"Well… Okay, if I have to."

"Yes, you have to." Becky retorts, pointing to one of the two love seats placed at right angles to the fireplace. "Please relax while I put

The Passions & Perils of the Prodigy

Christopher to bed, it may be a few minutes; I always read him a story at bedtime."

"May I listen in?" Ray requests. "Maybe I can learn something."

"Oh yes, we would both love that." Rebecca, using the large family Bible, reads the story in Matthew chapter nineteen where Jesus gathered the children around him. She always embellishes the stories and adds, "Jesus loves you too, Chris." With little effort, Chris repeats,

"Jesus loves you too, Chris."

Ray's face is serious, almost somber, when he takes Becky's hand, pilots her out of the boy's room, and asks her not to interrupt. Then he begins a well-rehearsed speech.

"Becky, you and this boy, the pair of you, have a strange effect on me. I am thirty-four years old and still single. Watching you tonight awakes a strong desire to change that. I did not dare to tell you, but I cared for you the moment I met you in that motel room. Your love and care for that child reveals so much about your character. The other day, when I answered your call about the birthday party, I pretended not to remember you. The fact is, I never forgot you. I even checked public records and found out that your husband passed away in 1949. I picked up the phone many times to call you, but I am not a forward person. What I am doing right now, talking to you like this, takes all the courage I can muster. Becky, would you consider being my wife? Please do not answer tonight. I want you to think about it until you are sure."

Rebecca, completely dumbfounded, opens her mouth to speak, yet never gets the chance. Ray interrupts her immediately, and says,

"One more thing, I do not want you to say a single word. Not even goodnight. I want you to think this over and call me when you have something to say." With that, Ray grabs his coat and leaves.

Rebecca tired and drained, nevertheless considers sleep a thing of the future. Now she has things to contemplate, possibilities to ponder, and decisions to make. She pictures a loving couple, raising this exceptional child together. 'Mrs. Ray Gordon' she fantasizes. It has a nice ring.

Chris has been repeating things he hears for some time. Will he be able to recognize numbers and letters in a storybook with large print? Based on the boy's interest in number and letters, Becky buys a child's storybook. With Chris on her lap, she first reads the whole story. Chris remains silent. Then Becky tries something new. She points to a letter in the book and calls out its name.

"B." Chris remains silent. Becky picks another 'B'. Chris remains silent. Becky cannot believe her eyes and ears when Chris points to another 'B' and pronounces the letter perfectly. He looks at Becky expectantly, as though he is ready for another lesson. Becky is not ready. She needs to verify that Chris really knew what he is doing.

"Where is the 'B', Chris? Chris remains quiet.

"I thought this is too good to be true," Becky concedes. Suddenly Chris points to several letters 'B'.

"B, B, B, B," he shouts. Becky is completely perplexed. She calls Hilda Ragford to share this new development. Hilda is thrilled and says,

"Do you remember my advice at the birthday party? You must take Chris to Dr. Pullman at the University." Becky agrees and plans to do that soon. She continues training Chris with books for young children.

A couple of weeks after the birthday party, Becky remembers Ray Gordon's proposal. A troubled sigh escapes her lips. How much does she really know about this man? Is he a Christian? Does he believe in the Almighty God she has come to revere and love? A Christian should not marry an unbeliever; the Bible is clear about that. I must settle this important issue first.

Ray is not home when his answering machine records Rebecca's call.

"Hi Ray, this is Becky, please call me." Nervously Rebecca waits for the return call. Agonizing over details of the upcoming conversation, she decides to have Ray come to her house so they could discuss things face to face.

Rebecca allows the phone to ring four times. Somewhere she read that a woman must not appear too anxious.

"Hello, Ray."

"Ray...? Who is Ray? Becky, this is Martin."

"Never mind, Martin; someday I will tell you about Ray."

"Okay. Will you be home this weekend so I can visit my son?"

"I think so, when would you like to come?"

"Saturday, around noon, if that is okay."

"Fine; we will be here, see you Saturday." Ray returns Rebecca's call as soon as he picks up her message. They exchange a few frivolities before Rebecca comes to the point and invites him for supper, Friday night.

"I am sorry, Becky. This Friday is our monthly family night. The Gordon bunch will be meeting at the folk's place; Saturday I have weekend duty at the station from 8:00 a.m. to about 4:00 p.m., but Saturday evening will be fine. You don't mind if I show up in uniform, do you?"

"Oh no, you look great in uniform. Saturday evening is fine. Martin is stopping for a while around noon to visit his son. He should be gone by three, or four, is five ok with you?" Ray does not reply immediately.

"Becky, I am not eager to run into Martin. I think he blames me for the outcome of the court decision. Why don't I come around six, would that be okay?" Something about this dialog bothers Rebecca, but she has not yet sorted it out when she answers,

"Six is fine, Ray. See you then." Rebecca leans against the wall near the phone, speculating what bothered her about that conversation. Ray was cordial and polite as always, so why the despondency? Christopher's wake-up call,

"Mommy, Mommy, Mommy." yanks her back to reality. She dismisses her musings and lovingly takes on her responsibilities with the baby.

Saturday late morning, after feeding the baby, Rebecca notices a bad stain on her blouse and disappears into the bedroom to change clothes. Her fresh blouse still unbuttoned, she quickly returns to the living room to watch the baby. Without warning Martin, using his key, lets himself into the house. Typical of Martin, he whistles and makes a snide remark about her unbuttoned blouse, prompting Rebecca's immediate demand for the return of her key. Reluctantly Martin submits.

"You are almost an hour early," Rebecca complains forcefully.

"So what," Martin shouts back. "I hope you are more patient with my boy." Little Christopher looks from one to the other and begins to cry, a signal to stop shouting. Martin sits on the couch and bounces Chris on his knee until he stops crying. He spends some time urging him on to say "Daddy." For half an hour Martin continues this effort with no result. Rebecca watches and decides it is 'brag time'. She sits next to Martin on the couch, so Chris can look at her, and whispers, "Mommy." Excitedly the toddler shouts. "Mommy, Mommy, Mommy." Martin's positive reaction is not what Rebecca expected.

"Wow, Becky, you made some headway with the kid. That's my boy," he says as he hugs the baby.

"Watch this," Rebecca brags. She has written the alphabet with large letters on a cardboard. Chris has learned to recognize letters A through M. He is calling them out as Becky points to them. Martin is overwhelmed.

"That is incredible. Do you think he has some special gift?"

"I think so, everyone is telling me to have him analyzed at the University. What do you think?"

"I agree. The kid might need some special training or something. I will go with you. When do you want to go?" Involved in the discussion about the boy's gifts and his testing, Rebecca loses track of time. She peeks at her watch; it is almost 5:00 p.m. . . .

"I'm hungry, Becky. Would you have a bite to eat for your favorite brother-in-law; maybe a bowl of soup or something?"

"I'm sorry, Martin; not tonight. I am expecting company. Maybe we can plan supper next time you visit, okay?"

"Company, what company? Do you have a boyfriend?"

"That is none of your business, Martin; now please go."

"Can't I stay and meet that lucky boyfriend of yours? I will behave, I promise."

"You are trying my patience. Please leave now."

"Okay, okay, but I warn you. Do not entertain hoodlums around my boy. I want him raised right." Not meaning to give anything away, Rebecca responds,

"Don't worry, my visitor is not a hoodlum, in fact he puts hoodlums in jail." Martin mumbles to himself. "Ray, Ray, Ray, where did I hear that name before? Is your visitor Sargent Ray Gordon?"

"Okay, now you know. Please go."

"Gladly; I want nothing to do with Gordon, and you should not either. If I meet him up close we will end up in a fist fight."

"Don't talk rubbish, Martin. Ray is a decent man. Now get out of here!"

Martin stomps off and slams the door behind him. Minutes later, Rebecca hears angry voices exchanging ugly accusations in her front yard. What began as verbal abuse grows into a major scuffle between Ray and Martin. It ends with a short fistfight, leaving Martin deposited on the ground with a nosebleed. Rebecca opens the door and sees Ray's hand extended to help Martin up. Martin spits into Ray's hand, gets up, and runs to his car. Moments later, he reappears, pointing a revolver at Ray and ordering him to apologize.

"Martin, I did not start this fight, I think you owe me an apology." Without warning, Martin pulls the trigger. The bullet misses Ray and, strikes Rebecca in the chest. Martin throws down the gun and rushes to Rebecca's side. He falls on his knees next to her body.

"Becky, Becky, I am so sorry. Please forgive me. O Lord. What have I done? Say something Becky."

Ray calls for an ambulance and an officer to care for the baby. Martin is barely cognizant of Ray's strong hands, placing handcuffs on his wrists, pulling him up and placing him into the back seat of the squad car. Then Ray rushes to Becky's side and checks for a pulse. It is very weak. He hates to leave Becky but must check on the baby in the house. Christopher is asleep in his crib. The ambulance and police car arrive at the same time. He shouts instructions to the officer, who gets the baby from the house and waits for Ray to transfer Martin into her squad car.

Finally, Ray is free to head for Emerson Hospital. The news that Becky has passed away in the ambulance hits him hard. A sensation of despair, such as he has never before experienced, wraps him in a cloud of hopelessness. His dream for a new beginning ends with Becky's death.

Chapter

10

Baby Christopher's situation after Rebecca's violent death, becomes front-page news. Martin Storm, the boy's father, responsible for Rebecca's demise, is in prison. The boy's grandparents, Roger and Doris Coulter, who lost both of their daughters within twelve months, are devastated. They feel unsuited to care for the toddler. However, because the child has no other capable relatives, the Coulter's are under pressure and dutifully accept the responsibility.

That marks the end of peace and quiet for this retired couple. New England readers have an elevated interest in Baby Christopher's future. They applauded the court's decision to assign the care of the child to his aunt, Rebecca Goodall. Now Rebecca is dead. New England wants to know what will happen next. Reporters view Roger and Doris Coulter as the fresh source of news and information.

Doris Coulter considers her life boring, lacking meaning and purpose. She welcomes her new responsibility to care for her grandchild. Becky has kept her well informed about Christopher's reading skills. Doris continues the training with new storybooks and is amazed at the boy's progress. By January 1953, Chris recognizes all the letters of the alphabet. He has not yet learned to recognize words. Doris makes that her next project. In March 1953, three weeks before his second birthday, he can read five-letter words and amazes everyone in the neighborhood.

Chapter: 10

Although he loves his grandson, Roger sees the boy as a burden and an invasion of privacy. With every passing week, the toddler becomes more active and Roger becomes less tolerant.

Two weeks before Christopher's second birthday, Roger, failing to notice the boy crouched on the floor, stumbles over him and, breaks his arm in two places. That day Doris receives indisputable orders to find a different place for the child.

The following Sunday, in the evening church service, Doris shares their predicament. Roger's pitiful arm cast reinforces her plea for help as she addresses the congregation,

"If anyone here is willing, and has the means to raise our grandchild, Christopher, in their home, please let us know as soon as possible." Nodding heads and sympathetic whispers are good indications. Will anyone actually want to care for the child?

By the time the Coulter's arrive back home, their phone recorder has registered four calls from church people willing to 'help out' and raise Chris in their home. Doris takes this news in silence and weeps privately. Those offers will put an end to her hope of extended care for her grandchild.

Roger cheers inside, but immediately dismisses two of the couples. He explains that they are the greediest of the greedy and probably see dollar signs in Christopher's future because of his rapidly growing fame.

The third couple wants to adopt the boy. Although Roger blames Martin for the death of his daughter, he nevertheless respects Martin's wishes to have his son carry on the 'Storm' name. Martin would not agree to a name change.

The fourth couple seems perfect; they are Pastor and Mrs. Ragford, the senior pastor of their church. Of their four children only the youngest, Tina, is still home and would be a great help to her mom in caring for the toddler. Tina is fifteen and has been an active babysitter for several church families. The Ragfords will become foster parents without changing the boy's name.

On April 1, 1953, little Christopher's second birthday, the Ragfords welcome their new family member into their home. To help celebrate this important milestone for Chris, they invite the Coulters, Bernice Storm, and a number of church families with children. Chris dominates the attention as he demonstrates memory tricks. He repeats the words of whole songs on the radio, hearing them only once. The more demonstrations Chris performs for the guests, the more they request.

Finally, Pastor Ragford decides it is time for the birthday child to open his gifts. This activity turns out to be an embarrassment for some of the givers, as Christopher fails to show interest in their gifts. Most two-year old children are not likely to fake gratitude and neither does Chris. However, he acknowledges every gift with pictures and printed matter. When he opens a hardcover book filled with giant letters, numbers, pictures of animals and people, he holds it up and screams,

"Thank you; thank you, thank you." Then he begins to read the letters and numbers on every page. Everyone is amazed with the performance of this two-year old. Someone uses the term 'Boy Prodigy'. Unofficially that term sticks and people use it often to describe Chris.

Now Chris names the animals on one of the pages. No sooner are all the animals identified, about twenty of them, when Christopher astounds children and adults alike by repeating all the animal names, looking at the page only occasionally. One of the children asks Chris whether he could name the animals with his eyes closed. Chris turns his back to the picture page and astonishes everyone when he accomplishes that difficult task. As the guests leave, they thank the Ragfords for a great, entertaining party.

Chris is a joy to the Ragfords and a special blessing for Hilda. She always enjoyed her children, but with the exception of Tina, now fifteen, all have left home. She dotes on Chris, the new addition to their family. She finds, however, that keeping up with Chris presents new challenges every day. The child constantly questions everything. He brings books and magazines to Hilda and asks her to read to him. He watches Hilda's lips and mimics her.

Often he brings a book, points to a word, and asks Hilda to read it. Then he says the word aloud and finds the same word throughout the book. This exercise enables him to know, read, and remember over 500 words by the time he is three years old. Hilda continues this method throughout 1954. By his 4th birthday, April 1, 1955, Chris easily reads simple children's literature. He amazes the family with his ability to repeat the words and pictures of children's books after reading them only once.

Pastor Ragford habitually prepares his sermons by reading the Bible aloud, then making notes for his sermon. He pays no particular attention to Chris who often sits in a corner listening to him.

Sunday morning, when Pastor Ragford's message deals with the story of the Prodigal Son, he inadvertently asks the congregation to turn in their Bibles to Mark chapter 15. A child's firm voice from the front row corrects him,

"No, no Daddy, that story is in Luke 15." The laughter of the congregation embarrasses the toddler. That incident stops demonstrations of his memory skills for several weeks. Often he quietly repeats portions of Scripture he hears in the pastor's office, but when encouraged to speak in front of people, he clams up.

Hilda had suggested years ago that the University should analyze Christopher to determine the nature of his gift. Now, with the boy's recent reluctance to speak publicly, she suggests to her husband that they make an appointment with Dr. Pullman.

"How old are you, Chris," Dr. Pullman asks as he offers his hand to the child. Chris pulls back and hides behind Hilda. Dr. Pullman expected that reaction. He explains that it goes along with his fear to speak in the presence of people. From behind a screen, Dr. Pullman repeats, "How old are you, Chris?" Chris answers at once,

"I am almost five."

"Do you know where my voice is coming from?" Instead of answering, Chris walks to the screen and points to Dr. Pullman.

"Will you shake my hand now, please?" Chris looks up, studies Dr. Pullman's face for a few seconds, and says,

"Yes, of course, Dr. Pullman." Professor Pullman is duly impressed, and believes that this exercise cured Chris of his shyness around people.

"Problem solved," he announces confidently.

"Problem solved," Chris, repeats.

"I am looking forward to this," Professor Pullman assures Rudy and Hilda Ragford.

Professor Pullman's office is a maze of tables with various types of testing equipment, musical instruments, blackboards, charts, and locked cabinets concealing the mysteries and intricacies of the human brain. Curious, Chris has been looking around. Finally, he gets up and heads to one of the tables. Hilda starts to call him back, but Dr. Pullman shakes his head and places a finger over his lips,

"This room is genius-proof," he teases and starts a video recorder. "We record all sessions," he explains. As is typical for Chris, he chooses the table with letters and numbers and fluently reads all of them. The next table has pictures of animals. Chris begins to name the animals, but unexpectedly starts crying. Hilda is baffled,

"He's never done that before," she remarks. Dr. Pullman displays an educated smile,

"That's because he has always known all the animals in the books at home. We have some rare creatures on that table; let me see what we can do about this." He walks to the table and pointing to every animal, he clearly pronounces its name. Without hesitation, the child repeats everything without an error.

"I think what we have here;" explains Dr. Pullman "is an advanced memory gift, probably something akin to Savant, Mnemonics, or Eidetic memory. Eidetic memory is the closest to the skill nicknamed

Chapter: 10

'photographic memory'. However, no official research has verified that true photographic memory exists.

Cases in recent history give credence to the existence of extraordinary memory skills. The one that comes to mind is the case of Laurence Kim Peek. Like Christopher, Kim Peek was born in 1951. He was an American savant, known as a mega savant. Kim could read a book in about one hour and remember details.

We will determine over time how Christopher's brain works. His memory works by sight and sound, probably in equal strength. If I am correct, you will be astounded with the next demonstration."

Dr. Pullman covers the table with the animal pictures. Then he begins naming the animals in the same order he has used before. "cat, dog, mouse"...by the time he gets to mouse, Christopher names the rest of them in rapid succession and proper order.

Hilda asks a question, which has bothered her since the child came to their home. She knows that most child prodigies have musical gifts, but when she plays the piano at home, Chris pays little attention. Dr. Pullman grins,

"You want to see him play piano right now?" he jokes. He walks over to the piano, which has a picture of a different animal on each key. Waiting until Chris is in a position to watch his fingers; he plays a simple tune with one finger. Immediately Chris repeats the tune several times.

"I believe the toddler's gifts may be limited to his exceptional memory. His IQ is probably only slightly higher than that of the average child. It is too early to tell, but I am convinced that Chris will eventually unwittingly be drawn to a favorite area in arts, science, or literature. Whatever field he selects, he will achieve excellent results because of his ability to recall information from books and articles that can prepare him for tests and final exams.

Try this at home; read a book to him, a chapter at a time, I am confident that he will repeat the entire chapter word for word. These gifts, if not exercised properly, can start to fade by the time Chris is six or seven, but with special training, they can continue into adulthood and make him an outstanding scholar in almost any field. He should begin special training at this University.

Now I want to do one more test. If he passes this, I will be glad to officially grant him Prodigy status. He would become the first Massachusetts child Prodigy in the last eighteen years. Earlier, Chris proved his memory skills with twenty-five animal pictures. To qualify, he must be able to do the same with fifty pictures in random order by sight only."

Dr. Pullman dumps a box of fifty animal pictures on the table and arranges them face up into five rows of ten each, allowing Chris to study the pictures.

The boy starts naming the pictures; Dr. Pullman stops him and instructs him to watch. Then he slowly turns all the pictures upside down. To show him how he must proceed, Dr. Pullman puts his finger on one of the pictures he has memorized, and names it before he turns it over. "Duck," he says and turns over the picture of a duck. Christopher is eager to copy Dr. Pullman. Obviously, he did not fully understand the rules. He places his finger on a card and proudly announces, "duck-horse," turning over the picture of a horse.

"Okay, little genius, I'll give you credit for that one, let's try it a bit differently." Now Dr. Pullman places his finger on a card without making a sound. "Cow," Christopher says firmly.

Dr. Pullman has not placed the pictures in any particular order. He and the Ragfords are eager to see the result. It is the picture of a cow. This continues without error until the doctor's finger lands on the 40th picture, Chris says, "Turtle," but the picture is of a porcupine. "Turtle," Chris repeats, pointing at the picture of the porcupine. Dr. Pullman is puzzled. He took the toddler back to the table of the twenty-five pictures where he has pronounced every animal for the child. The board does include a picture of a porcupine, but no turtle. Chris points to the porcupine and determinately he insists, "Turtle."

"Unfortunately, we are running out of time. After testing him on the remaining pictures, I will discuss the outcome with my colleagues. The

University is strict about the results of these tests and does not want to have its name associated with a false reading. I cannot determine why Chris misread the one picture. I will call you soon."

Christopher identifies the remaining ten pictures effortlessly. The next day, Dr. Pullman calls with great news,

"I owe Chris an apology, he says, "playing the video tape clearly shows that I made the mistake. I pointed to the porcupine, yet clearly said, 'turtle'. He passed! We will issue official documents that the boy is a child Prodigy in the area of visual and auditory memory."

Dr. Pullman, representing the University, makes an official announcement to the press, describing the type of memory skill involved in granting Prodigy recognition to four-year old Christopher Martin Storm. The Professor includes his personal opinion that Chris has a bright future and predicts outstanding achievements in any academic field.

Headlines reporting the Prodigy recognition of a local child results in a media circus. Christopher Storm, already well known to the readers, becomes their hero. As his guardian, Pastor Ragford receives offers from entertainment agencies amounting to hundreds of dollars for one-hour shows with the child displaying his memory skills.

At a board meeting of Pastor Ragford's church, the trustees have conflicting opinions. Some insist that the church could use the money and that they should allow the child to do demonstrations. Others consider it wrong and greedy to use the child this way. Finally, Rudy Ragford firmly states that they will not expose the child to the traps of the entertainment industry.

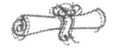

Chapter

II

One leisurely afternoon, Chris, now almost five, is visiting the friendly neighbor. Mrs. Palmer walks her dog every day up and down the sidewalk past the parsonage. She loves talking to Chris and often encourages him to pet the dog. Chris always refuses, explaining that he is afraid of dogs. Mrs. Palmer reasons with him that he is older now and that the dog is gentle. Finally, she convinces the child, but as Chris extends his hand, the dog retreats violently, jerking the leash out of Mrs. Palmer's hand. The animal runs into a passing car. The dog is dead. The driver never stops. Chris screams at the top of his little lungs, running into the house, seeking comfort in Hilda's arms, but nothing stops him from crying bitterly.

Repeatedly he cries the words,

"The puppy is dead." In addition, Chris repeats meaningless letters and numbers. For over two weeks, the child cries spontaneously. At her whit's end, Hilda calls Dr. Pullman.

"Do you remember my advice about special training for the child," he demands sharply." A child with his gift remembers every ugly detail of that accident. He needs to learn how to forget unpleasant experiences. Please bring him in."

The visit to Dr. Pullman's office is beneficial on many levels. He determines that the letters and numbers repeated by the child are from the license plate of the hit-and-run vehicle. He administers a complicated mental exercise aiding the child in dealing with this frightful experience. In addition, Dr. Pullman convinces the board that a scholarship for this boy would benefit not only the child, but would also result in excellent public relations for the school.

On Monday, May 21, 1956, Christopher Martin Storm begins special training for gifted children at the Boston University.

Nothing escapes the headline-hungry reporters in Massachusetts. With Melanie Mouth Marcus leading the pack, they converge on the campus staff like wolves. Every demonstration of Christopher's enormous memory gift ends up in print. So does Dr. Pullman's statement that he has never encountered a child with Christopher's passion for reading, learning, and memorizing. Soon the news finds its way to distant shores. Scholarship offers from some of the most prodigious schools in England compete with the offers of the fine universities located right here in Boston. Chris remains at the U under Dr. Pullman's tutelage.

He grows rapidly in stature, knowledge, and wisdom. Every year he accomplishes what takes others three years.

Near the middle of March 1958, Chris baffles Pastor Ragford with an unusual request.

"May I say something from your pulpit on a Sunday morning?"

"What would you like to say to the people?" Ragford asks.

"I want to tell them about God, like you do."

"You mean, you want to preach, like I do?"

"I want to tell people some important things from the Bible."

"I will have to talk to you later about this, Son. It is my responsibility to make sure that the speaker in the pulpit says the right words."

"But Dad, all the things in the Bible are right. I only want to quote the Bible from memory."

Soon, a rumor spreads that Chris, now seven years old, will preach at his foster father's church on Sunday, April 6, 1958. Hundreds of phone calls inundate the receptionist. Pastor Ragford solicits help from his congregation to answer the phones.

Sunday, April 6, 1958, marks the worst traffic disaster in the neighborhood of the church. The morning service starts at 10:00 a.m. By 8:00 a.m. the church is crowded to capacity. Motorcycled police officers direct traffic and ticket half a dozen fender benders. They inform people that the church is full and urge them to leave. People find parking places as far away as two miles, hurrying back in hopes of an encounter with the famous Prodigy. This is the little hero they have read about, but never met; the toddler whose mother died in childbirth; the boy whose aunt kidnapped him and cared for him deeply, until his father shot her to death.

People, determined to meet the young genius come from New Hampshire, Rhode Island, New Jersey, and many areas in New York. Nobody will convince them to leave now. However, the church is full. The executive of a media equipment company has the solution. Trucks deliver and set up loudspeakers all around the church grounds with microphones inside the church.

Promptly at 10:00 a.m., Pastor Ragford welcomes everyone. The choir opens the service with a simple, meaningful chorus.

'We have come into His house and gathered in His name to worship Him.' A hush falls over the crowd of thousands and simulates an attitude of true worship.

Inside the church, a piano bench functions as a platform for Chris. The crowd explodes in wild applause, before Chris reaches his bench. Chris signals for silence. With bench and all, Chris is about five feet tall. He remains silent and stares at the audience. His eyes move back and forth for almost a minute. The atmosphere resembles the silence before a storm. Finally he speaks,

"O the depth of the riches both of the wisdom and knowledge of God! how unsearchable are his judgments, and his ways past finding out! For who hath known the mind of the Lord? Or who hath been his counsellor? Or who hath first given to

him, and it shall be recompensed unto him again? For of him, and through him, and to him, are all things: to whom be glory for ever. Amen.»

Again, Chris pauses and peruses the audience. Nobody knows that every time he pauses, he actually compares the faces he encounters this moment, to the faces he saw moments ago. He believes that when a powerful Bible message affects listeners, it changes their countenance.

These pauses and gazes become his hallmark. He continues, "I believe God had a purpose when He designed my brain. A brain that remembers almost everything it hears and everything it sees. Because of that gift, I am able to memorize everything in the Bible about Jesus. When you know everything about Jesus straight from the Bible, nobody can fool you. You can stop looking elsewhere. You are on the right page and the right road. Nobody can sell you some other weird, powerless god. It is extremely important to get the message of the Bible right. Never brag about getting the Bible message *almost* right. Something, which is *almost* right, is actually always wrong. Do you want your surgery to go *almost* right? Is it okay if the freight train *almost* misses you? If you are stuck in quicksand, do you want somebody to *almost* pull you out?"

As Chris returns to his seat, the crowd goes wild with applause. Chris whispers into Pastor Ragford's ear and Pastor Ragford announces that the applause embarrasses him and he would like it to stop. That results in another, but shorter round of applause.

Monday morning, front-page photographs of the church, the surrounding grounds, the crowds, Police officers, and double-parked cars become the envy of neighboring pastors who recognize members of their own congregations in the crowd. This event starts an unfortunate attempt to compete by featuring special guests, some of whom would come only if paid well.

As Dr. Pullman had predicted when he first met Chris as a five-year old, Chris has chosen his fields, Theology and Science. He achieves excellent results in tests because of his ability to remember study material. He earns an Associate degree in Theology in April 1960 when he is nine years old. By 1962, at age eleven, he earns a Bachelor's degree in Theology and begins working on his Masters.

Always reading and studying, the young man is knowledgeable in dozens of scientific subjects. Several publications carry his regular articles on special, little-known places on earth, the wonders of nature, and the incredible accuracy of the earth's annual orbit around the sun, always taking 365.242 days.

All of his work reflects his knowledge of the Bible, and the wisdom found in its pages. These publications add to his fame around the world, especially among Christians and Theologians.

Jealousy among other students and even instructors often causes friction. Chris, quickly maturing in spiritual strength, never recompenses evil for evil and humbly leaves everything in the Lord's hands.

Chris makes a few enemies among scientists who leave God out when they discuss evolution. His argument for creation is iron clad. If you reject the account of creation, you must reject the whole Bible. When challenged on this point, he simply states,

"If the creation account in Genesis is a lie, why would I believe the rest of the Scriptures?"

CHAPTER

12

Everything is of interest to Chris, except politics; but when the assassination of Present Kennedy in Dallas, on November 22, 1963, stuns the whole world, he begins devouring war histories and political journals. Chris is able to scan eight to ten books, journals, and magazines every evening after school. He recalls the main contents of everything he reads, and compares publications for agreement. He contacts some of the authors, and then uses that data to shape his publications.

He publishes his first work on American politics in March 1964. His creative arguments on political issues gain a wide following. Among journalists, he is a major competitor. His work raises Chris' fame to new heights. It also results in formidable financial compensation.

At the request of several resident professors, on Monday, April 12, 1965, the university holds a special staff meeting. They bring an unusual concern to the conference table. Chris, now fourteen, has become a nuisance in their classrooms. He often corrects Professors when their curriculum varies from newer information in science books or journals. This embarrasses them. The complaint does not attack Chris' character. They admit that he suggests corrections sincerely and without arrogance. His passion and devotion to truth require accuracy in the classroom. His arguments are so effective and convincing that his Professors have come to detest his presence in their classrooms.

After a short discussion, all the staff members agree. They settle the matter when the chair, Dr. Elwood, makes a motion.

"I move that we present Chris with his MA of Theology at the upcoming graduation in May and then dismiss him." The motion carries.

Chris thoughtfully listens to Dr. Elwood, as he shares the board's decision with him.

"I must discuss this with my parents." He suggests. Dr. Elwood reiterates that the board's decision is final and that the only thing Chris needs to consider now is where to go from here.

"You will have your Master of Theology, Chris. If you decide to pursue further studies, I can suggest other schools."

"I know." Chris agrees. Several schools, even some in Europe, have offered scholarships. God will show me how to proceed."

"Okay, my boy. Good luck with that."

"Sir, luck has nothing to do with it. God faithfully guides the way. We will talk again soon."

"I wish I had your faith, Son."

"I do too, Sir, because without faith it is impossible to please God. Goodnight."

That evening by the fireplace, the Ragfords have a family discussion about the young man's future. All agree that Chris is too young to hope for a meaningful job opportunity. He should pursue further studies. At this point, Rudy asks a question that rekindles a desire Chris first detected as a five-year old.

"Have you considered the ministry, Chris?"

"Oh yes, Dad, but how, and where and when?"

"Let's wait on the Lord, Son. He will provide the answers to all three questions." Rudy and Hilda hug their boy and bid him goodnight.

Early Tuesday morning, Chris sits at the kitchen table, covered with books and journals about schools and seminaries. He flips a few pages

Chapter: 12

in a book, shakes his head, and puts the book aside to his left. He nods his head at another and places it to his right.

"I like this one," He blurts out decidedly, when Rudy enters the kitchen. Rudy peers over the boy's shoulder.

"You realize that one is in Minnesota, don't you, Son?"

"I paid no attention to location." Chris admits. "I studied their curriculum and their mission statement. I like this one," he repeats.

Dozens of reporters cover the graduation ceremonies at the University. Once again, Chris is their star. His grades and early graduation with a Masters in Theology draws nationwide attention. New scholarship offers pour in from universities all over the country. Chris and his family spend a few evenings cataloguing them and finally decide on the University in Minnesota, which Chris had picked in the beginning.

Chapter

13

Tuesday, August 17, 1965 is a warm day in Minnesota. If there is a way to move without alerting the press, Chris has not yet discovered it. Throngs of reporters flash their cameras, mimicking a 4th-of-July party at the Minneapolis-St. Paul International Airport. Chris hates all the attention. He methodically answers questions and tries to locate the expected University contact. An elegant woman steps forward, and shakes Chris' hand. Then she addresses the reporters,

"I am Dr. Lillian Crane, the chancellor of Roseville University. Mr. Storm is now our responsibility. He transferred to us from Boston, where he earned his Masters of Theology. He will continue his studies at our University towards a PhD in Theology.

Now, if you stand back and allow us to pass, I will hold a press conference on Tuesday, November 1, at 2:00 p.m. at the main entrance of the University. At that time, I will personally answer your questions. Good day, ladies, and gentlemen."

Dr. Crane and Chris escape the beckoning reporters and take refuge in the University limousine. Chris has not said a word to Dr. Crane. Lillian Crane smiles at her new student and starts a conversation.

"Chris, your reputation around the country is impeccable and I am honored to finally meet you."

Chapter: 13

"Dr. Crane, you came to my rescue at the airport and now you corner me in the back seat of this car and embarrass me. I am honored to be here. You see, I meticulously researched the staff of the University and probably know more about you than you remember about yourself. You are one of the reasons for my choice. Your strong testimony, published in your brochures, is an encouragement. Can I count on your school to develop my passion for the truth of the Scriptures?"

"Chris, your devotion to Bible truth is commendable. Roseville University is established with exactly that mission in mind."

"Chris, in the next couple of weeks, will you accept an invitation for dinner with my family at our home?"

"Yes, I would enjoy meeting your daughter and having dinner at your home. Is Dr. Gordon Crane in town or is he still in Egypt?"

"You seem to know a lot about my family. How did you know that Gordon is working in Egypt? And how did you know that we have a daughter? I suppose you even know my daughter's name?" Chris pauses for a moment.

"Yes, your daughter's name is Pamela."

"Now I am really stumped. How can you possibly know that? University brochures do not mention her."

"No, they do not. Neither do they mention that she is a Sunday baby, born on September 4, 1949."

"Chris, are you some kind of mind reader?"

"I am working on that; but so far I have only learned to read and remember books, journals, magazines, and newspapers."

"Then out with it, how do you know details about my daughter?'

"Dr. Crane, do you read some of your husband's articles in Archeology News?"

"I read all of them. How does that figure into your acquaintance with my daughter?"

"Okay, I don't want to tease you any longer. The August 1963 issue carried an article by your husband in which he mentioned your daughter's name and birthday. In fact, it included a photograph of him holding up the birthday card he was sending to Pamela. Are you okay now?"

"I heard these things about you, Chris, but how can you possibly remember an article you read two years ago about a girl who means nothing to you. That boggles my mind."

"If I knew how I recall things so easily, I would give seminars on the subject. The fact is, I seem to store everything I hear and see, without any effort on my part."

Dr. Crane and Chris discuss various subjects from science to social issues. Before the limo reaches the University, Dr. Crane realizes that this fourteen-year old boy so advanced in academic accomplishments, is seriously deficient in social graces and relationships.

"Chris, do you have a girlfriend?"

"I have many girlfriends and boyfriends. Most of the students at Boston University are my friends."

Dr. Crane takes a deep breath, shakes her head, and announces. "We are here. This is your new home, Chris. Because you are a minor, I have assigned a counselor to assist you. His name is Gary Wilson. Gary will share the dorm room with you until further notice. He has been a staff member here for two years and can show you around. He also has a University vehicle. Enjoy getting to know the neighborhood. Classes start on Monday, August 23. I will see you then. I am so proud to have you in our school."

A greeting committee of several staff members, including Gary Wilson, provides another round of embarrassment for Chris who has always been shy. Finally, Gary accompanies him to their dorm room, which Chris finds more than adequate.

Chris is impressed with the Roseville University library. The Boston University library is large and has a substantial inventory of books and other literature, but Chris did not expect to find such a diversity of literature here in Minnesota. He need not fear that his inordinate craving for the printed word might run the well dry.

"God wants me here, "he whispers to himself. Gary watches as Chris picks a few books, pages through them and puts them back on the shelf.

"Don't you like any of them?" he probes.

"Oh yes. I do. This is a great library."

"Then why don't you read them? Why do you put them back on the shelf after paging through them?"

"Gary, I did read the first two, but found the third repetitive. This library is extravagant. It has a much larger collection of religious literature. God has a plan for me here, Gary." Chris catches a strange expression on Gary's face. "What about you, Gary, where is God leading you?"

"I am not sure that God is leading me anywhere, Chris. I have four years of college with nothing to show for."

"You are on the staff of this University, aren't you?"

"I don't mean to offend you, Chris, but look at my job here. I am babysitting a fourteen-year old boy. Since it is you, a famous boy genius, this might be a step up from the regular job of giving guided tours around the campus. You call this the leading of God?"

"Everything a person needs to know to live a successful life at peace with God is in the Bible. Do you believe that, Gary?"

"Of course, I believe everything you said. I have been a Christian since 1960 when I was nineteen."

"Well, then all we have to do is to find the words in the Bible that you missed when you were looking for God's direction for your life, right?"

"I think you are oversimplifying things, Chris."

"I am not, Gary. It is obvious that you sailed right past the passage in the Bible meant for you. You have to start over and find it. The first time I read the New Testament from cover to cover was on August 11, 1956. I will never forget it. It was a hot and humid Saturday afternoon. I found a shady place under an oak tree and decided to read the New Testament. It would have taken only about two hours, but when I got to Acts chapter nine, something stopped me. In verse 1, Saul is determined to slaughter Christians. In verse 5 he cries, *'Who art thou Lord'?* Gary, I was jealous of Paul. I said, Lord, if you could use that hater of Christians, please use me too."

"Then what happened, Chris?"

"Well, not much. It seemed as though God did not want me. Everything stayed the same. I did not see a light, or hear a voice or go blind. I guess God had that conversion package reserved for the Apostle Paul. I kept reading and then it was the Apostle himself, in his letter to the Romans where he says that we all have sinned and fallen short of the glory of God. A light came on. Minutes earlier, I had offered myself to God as though I was some gem he could not do without; but when I came to him as a repenting sinner, everything changed. I told my foster dad what happened to me. He baptized me the next Sunday.

I cannot figure out why people try to live without the assurance that God has forgiven them. When I grow up, that's what I'll be preaching about, Gary."

"Wow, Chris, if you never preached before, then you just delivered your first sermon."

"Gary, have you ever read this verse. "Seek, and ye shall find?"

"Don't make fun of me, Chris. Everybody knows that verse."

"But do you believe that verse?"

"I never really thought much about it. It also says, 'knock and the door shall be opened', but isn't all that sort of symbolic, a metaphor or something?"

"Gary, I don't think the Bible is for entertainment. It is God's very voice. When a person reads the Bible audibly, their own voice turns into the voice of God, because He inspired the book."

"I never thought about it that way before, but I suppose you are right. I am twenty-four years old and have wasted a lot of time. From now on, I am going to read the Bible as though God is actually speaking to me. Where do you think I will find the section that is meant for me?"

"Gary, only God knows the answer to that. I know that you will find it somewhere between Genesis and Revelation."

Chapter: 13

"Chris, I still want to know about your claim that you read books when really you only page through them."

"One can't really call it reading. I had special training at the University in Massachusetts. They based the training on the ability to remember everything I see and hear. They put me in a room with a professor and a projector. One word at a time appeared on the screen and a voice would pronounce the word. In three months, I had learned 100,000 words, the way they look, and the way they sound.

During the next three months, they did the same with sentences. I had no perception of punctuation until I saw sentences. It was all rather monotonous. Nevertheless, now I can look at a page in a book and remember everything on that page. It seems as though my brain takes a picture and stores it for later retrieval. I do not read as everybody else, a word at a time. When I read aloud, I picture the whole page and then repeat the words from memory."

"Have you memorized the entire Bible?"

"Yes, but it is not the way you would memorize a verse of Scripture. If you ask me to quote Psalm 23, which you probably know by heart, I have to process that request by picturing the page the way it looked when I read it. That picture pops up in a few seconds and then I quote the page."

"You want to grab a bite to eat, Chris?"

"Sure, I could eat." The restaurant is busy. Gary leaves his name with the host. They find a seat in the waiting room. After about fifteen minutes, Chris turns to the man on his left and says,

"You're next, Sir." Before the man can respond, the host calls out. "George, for three." The man looks at Chris,

"How did you know, young man?"

"I saw the signup sheet and I heard your wife call you George." The family leaves with the host. Gary is shaking his head,

"You do this sort of thing a lot, Chris?"

"What sort of thing?"

"Memorizing stuff that is of no particular interest or value?"

"You don't understand my problem, Gary. I made no effort to memorize the list. I actually have to make an effort to avoid looking at things so my brain does not get plugged up with useless information."

A short time later, a loudspeaker calls out the license plate of a car in the parking lot with its light on. One man mumbles,

"I don't know my license plate."

"It's a black Lincoln Continental." Chris offers. A man in the far corner of the waiting room gives Chris a strange look, and leaves the restaurant to turn off his lights. Again, Gary shakes his head,

"You're too much, man."

"We passed the car on the way in here," Chris explains.

"I suppose you know every license plate in the parking lot?"

"Of course not, only yours, the Lincoln, the red Buick and the white Olds. I never look at plain Fords and Chevys," he jests.

"What will you have today," the waitress asks. Gary is still studying the menu. Chris is ready.

"I'll have number 12, your rib special with mashed potatoes, gravy on the side, a side salad, and a coke."

"And you, sir, what can I get for you?" Gary looks at Chris,

"What do you suggest, Chris?"

"If you like fish, Gary, I suggest number 18, the tilapia dinner, choice of baked, mashed, or house potatoes. Comes with a dinner salad and includes desert, your choice of, ice cream, brownie, or tapioca pudding." The waitress gawks at Chris,

"What did you do, memorize the menu?"

"Yes, he did," retorts Gary. "I'll take the tilapia with mashed potatoes."

While waiting for their food, Gary pages through the newspaper a previous customer had left on the table.

"Do you do crossword puzzles, Chris?"

"No. I guess I consider them childish and never took time away from studies to play games."

"Thanks' a lot buddy. I love crossword puzzles and find them challenging." Gary tears a puzzle from the paper and hands it to Chris. "Try it."

"Okay, Gary. I read a book about World War II, which claimed that Alan Turing loved crossword puzzles. I guess if they are good enough for Turing, they are good enough for me."

"Who is Alan Turing?"

"Alan Turing worked at Bletchley Park in Britain and was the mastermind behind the machine that broke the Nazi code. It helped shorten the war. I would have loved to meet him. Unfortunately I was only three years old when he died in 1954."

Looking at the crossword puzzle, Chris appears lost. "I see a bunch of black squares and empty spaces between them. Give me a hint."

"Come on, genius," Gary teases. "Clues under ACROSS are for the horizontal spaces and the clues under DOWN are for the vertical spaces. Just write answers in all the blank spaces. Have fun." Gary is amazed when Chris barely stops to think and finishes the puzzle before the food arrives. He comments,

"Crossword puzzles could serve as brain exercises if they challenge a guy to study. This one, about world geography, is too simple." As they leave the restaurant, two young women enter. One of the girls stares at Chris.

"Do I know you from somewhere?" she quizzes.

"Maybe; I am not a mind reader," counters Chris. You know if you do, or do not know, whether you know me, why would you expect anybody else to know whether you know me, you know?"

"That is a mouthful, boy. Just tell me whether you are from Massachusetts..., now I remember. I saw your picture in one of Dad's magazines. He is a member of the Mensa Society. I guess it's a bunch of geeks with high IQs, whatever that means."

"You know this is a really boring conversation. I would rather talk about your"…..Gary grabs Chris' arm and hustles him away.

"What were you going to say to her, Chris?"

"Nothing bad; I wanted to tell her that her friend is pretty. Isn't that okay either?"

"Chris, my boy, I see a great labor of love ahead of me with you. Never tell a girl that her friend is pretty. She would feel left out. If you do not think that they are both pretty, leave it alone." Chris is obviously struggling with that idea and says,

"I think I have a lot to learn because too many people are faking too many things about too many real issues." Gary shakes his head.

"Chris, you need to read the book by Dale Carnegie 'How to win friends and influence people'."

"What's it about?" Chris asks. Gary stares at him,

"Sometimes I wonder about your genius. The book is about winning friends and influencing people." Embarrassed, Chris says,

"Gary, I can read fast and I remember everything I read or hear, but I am not getting the point of this conversation. Just explain to me in plain words why I should treat girls and women different from boys and men."

"Chris, have you not noticed the many differences between boys and girls?"

"Of course; girls sometimes walk arm in arm. They often go to the bathroom together. They cry easily. Also girls giggle, but when guys laugh at a good joke, they sound like a bunch of hyenas."

"Is that it, Chris?"

"And also, some girls wear skirts or dresses."

"I think your intellect makes it hard for me to remember that you are only fourteen years old. It seems that nobody has taken the time to explain things to you about relationships. This is an area where I shine. In the next few days you will mature four years."

This is the weekend when Christopher Martin Storm gains a new perspective on the world. Heretofore the world consisted of people. To his great delight, his new world consists of males and females. He marvels how he could have missed the special beauty God has bestowed on women. How their bodies are entirely different from his body. How their smile could cause his face to turn red and his mind to play tricks.

The University in Boston was Chris' initial training ground where he grew content with the fact that everyone is older and treats him like a kindergartener. The challenge at this University is greater. These students read his recent articles. They know who he is and want to meet him to see demonstrations of his phenomenal memory skills. Nevertheless, with time, things shift into normal and he is merely another student.

It's Sunday, August 29. The long Labor Day weekend is ahead. After attending the worship service at the beautiful University chapel, Chris and Gary, over lunch at Perkins, are trying to plan a fun holiday, but come up empty. Back at the dorm, Dr. Crane's call is waiting on the answering machine.

"Chris and Gary, this is Lillian Crane, would the two of you be willing to help us celebrate Pamela's sixteenth birthday on Saturday, September 4? Please call me back." Both men immediately approve this marvelous idea.

Chris grew up in a modest home. He is overwhelmed with Dr. Crane's residence in Stillwater, Minnesota. The home is set on a hill, overlooking the St. Croix River. Acres of manicured lawns, trees, flowerbeds, and water fountains surround it. Only after the last curve does the long, winding, and tree-lined driveway give up its secret of the mansion details.

The doorbell honors guests with a fifteen-second selection from the Hallelujah Chorus from Handel's Messiah, and as the boys learn later, the system randomly selects other classical tunes. A young man in formal attire opens the door and introduces himself as Foster, the butler. His gesture invites the befuddled young men into the huge, marble floor foyer where they now spot Dr. Crane, with outstretched hand to welcome them. It is all a bit much and both men are unprepared for such extravagance. Gary recovers quickly, but Chris is overawed. He secretly wishes he could turn around and seek the comfort of his dorm room. Nevertheless, Lillian's friendly welcome and handshake restore his composure.

"Come to the parlor, I want to introduce you to the other guests. I purposely invited you one hour later, so I could introduce you to everyone at once."

The parlor, furnished with couches, stuffed chairs, and hassocks would easily hold at least sixty guests. About thirty guests, mostly young women, are engaged in conversation and occasionally laugh aloud in appreciation of well-delivered jokes.

As Dr. Crane enters with the two new guests by her side, a hush replaces the happy noise in the room.

"Listen up everybody. Allow me to introduce our new guests. This is Gary Wilson. He has been on our staff for about two years. And this is Christopher Storm, who transferred to us from a University in Boston."

Dr. Crane has prepared her guests about Christopher's shyness. As a result, the room remains silent. No one speaks, creating a few moments of awkward stillness. Then Chris hears behind him, the booming voice of Dr. Gordon Crane, who has recently returned from excavations in the Holy Land, in time for Pamela's all-important sixteenth birthday.

"Okay," he announces. Everyone is here now; let's get on with the birthday party." Chris finds a seat by himself near a window. To his horror, one of the girls approaches him and introduces herself as Pamela Crane. With a rich dose of naughtiness she demands,

"Move over." Chris wants to crawl under a rug. He stammers. "Pamela, there is no room for two on this chair."

"How much do you want to bet?" She flirts, and plops on his lap. Chris considers dropping her off, but this is Dr. Crane's daughter. He must be civil toward Pamela. Once again, Lillian comes to his rescue. "Pam, please behave. Get off Chris' lap." Pamela reluctantly obeys her mom, leaving Chris, his face the color of a ripe tomato, in a heap of pitiful boyhood.

"Women are terrible," he silently assures himself. "I will never understand the riddles surrounding their world."

Chapter: 13

Later, he catches Pamela's pouting stare and decides to talk to her. Edgy, but determined, Chris approaches Pamela and asks her to walk him around the room and introduce her friends. She forges a forgiving smile, takes his hand, and starts the introductions. He copes with some of the eager questions coming at him and answers them politely. A young woman questions him about his birthday and the related astrological sign. Chris gives her a determined look and politely asks whether she would not rather get her guidance from God, who made the stars. He quickly moves on to shorten her embarrassment.

Foster, the butler, briefly rings a porcelain bell, and announces, "Dinner is served." Everyone finds his or her place card at the two long tables. Dr. Gordon Crane calls for silence and thanks the Lord for His generous provisions of food and drink. During dinner, several young people ask Chris to speak about his special gift of memory. Finally, Chris concedes and asks Pamela Crane to find a few Bibles. Pamela returns with ten Bibles.

"Hand them to some of your friends," he directs. "Now open your Bible anywhere, Old Testament, or New. Name a book, chapter and verse. I should be able to quote the verse, but be sure to correct me if I get something wrong. Pamela keeps one of the Bibles, but starts out with a trick question. "How many times does the name of God appear in the book of Esther?" Chris frowns,

"You are not following directions, Pamela. You are supposed to give me a passage, not a trick question." Chris asks,

"Who knows the answer to Pamela's question." Six hands go up, all girls. Chris is not surprised, but he wants to challenge the men.

"How many guys know the answer to Pamela's question?' No hands come up. Chris turns to Gary,

"Do you know, Gary?" Gary quips. "With roommates like you, who needs any enemies? All I can do is guess. I will say twelve times." Chris shakes his head.

"Are you guys going to let the girls beat you in Bible quizzes?"

"So you all know, God's name occurs 4094 times in the KJV of the Bible, but not once in the book of Esther." One of the boys raises his hand and asks,

"How many times does the name Jesus occur in the Bible?" With a sneaky grin on his face Chris asks,

"Old or New Testament?"

"Both please."

"Okay, the name of Jesus occurs 942 times in the New Testament and zero times in the Old. If you add those two numbers, you have your answer for the whole Bible." The young people are really enjoying the game and presently the ten boys and girls with Bibles open them and appear to be searching for difficult passages. Pamela is first. Unable to hide her mischievous boldness, she grins wickedly and calls out "Proverbs 5:19." Chris blushes.

"That particular passage gives instructions to husbands. You are not a husband, Pamela. Does anyone else have a verse," Chris asks, but finds everybody paging through the Bible to locate Proverbs 5:19. A couple of boys start giggling and one declares,

"I ought to read the Bible more often."

"I think this game is over, guys,' Chris says decidedly." By the way, Keith, Wayne, Craig, Bill, Dale, Dick, Andy, and Doug, you need to get serious about studying your Bibles. Let's turn this game around for a second, I will give you a passage, and you tell me what it says, 2 Timothy 2:15." A girl at the back table raises her hand. *"Study to shew thyself approved unto God, a workman that needeth not to be ashamed, rightly dividing the word of truth."*

"Thank you, Cindy."

"How did you know my name is Cindy?"

"Pamela told me your name when she introduced you to me, remember?" An appreciating applause follows that comment and there are new demands for demonstrations. Chris obliges and suggests,

"Everyone write one sentence on your napkin, but remember, I will not repeat anything gross or vulgar, so please behave as good little boys and girls, and please print in bold letters." Pamela finds a few pencils and soon the players are ready. Chris gives final instructions.

"I will walk behind you and look at your napkin. Then you will put it upside down on the table in front of you. I will attempt to repeat what you wrote."

"No way, someone expresses, there are too many of us. Nobody can do that."

"You may be right, Andy, but how will we know unless we try." With the encouragement of a short applause, Chris begins his rounds. Beginning at the back table, he states. "Cindy wrote *I love parties*. Dale wrote, *I would rather be fishing*. Becky wrote, *I want Chris at my birthday party on November 14*. She also left a bright red lip imprint on her napkin. Nancy wrote, *I need a new car*. Loretta wrote, *I can't wait for the first snow fall.*"

When Chris finishes, laughter and applause reward Chris for his performance. Chris raises his hand to silence everyone and states that putting all these sentences together makes up a fine story. With that, he begins.

"On November 14, I will be at Becky's birthday party. Cindy will be there because she loves parties, she will pick up Nancy, who needs a new car, but Dale would rather be fishing, and Loretta stays home waiting for the first snowfall….." The applause is loud and long. Chris is an instant celebrity.

As people begin to leave, Gary and Chris exchange a telling look and both rise at the same time and head for the exit. Lillian Crane catches up with them and gives both men a hug. She thanks Chris for making her daughter's party a great success. Pamela calls from a distance. "Chris will I see you again?" Chris grins, but offers no reply.

Chapter

14

As promised, on Tuesday, November 16, at 2:00 p.m. Dr. Lillian Crane holds a Press Conference. Minnesota winter weather is famous for re-scheduling meetings. Cold winds, gusting to twenty-six mph, and a few inches of snow, however, do not stop reporters and journalists from Minnesota, Wisconsin, Iowa, South Dakota, and North Dakota, to make the trip.

Dr. Crane takes her place on the platform and the reporters respectfully quiet down.

"Ladies and gentlemen, let's try to do this in an orderly fashion. I will make a few statements concerning Mr. Storm's curriculum and then open it up for questions." One reporter interrupts,

"Will we get to meet Mr. Storm today?"

"I am afraid Mr. Storm has declined. Remember he is only fourteen years old and rather shy. Please allow me to provide the information for you. Christopher Martin Storm is one of the finest scholars at this University. He is also the youngest in the history of this school. We had to adjust his curriculum on a monthly basis because of his unprecedented ability to remember everything he reads. At the airport back in September, I mentioned that he would pursue his PhD in Theology, which includes Latin, Greek, and Hebrew. His second goal now includes a PhD in Philosophy. Mr. Storm believes that he can pass all the tests required to earn his Doctorate of Theology by the end of this semester and his second PhD next year. To refresh your memory, a semester at this University, is two periods of fifteen weeks each, dividing the academic year. In addition, after earning his first PhD, Dr. Storm will add a European language to his studies. He has chosen German, because a visit to Europe is in his plans sometime in the next few years."

A reporter from North Dakota, who was not present at the airport in September, has a request dittoed by many reporters,

"Dr. Crane, can you elaborate on the special gift Chris possesses? How can he learn difficult subjects so rapidly?"

"Yes, I will tell you what I have learned from conversations with Mr. Storm. The University in Massachusetts recognized his child Prodigy status and provided specialized training. They established his gift to be an inexorable memory of sounds and visions. He never learned to read the hard way as you and I did. In fact, he actually has trouble reading one word at the time. He reads a page at a time. As he put it, 'It seems that my brain takes a picture of the page and makes the information available for future use.'

If he were here reading an article to you, he would look at both pages of an open book or magazine and then look at his audience and quote from memory what he saw. When he takes tests, he closes his eyes, pictures the information he has studied on the subject until the answer becomes visible in his mind. He said that if he cannot visualize the answer, it means he has not read anything on the subject. The test question would remain blank. He never guesses. I can vouch for the fact that Mr. Storm leaves very few test questions blank."

"Please Dr. Crane could we please meet this young man, we will be gentle and won't embarrass him."

"Ladies and Gentlemen, I will ask him. Relax and I will see you in a few minutes. One request, if Chris does come, do not applaud when he enters. He accepts applause after demonstrations, but is embarrassed when people applaud his entrance. Simply say hello Chris."

Minutes later, Dr. Crane returns with Chris in tow. A couple reporters short on memory, start applauding, others call out, "Hi, Chris." Soon the room is quiet.

To Dr. Crane's astonishment, Chris walks to the reporters, shakes everyone's hand, and calls them by the name on their Press ID tags. Then he returns to the podium and says,

"I know that you want to learn how my unusual memory works. I have no idea. I cannot explain it. Perhaps a brief demonstration will help." Chris scans his audience and says,

"I am going to ask all of you to turn around with your backs to me, please." Puzzled, every reporter obeys and soon all of their backs are turned. Demonstrating, his keen sense of humor, in a loud whisper Chris suggests to Dr. Crane that they should sneak out while their backs are turned. The reporters laugh and begin turning back when Chris says, "We are not done. Please keep your backs turned. You may turn around as I call your name."

One can hear an expectant murmur among the reporters. One by one, Chris recalls their names from memory. With only one reporter still not called, Chris playfully discomfits the young woman.

"Let's see now, one name left, I remember a slight German accent, blue eyes, a cute turned up nose, lips without lipstick, a lock of blond hair nearly hiding her left eye."

"I'm turning around now, Chris, you are embarrassing me." As the woman turns, Chris calls out her name.

"Ursula Merck, thanks for being a good sport." As Chris leaves, applause echoes through the closed door behind him.

The call volume to the University reception desk has been rising to inordinate levels. Dr. Crane orders a separate phone line featuring a weekly, recorded announcement of newsworthy events at the University, including reports regarding Christopher's achievements. The week of February 21, carries the announcement of special interest to reporters

Chapter: 14

and journalists. Dr. Crane will hold another press conference shortly before Spring Break on Tuesday, March 8, 1966 at 2:00 p.m. .

Dozens of Press personnel never before seen on University grounds are now swelling the crowd of news-hungry reporters and journalists. As Dr. Crane and Chris enter the room, they are welcomed to the podium by lively applause. A quick look, assures Chris that nearly all the reporters present at the last press conference are also present today, including Ursula Merck. As their eyes meet, they exchange a smile loaded with mystery.

Dr. Crane taps on the microphone and opens the meeting.

"Ladies and Gentlemen of the press, a few ground rules will make this conference a success for all of us. I will highlight some of the events at this University since our last Conference. After that, the floor is yours. Mr. Storm and I will be happy to answer your questions.

The University has experienced the largest number of admission applications in its forty-year history. We have added four Professors and expanded our curriculum as requested by the student body. The most exciting announcement I am making today is that Christopher Storm is completing his studies for the Doctorate of Theology. If he turns in a passing grade on the final exam, he will earn his PhD.

One more announcement and then I will hand the mike to Chris. In fact, this announcement concerns Chris and I did not forewarn him. Let us see how our genius handles surprises. In a meeting held two weeks ago, taking for granted that Mr. Storm will earn his PhD, the staff voted unanimously to offer him a faculty position at this University." As everyone begins to cheer, Dr. Crane signals for silence,

"Because Chris is a minor; we contacted the proper authorities and received certification that allows Chris to hold such a position as long as he has an adult sponsor and counselor. I have personally volunteered for that job."

Dr. Crane shakes Chris' hand to congratulate him, but he meets her delighted expression with a gaze she cannot interpret. She motions for Chris to respond at the microphone.

"Dr. Crane is the finest educator I've met in the ten years of attending schools and Universities. That is why it will be hard to say what I must say right now. The media has covered every moment of my young life, so nobody should be startled to learn that I was raised in several different homes, but eventually spent the majority of my upbringing in the home of Pastor and Mrs. Ragford in Massachusetts. In that home, I was constantly encouraged to study the Scriptures. The Bible is the word of Almighty God. I have a brain that allows me to read and remember volumes of printed material. It is a gift. I did not receive that gift from my parents, or from Pastor Ragford, or from Dr. Pullman at the University. I received that gift from God. I am obliged to use that gift to glorify Him."

A number of hands go up and three or four reporters speak at the same time. Everyone is eager to know the details of Chris' plans.

"The details are up to God, I dare not run ahead of Him. I must determine His will for the future. As He has in the past, God will reveal clear steps in His timing."

"Does that mean you are turning down Dr. Crane's career offer?"

"Right now, whether Dr. Crane and this University will remain part of my future is unclear. Unless God removes me from here right away, I intend to complete a course in German and a fine reporter in your midst will agree to assist me. Her name is Ursula Merck."

Several reporters whip around to locate Ursula, whose rosy face expresses total shock. Her mouth is half-open, but no sound escapes.

"Look folks," Chris teases "a speechless reporter!" As everyone laughs, Ursula yells,

"You obviously grossly underestimate the revengeful powers of a German woman."

"Now hear my first sermon, Ursula. Vengeance is mine, saith the Lord." The joking continues a few minutes. Then Dr. Crane returns to

Chapter: 14

the podium and adjourns the meeting with words that express hope for Christopher's continued stay at the University.

"Perhaps Chris can serve in the capacity of the chapel minister, since the current minister is seeking a different position," she forecasts.

As the crowd of news people moves toward the exit, Ursula makes her way toward Chris.

"How is it that you can lie with a straight face, Reverend Storm," she demands with an endearing grin.

"When did I lie?" Chris counters.

"You lied when you said that I would agree to assist you with German lessons."

"Ursula, whether that is a lie or not is really in your ballpark, isn't it? Just say yes, you will assist me, and our friends will have heard the truth and nothing but the truth."

"Okay, Chris, I suppose I can spare a few hours here and there with the correct pronunciation of difficult German words."

Ursula hands Chris her business card and leaves with a reminder to call her any time.

It is Sunday, March 27. After church, Gary and Chris have lunch at Applebee's. Gary has a date with his steady girl. He is taking an engagement ring with him. He is nervous about popping the all-important question because it will be a surprise to Carolyn. He spotted this beautiful ring in the window at Zale's Jewelry store and could not resist it. He drops Chris at the dormitory and leaves to carry out his mission.

As is typical, Chris is knee-deep into the works of well-known preachers and Theologians. He comes across a list of Evangelist Billy Graham's crusades and finds it overwhelming. Chris recalls that in 1964 members of Pastor Ragford's church attended the crusade in Boston. Some of them sang in the huge choir, a cooperative work of several neighborhood churches.

Chris regrets that he missed that crusade. He was living at the University under the care of Dr. Pullman, who is not a Christian. Chris learned of the crusade too late and remembers that he held it against his foster father, Pastor Ragford, for not informing him. Pastor Ragford cleverly turned it into a lesson on forgiveness.

Deep in thought about missed opportunities, the silence-breaking peal of the phone propels him to his feet.

"Hello, this is Chris."

"Hi Chris, this is Ursula. Do you remember….," Chris interrupts. "Ursula, I think you have me confused with somebody else. When people say to me, 'Oh forget it' I always answer, I wish I could; and when people start a conversation with 'Do you remember? I always end up saying 'Yes' before they finish the question. Yes, I remember you, Ursula. Ursula continues,

"Chris, I found out that we were both born on April 1st. What are your plans for your birthday?"

"I have no plans for my birthday. Do you have plans?"

"Yes, I do and they include you. Would you consider celebrating our birthdays together at my house? I have already invited a few people that you know from press conferences, plus a couple of girlfriends. Will you come?"

"Ursula, I have no transportation and Gary is not here, so I can't ask him."

"That's no problem. I can pick you up. Will you come? You do not have to bring anything. Several of us have decided to skip the birthday gift routine and enjoy the company. Will you come? Please? Chris, promise you will come. I will pick you up at 6:00 p.m., okay?"

"What is everybody wearing to that kind of a party?"

"Casual, Chris; the more casual the better. See you Friday, bye."

Ursula's birthday party is different from Pamela Crane's celebration. There are no formal gowns or suits; no butler and no long dinner tables. As Ursula and Chris arrive, they find men and women, squatting on the floor, drinking beer and devouring half-moons of pizza. Ursula tries to introduce Chris, but someone told a clever joke, resulting in thigh-slapping laughter. Only one or two individuals turn and acknowledge

Chris with a casual wave of the hand. Ursula apologizes to Chris, who responds with a sympathetic grin and claims to understand. He can see that the behavior of her birthday guests embarrassed her. Ursula leads Chris to the kitchen, offers him a Coke, and points to the coffee table covered with boxes of pizza.

"After you," Chris says. Ursula obeys and leads the way to the coffee table. As they near the table, Chris recognizes one of the reporters.

The man has his arm around the girl next to him.

"Jerry," Chris interrupts. "Is this your wife?" Everybody giggles, as though Chris had told a new joke. Ursula fixes a stern look at Chris and shakes her head.

"Let's have some pizza, Chris," she urges. Now Jerry turns to Chris. With a drunken accent, he asks,

"Hey boy, why did you think that Emily is my wife?"

"Because you were wearing a wedding ring at the press conference." This time the crowd responds with silence, the girl moves away from Jerry and starts to say something, but Jerry bellows back,

"How would you know that I was wearing a wedding ring?"

"Because we shook hands and you were wearing a wedding ring."

"Hey wunderkind, don't people shake with their right hands; and are wedding rings not worn on the left hand? Hmm?"

"Yes, normally they shake with their right hands, but you were holding a camera in your right hand and offered me the left."

Chris catches accusing stares all across the room. He recalls Christ's warnings for his disciples. *In the world, you will have trouble. But be of good cheer I have overcome the world.* He takes a deep breath and asks, "May I say something to all of you, please? The Bible teaches a completely different life style from what I observe here. You are behaving as though you never considered the idea of a clean, victorious, and righteous life. Think about it. Ursula would you be kind enough to take me back to the dorm?"

Chris follows Ursula as she heads for the door. They reach the car when they hear Jerry yell,

"Wait Chris, please wait." The man sounds completely sober. When he reaches Ursula and Chris, they are amazed to see that he is crying.

"Chris, I was raised in a Christian home. I am aware of what you shared in there. I was an active member in the church, where I met my wife, Wendy. We had been married about ten months when I learned about Wendy's affair with our family doctor. I was devastated and blamed God for allowing such a thing. Wendy claimed she broke off the affair and we tried to make a go of it again. Two months later, a reporter friend spotted her in a downtown Minneapolis restaurant with a known politician. He took some pictures of them holding hands. This was in November shortly after the Press conference where we met. This time I did not recover. I stopped going to church, threw the wedding ring at Wendy, and left the house. We never got divorced. Wendy still lives there and I rent an apartment in a poor neighborhood in South Minneapolis.

I want to thank you, Chris. Your testimony has put me to shame. Tomorrow I will be on my knees, asking God for forgiveness."

"Jerry, you have no way of knowing whether you will be alive tomorrow. Ursula, would you mind if Jerry joins us in your car for a few moments." A completely confused Ursula nods and unlocks the car. Jerry crawls into the back seat and with tears; he confesses his sins and begs for forgiveness. His confession continues for several minutes, Chris carefully interrupts and asks,

"Jerry, do you know the passage in I John 1:9?" Jerry pauses; I think I memorized that one, but help me out, Chris." Chris quotes,

"If we confess our sins, he is faithful and just to forgive us our sins, and to cleanse us from all unrighteousness. Believe that, Jerry and enjoy your forgiveness. Now, as Jesus would say, go and sin no more."

Jerry grabs Chris' hand with his left and Ursula's with his right and with his face beaming; he thanks them both profusely before leaving.

Ursula starts the car, and turns it off again. She gawks at Chris as though she has something to say. Then she starts the car, drives two blocks, pulls into a parking lot, and repeats her staring maneuver. Chris does not say a word and neither does Ursula. Ursula starts the car, pulls

Chapter: 14

out of the parking lot and does not stop or speak until they reach the University grounds. There she pulls into the parking lot away from the dorm. She turns off the engine, stares at Chris, and finally spills her mind,

"Chris, I am not like Jerry. I did not grow up in a Christian home. Father was a Nazi officer and believed only in Hitler. He hates Jews and Christians and will strike Mother any time she mentions anything about the church.

My brother, Egon, served as an officer on a German submarine and received medals for sinking a number of British Merchant ships and even a British destroyer. In 1943, he and his entire crew died when a British destroyer, sunk his U-boat with a new type of circular depth charge. He was only twenty-one years old. Mom said she cried for days over his loss. Mom married young, but was thirty-nine when Egon died. My birth, three years later, was unexpected and, I think, unwanted. I never felt loved by either of my parents. Twenty-three years after my brother died, my mother still mourns his loss, but never expresses any interest in me or my work, or anything I do." Ursula hangs her head and weeps quietly for a few minutes. Chris is surprised at Ursula's openness.

"Why did you tell me about your family?"

"I don't really know. In case you ever learn about my dad, Walter Merck, you are forewarned. I feel so out of it. I have never gone to church. I never even considered it. When you and Jerry talked in the car, you seemed so knowledgeable and comfortable with the subject. There seemed to be a bond between the two of you, yet you hardly know each other. It made me feel as though I am missing out on something."

"Ursula, Jesus Christ is the head of the true church. If two people know Him, they know much about each other. Jesus provides that bond you mentioned. Jerry is a Christian, but like a sheep, that loses its way, Jerry wandered off the narrow path where Christ's sheep follow their shepherd. He was lost for a season and is found again."

"Chris I am totally confused. I am trying to figure out what people must do to become like you and Jerry and you are talking about sheep."

"I am sorry, Ursula. I am so accustomed to church jargon. Have you ever heard of the 23rd Psalm?"

"I don't think so. Wait; Uncle Werner took me to my aunt's funeral and I kept the little brochure. I remember reading it and thinking that it made no sense because it was talking about sheep and pastures.

Uncle Werner is Dad's brother, but they are completely different. Uncle Werner is nice. He goes to church and has asked me to go with him. He lives in Moorhead, and we never got together."

Chris presents the plan of salvation in such a easily followed manner that Ursula ends up bowing her head and in tears repents of her unrighteous actions, asking God for forgiveness and thanking Christ for dying on the cross for her. Chris takes Ursula's hand,

"Now we are brother and sister in Christ."

"We are? I have a lot to learn, she admits."

"Yes, you do and I have a proposition for you. I will teach you the Bible, and you help me with German."

"Chris, that sounds wonderful."

Chapter

15

As expected, Chris aces the final exams. He is now Dr. Christopher Martin Storm. Friends and family from Massachusetts join the commencement ceremony. To honor their top student, the school asks Chris to speak at the ceremony. The faculty has learned that Chris has memorized the entire Bible. Dr. Lillian Crane introduces him as Dr. Christopher Storm, the Biblicist. Reporters use that title in their columns. Soon people around the world know Chris as the Biblicist.

Chris' valedictorian speech will remain in the memory of all who hunger for the deeper points of the Scriptures. It is about his passion to live for God. Even as several of the most liberal folks walk out to continue their travel on the broad path of destruction, Chris finishes his speech and receives a standing ovation, which he attempts to silence without success.

Dozens of reporters, including Jerry and Ursula, cover the ceremony and once again, the name of the fifteen-year-old Dr. Christopher Storm is in the headlines. Dr. Crane announces that Chris has signed two 3-year contracts with the University; one to fill the chapel pulpit, and the other as Professor of Theology.

When those contracts expire, Chris will be eighteen years old and considered an adult for most opportunities open to Theologians of his caliber.

The only additional training he will be completing before occupying those positions will be the German class he had planned some time ago. Ursula remains his faithful friend guiding him safely through the proper pronunciation of German words.

Chris rejoices, watching Ursula grow into a serious student of the Scriptures and a surrendered follower of Christ.

Chris' and Gary no longer share a room, but Gary attends every chapel service when Chris is preaching. Spending much time together, they have become true friends. Chris felt sorry for Gary when he returned after his meeting with Carolyn with the engagement ring still in his pocket. Carolyn had turned him down.

Ursula also attends the chapel services. Often Ursula and Chris share lunch after the service and many times, Gary joins them. A special bond develops between the three young people and Chris is not surprised when, a year later, Gary and Ursula announce their engagement.

The wedding day, scheduled for July 22, turns out to be the hottest day of the 1967 summer in Minneapolis, reaching ninety degrees. It is hot and humid. A few guests fail to show up, but as long as Gary, Ursula, and Chris are on hand, the wedding can proceed. Ursula's Uncle Werner gives away the bride. Chris preaches a convincing sermon about true love for the couple and the simple plan of salvation for the unsaved guests. Hugs, tears, joy, and laughter all find their proper places and the wedding is a memorable triumph.

The happy couple has reservations on a cruise ship leaving from New York, bound for Germany. Ursula and Chris will visit her parents for several days before continuing their tour on sightseeing vessels throughout Europe. Monday morning, July 24, Ursula's Uncle Werner, followed by a couple of vehicles carrying well-wishers, drives them to the airport. Bon voyage.

Ursula had made contact with her mother, Else Merck, before leaving the States. Else convinces a few friends to join the welcome party to greet Ursula at the harbor. Else is devastated when she learns that Ursula has

Chapter: 15

become seriously ill on the ship. Recently, Else had reevaluated their relationship and pondered how to patch things up with her Ursula.

At the hospital, Ursula is conscious, but weak. She looks peaceful, her eyes fixed on the ceiling as though she is expecting her soul to rise any moment to meet the Lord. Gary is holding Ursula's hand and senses a very weak touch. He has tried to remain strong for his beloved Ursula. Now, with the inevitable separation only minutes away he kneels beside her bed and falls apart.

"Ursi, Ursi, darling, please don't leave me. I love you so much. I do not know what to do. How can I go on without you? Ursula, stay with me. Please, Ursi, please don't die."

Slowly, Ursula turns her head. Their eyes meet, filled with love and tenderness .They do not need words now. This moment, written in the language of true devotion, belongs to the chronicles of eternity.

In the presence of her husband, her mother, and a few friends, Ursula's soul breaks through the confines of this plagued universe and ascends into the realm of the peace that passes all understanding. Wrapped in the splendor, foreign to this planet, she ascends into the glorious presence of the only true God.

Early Friday, August 4, the Western Union telegram shakes Chris' world. He puts his head on the desk and weeps bitterly. Ursula became ill on the seventh day of their journey and died in a German hospital today, August 3, 1967. Ship doctors suspect Salmonella poisoning.

Though severally limited by language barriers, together, Ursula's mother and Gary make funeral arrangements. Mrs. Merck has not seen her husband for several days and is unable to reach him. Gary calls Chris and shares funeral plans. Chris insists that he will officiate at the funeral and Gary is ecstatic to accept his offer.

Chris arrives by plane at 10:15 a.m. on Saturday, August 5. Mrs. Merck finally reaches her husband and convinces him to fetch Chris from the airport. Both wearing nametags they meet and study one another for a few seconds before shaking hands. Chris is aware of this man's Nazi background and trust's God for an opportunity to share the Gospel with him.

Walter Merck is well mannered, but not friendly. He leads the way to the car. The two men do not speak. In the car, Chris starts the conversation, a chance to practice his newly acquired second language.

"Ihre Tochter war eine gute Freundin. Es tut mir leid, das Sie gestorben ist." *(Your daughter was a good friend. I am sorry she passed away.)*

The hardness of the man's heart is evident when he replies. "Na Ja, all Menschen müssen ja sterben. *(Oh well, everyone must die).*

The funeral is on Monday, August 7. Only twenty-four people attend, mostly friends of Else Merck. A few young women, who knew Ursula before she left for the USA, are sitting together in a back row. They are the only ones not wearing black armbands, but their countenance reflects their earnest sympathy. A soloist sings from a book of German Folk Music. It is a beautiful tune, but has strictly secular wording. Chris is beginning to wonder whether someone will forcefully remove him from the funeral home if he speaks of Christ and His plan of salvation. For a few seconds he toys with the idea of leaving Christ out of the message, but ashamed, he assures himself that the Spirit will guide him. A Bible passage jumps in the forefront of his vast memory. *'But whosoever shall deny me before men, him will I also deny before my Father which is in heaven.'*

"Okay, Lord, got the message. Appreciate that tender nudge!"

(Chris 'sermon, delivered in German, is recorded below in English.)

"I will begin with a quote from the book of Hebrews, chapter 9 and verse 27. *'It is appointed unto man once to die but after that the judgement.'* Ursula's dad, whom I met for the first time upon my arrival at the airport, is in complete agreement with this verse. He acknowledged that everyone must die. Of course, he left out the part about the judgement. I am here today to fill in the blanks."

Walter Merck, his face twisted with anger, abruptly storms out of the building. Mrs. Merck jumps up and excitedly warns Chris. "Er wird mit einer pistole zurück kommen." *(He will be back with a pistol).*

Chapter: 15

    Chris pauses, but then continues his sermon. One of the young boys in the second row demonstrates his skill with bubble gum. Chris gives him a stern look, which the boy answers by sticking out his tongue. Chris, never too shy to speak the truth in love, switches to a different subject.

    "There is a verse for parents in the Scriptures that, I think, is helpful. You'll find it in Proverbs 22:6, *train up a child in the way he should go: and when he is old, he will not depart from it.*" Looking straight at the parents of the wayward boy, Chris continues. "Mom and Dad, you have a head start on raising a boy who will still blow bubbles at funerals and stick his tongue out at pastors, when he is forty."

    At that moment, Walter Merck thunders into the room, pointing a pistol at Chris. Else cries out. "Mach das nicht, Walter" *(Don't do that, Walter)*. Two police officers, who watched Walter fetch the revolver from his vehicle, rush him from behind as the gun discharges, turning the small chapel into an echo chamber of explosions. Everyone studies Chris. Gary races to the podium. Blood is dripping from Chris' left hand. The bullet struck his arm.

    The police officers handcuff Walter Merck and one of the officers examines Chris' arm. He determines that he may need some stitches and calls an ambulance. Then he inquiries about the details of the incident. Chris points to Else. "Bitte sprechen Sie zu seiner Frau." *(Please speak to his wife.)* As Else follows the officer outside, some of the people are getting up to leave.

    Chris, feeling a bit faint, nevertheless encourages everyone to remain seated and states that the last few minutes have been an excellent lesson about the uncertainties of life on this earth.

    Chris closes with a short prayer, which includes a petition for Walter Merck. To his astonishment, everybody stays in their seat, including the parents of the misbehaving boy.

    The ambulance arrives. Medics do not find the bullet in Chris' arm. It only grazed him. They tape and bandage his wound, provide some pain medication, and leave.

Chris smiles at his audience. You are free to leave. I have said the closing prayer. The father of the boy raises his hand. Chris nods his head encouraging him to speak.

"You do not preach as other preachers in Germany," he begins. Chris laughs. "I probably do not preach as any other preachers anywhere in the world," he admits.

"You pointed out our son's misbehavior right to our face. Nobody's has ever done that before."

"That's because I cannot see the wisdom in silencing the words of the Scriptures, which is the voice of God, to protect the feelings of people who need correction. God changed the course of Walter's bullet. He must have more work for me. The bullet wound on my arm will become a heaven-sent reminder of God's grace."

Chris' round-trip ticket would take him home tomorrow, but at Gary's urging, he changes the return date to Friday, August 11.

Mrs. Merck is a great cook and the guests enjoy her hospitality. Without saying so, Mrs. Merck appears to be relieved that her husband is incarcerated, awaiting trial.

When Mrs. Merck learns of Christopher's Prodigy status and the fact that he, at age fifteen, has earned two PhD degrees, she pulls the same trick which Chris experienced dozens of times. Without warning Chris and Gary, she invites some young people for dinner Thursday evening.

Dr. Roland Lauterbach, a Professor at a prodigious London University, accompanies his daughter, who is one of the young women invited. All the dinner guests have arrived and introductions are finished. Mrs. Merck apologizes for the earlier, improper introduction of Dr. Christopher Storm. Dr. Lauterbach whips around and ogles Chris.

"I saw your picture in the June 1966 issue of Mnemonics Magazine."

"That may be so, Dr. Lauterbach; they don't tell me what happens to the hundreds of interviews and pictures of me that are floating around.

Chapter: 15

The articles I have read typically exaggerate my abilities. I have a hard time living up to them."

"Well, Dr. Storm, I am overwhelmed by this opportunity to meet you. A few associates were hoping to invite you to our University for a demonstration of your gift. Would you consider such a visit, all expenses paid, of course?"

"It is a tempting proposition, Dr. Lauterbach; I would have to work that into my schedule at Roseville University, where I have signed a three-year contract. As you know, I am still a minor and under the supervision of Dr. Lillian Crane. The final decision is up to her."

"Fine, now are you willing to demonstrate your gift this evening?"

"Not on an empty stomach," Chris replies and lists the details of all the meals Else Merck had prepared since Monday. A sumptuous dinner and lively conversation follows the enthusiastic applause. A few of the guests take their leave shortly after dinner. Dr. Lauterbach, his daughter Ingrid, and a few young people enthralled with Christopher's abilities, stay for more demonstrations.

Chris hints that his favorite demonstration is to quote from the Scriptures, but that suggestion meets with an immediate opposition.

"You did that at the funeral," argues a young man.

"So, you also have an excellent memory," Chris teases. "Do you remember anything I said at the funeral?"

"I think you said *ouch* when that bullet hit your arm," is the boy's juvenile reply. Chris precipitously gives him a serious look. Calling the boy by name, he says,

"Thank you, Manfred. You have assisted me in making an important decision. Today there will be no demonstration of the gift God has provided, to glorify His name. Now I want to get some fresh air. It was nice meeting all of you. Goodnight."

A large, white rock in the backyard has become Chris' favorite spot over the last few days. He is not sure why, but this time, when he reaches that rock, tears of sorrow overcome him. Is it a late reaction to Ursula's death? Is it the indifferent behavior of those lost people in the house? Is it his impulsive decision to stop the demonstration? Chris sinks to his knees and with tears soaking the ground, he prays,

"Oh Lord God, Creator of heaven and earth, You have placed me in the center of corruption. My memory, this gift of unnatural ability, is saturated with evil words, sights, and conduct. Father, help me to forget, lest I perish in the mire of such memories. I know every word of the Holy Scriptures, but I constantly fail to sort them properly. Words that condemn me and sting my soul, words that comfort me last only until I look around..." Chris stops. Did Peter not begin to sink only when he started looking around? Is that not what robbed him of the power to walk on the water? Chris wipes tears from his face with the back of his hand. "Some theologian I turned out to be, falling apart before the real battle has even begun. Lord, from this moment on, I am completely surrendered to you. Forgive my doubts and weakness."

Years later, Chris testifies that this moment at the large, white rock in Mrs. Merck's back yard was a turning point in his young life and that whenever fear or anxiety threaten; he finds peace recalling his white rock encounter with God.

When Chris returns to the house, everyone is gone. Else Merck, an educated, strict German woman, is about to council him about his improper behavior of leaving the house full of guests. However, something in his countenance stops her.

"Where were you, Chris, she asks simply."

"I am sorry for leaving so abruptly, Mrs. Merck, but I had a meeting with God at the white rock in your back yard."

"I hate to argue with you, Professor Storm, but I sit on that rock all the time and never see God there."

"Dear Mrs. Merck, perhaps next time, if you kneel and tell God about some of your carnal thoughts, words, and deeds, write me and let me know how that turns out."

Chapter: 15

Gary, struggling to recover from Ursula's death, confides in Chris that he is angry with God. Chris gives him a tender, but candid look. "You're a smart fellow, he asserts, and what do you hope to gain from God in return?"

"Don't be so, so, so right all the time, Dr. Freud."

"Don't call me Freud," Chris counters. "call me 'Freund.'"

"Who is Freund," Gary questions.

"Nine days in Germany and you have not learned the word 'Freund?' Let's fix that right now, my Freund."

"Oh, you are so clever. Of course, 'Freund' means 'friend'. In case I have not mentioned it lately, Chris, I don't know what I would do without your 'freundship'." Chris laughs,

"German is not that easy, Gary. It is not 'Freundship." It is 'Freundschaft'." Gary shakes his head. "Forget it Chris, I will never keep my 'ships' and 'schafts' straight.

Gary's cruise ship is due tomorrow, the same day of Chris' return flight. He cannot see himself alone on that cruise. Gary decides to return by air. Perhaps he can get a seat on Chris' plane.

"Let me see your ticket, Chris," Gary picks up the phone.

"This I have to see," Chris cheers.

"See what?"

"You making airline reservations in German; the same fellow who is still working on the word 'Freund'. Gary slams the phone back on the hook. "Hilfe bitte! *(Help please)* See, I know some German."

Chapter

16

The recently hired University limousine driver holds his sign at the Minneapolis Airport: WELCOME HOME Chris and Gary. Chris recognizes a few reporters behind the chauffeur.

"Let's circle around and walk past them," he whispers to Gary. "I don't want to talk to reporters today." It works. They pass unnoticed. Chris spots an airport service volunteer wearing a red hat. He exchanges a few words with the man, hands him a $5 bill, and a note addressed to the limo driver holding the sign. Gary laughs when he observes the limousine driver head for the closest exit, leaving confused reporters behind. The driver meets them at the parked limo.

Mourning Ursula's death together draws Chris and Gary closer. The self-confessed ladies' man is not dating and tells Chris, he may never love again. Chris offers no answers, but he prays for his friend daily. Gary's pain is his pain. This turns out to be quite literal when Chris meets Meredith Pike, a Christian woman, who wants a relationship with him. Chris is impressed with her character, but decides not to pursue female companionship until Gary finds someone first.

On August 17, 1969, during a Sunday chapel service, Chris recognizes a woman from the drunken birthday party at Ursula's apartment over

Chapter: 16

three years ago. She is the woman who hung on Jerry's arm when Chris confronted him. After the service, Chris introduces Gary to Emily.

"Good morning, Emily, do you remember me?"

"That question hardly deserves a serious answer, Chris. I will never forget you. After your confrontation that day at Ursula's place, I reexamined my life. Now I attend church regularly with some Christian friends. I trusted Christ for my salvation during an evangelistic meeting."

Emily turns to Gary,

"I am so sorry for your loss." Gary marvels at the sincere tone in Emily's voice. Emily continues,

"Ursula had many friends here, but most of them are unsaved. I have tried to witness to some of them, but they remember my partying days and walk away. I can't get through to them."

"Emily, I think you should take someone with you. Someone who will vouch for your character change," Gary suggests.

"Well, I'm ready when you two are," Emily pledges. Are you taking me to lunch," she quips. Gary responds hastily,

"It will be our pleasure." He finds Emily charming and intelligent. It has been more than two years since Ursula passed away. Gary is comfortable in Emily's company. He wonders whether she could become more than a lunch companion.

Chris, reading Gary's body language and facial expressions detects a fresh spark in his friend's eyes that had lost their radiance since Ursula's death.

"What would you two say if I asked to be excused from this rendezvous?" Chris asks sheepishly. Gary responds only with a grin.

"So, then it's settled," Chris determines. "I trust you and Emily will get along fine and make plans to go witnessing together. See you later, Gary. So long Emily."

Monday morning, when Chris meets Gary in the hallway, he is a different man. He is humming a tune and smiling from ear to ear. Before Gary gets a chance to say anything, Chris insists,

"You'll have to tell me all about it tonight."

"Okay, Daddy," Gary teases. For the next few weeks, Chris does not see much of Gary. He and Emily are dating steadily. Every Sunday after the service, the two disappear quickly, sampling different restaurants in the area.

Chris considers Gary's new circumstances an open door to his own endeavors in the area of intimate relationships. The only woman he has ever seriously considered as a soul mate is Ursula. The age difference put a halt to that dream and when Gary fell in love with Ursula, Chris was emotionally ready to give her up. Nevertheless, he feared that a piece of his heart might always belong to Ursula; making a new relationship unfair to any woman, he would choose as a life partner. Perhaps young women sensed a restraining message in Chris' attitude toward them. The message seemed to warn, 'I am not available.'

Pamela Crane confides in her best friend, Tracy Logan, that dating is overrated. She claims the men she has dated so far are immature, selfish, and certainly not marriage material.

"As far as I am concerned," she confesses. "There is only one man I really admire."

"Let me guess, Pammy...Christopher Storm."

"Of course. Who else?"

"But he's only eighteen."

"Sure, he is eighteen in years, but thirty-six in accomplishments. He probably does not remember that I exist. Since the birthday party, I have only seen him a few times at the U when I visit my mom. I hear much about him from mom and, of course, by reading about him."

"Well, what's stopping you, girl? Go after him!"

"Chris is so proper all the time. I am not sure what bait to use to reel in that big fish."

"Are you kidding, Pam, if you don't have the right bait, who does? You are gorgeous by every sense of that word. Perfect face and perfect figure; what else could the man want?"

Chapter: 16

"Tracy, this guy keeps saying that God looks at the heart. I think he does the same. I have shown him my naughty side the first time we met. Chris never forgets anything."

In early March 1969, Dr. Crane spots Chris in the library.

"In a few weeks you will turn eighteen," she whispers as though she is divulging a well-kept secret. "What are your plans for that historic day?"

"I have not even thought about that, Dr. Crane. Why do you ask?"

"I want your birthday party to be at our house with some of our mutual friends. Not only will you become a legal adult that day, but also your contract with us expires on April 1. We want to hear about your plans for the future."

"I am sorry; Dr. Crane, but you caught me completely off guard. The future is uncertain. However, your offer to celebrate my birthday at your residence is gratefully accepted."

"Okay, Chris, since April 1st falls on a Tuesday, a school day. Let's have the party on Friday, April 4th, okay?"

Reminiscent of Pamela's birthday party, the butler greets Chris at the door. However, it is not Foster, the young butler; it is an older, distinguished looking man by the name of Ramon. Chris remembers many birthday wishes, but never has he been congratulated in a more awkward approach than Ramon parades,

Sir, I have been informed of your birthday and have been ordered to congratulate you upon your arrival. I am to wish you a most blissful birthday."

"Chris is amused,

So, Ramon, are you going to wish me a most blissful birthday?" Noisily Ramon clears his throat,

"I wish you a most blissful birthday, Sir."

"Thank you, Ramon. What happened to Foster," Chris inquires.

"That is not my concern, Sir," Ramon replies stiffly.

"I suppose it is none of my business either," Chris admits.

"I can't say, Sir. Perhaps it is and perhaps it isn't." Ramon directs Chris to the parlor. Chris recognizes several guests from Pamela Crane's sixteenth birthday party, which is almost four years ago. Of the forty-two guests, twenty-eight are young women, Pamela's friends. Gary and Emily draw attention to themselves by their observable affection for one another. Several prying guests, finding no ring on Emily's finger, press for statistics on their relationship. When and how did they meet? Are they planning to marry? Will Gary soon pop the question? Gary and Emily handle it prudently, but give nothing away. A few minutes later, Gary whispers to Chris that he has ordered the engagement ring and that they will soon announce their engagement.

Chris is wondering whether now, at age eighteen, and with Gary taken care of, how he would change his behavior toward women. However, he is sure that it must change. He senses a new passion for romance and love and must learn to be open to God's leading for a relationship with a godly woman.

Things change rapidly for the handsome young Dr. Christopher Storm. At the party, he is aware of the looks coming his way from several of the young women, including Pamela, who is now almost twenty. Chris remembers her as a forward, a bit naughty sixteen-year old who sat on his lap; but now Pamela seems more refined, almost quiet. Chris learns later that Foster, the young butler, had tried to take advantage of Pamela the day after she turned seventeen. Pamela refused him and reported his advances to her dad.

The seating arrangements at the dinner table, which Dr. Crane had left to Pamela's imagination, favored the fourteen male guests each of whom shared the company of two women, one on each side. Pamela claims coincidence that she sits on Chris' right and a woman in her forties on his left. Across the table from Pamela is her best friend, Tracy Logan, who is bombarding Pamela with disgusted looks, so obvious that Chris finally questions Pamela about it.

"She is upset because she wanted to sit next to you," Pamela admits.

"And why isn't she sitting next to me?"

Chapter: 16

"Because!"

"Because she is pretty?" Chris pokes.

"Yes, because she is gorgeous and smart and witty and I want you for myself." Chris looks at Pamela and simply states, Pamela, I like you too and am honored that you chose this seating arrangement."

"How did you know that I arranged the seating?"

"Because I have a PhD in Philosophy, Chris teases."

Comparing the Pamela Chris met at her sixteenth birthday party, to the Pamela seated next to him, he much prefers the later.

At a prearranged signal from Lillian, everyone in the room joins in singing "Happy Birthday" to Chris and end the song by demanding a speech. Chris expresses his gratitude for the well wishes and thanks Gordon and Lillian for their hospitality. As is his long-established practice, he adds some favorite Bible verses and ends his short speech with a sincere wish that everyone in the room would submit their life to Christ.

After dinner, Chris and Pamela stroll through the garden, and freely exchange complimentary words and looks. Chris is surprised at his attraction to Pamela. Since her sixteenth birthday party, he has seen her only a few times, when she is visiting Dr. Crane at the University. He has known her for almost four years, but only as an acquaintance. So where did this attraction come from?

As Pamela reaches for his hand, he is happy to accommodate her and answers that gesture with a pleased smile and a firm grip. They discuss many subjects and both find that they share many thoughts and ideas about life and courtship.

They reach the lovely gazebo at the south end of the garden. Pamela stops and turns toward Chris. She had been attracted to him right away when they met four years ago. Now, at twenty, she wonders whether Chris is serious about their relationship. She decides that this is the moment. She must find out right now.

"Chris, we are walking hand in hand like a couple in love. I do not really know how you feel about me. Is this just a stroll in the garden or is

The Passions & Perils of the Prodigy

it more than that?" Chris looks into her eyes, he perceives a young woman in love. He is not comfortable with making sudden decisions. He needs time to seek the Lord's will in matters as important as a relationship with a woman. He has always considered Pamela a little wild and immature, but she is different now. He finds her thoughtful and kind. Now she is more to him than just Lillian's daughter. He responds,

"Pamela, I really like you. We seem to see eye to eye on so many things. I think you are wonderful. I know that I want to see you again. Could I call you and take you out to dinner?"

"Of course, Chris, please make it soon."

Two weeks after the party, Gary and Emily announce their engagement. Together they had witnessed to Emily's old friends. Some of them are now part of Gary and Emily's Christian group of friends. Chris is grateful to God for the joy his best friend is experiencing and tells Gary that he reserves the right to officiate at their wedding when the time comes. To show his agreement, Gary answers Chris with an embrace.

Chapter

17

None of the invited guests will soon forget Gary and Emily's wedding on Saturday, July 18, 1970. A radiant glow covered the faces of the loving couple and their pastor, Christopher Martin Storm, nicknamed the Biblicist. As always, Chris scans his audience, then quotes Scripture from memory,

"Let no corrupt speech proceed out of your mouth, but such as is good for edifying as the need may be, that it may give grace to them that hear. And grieve not the Holy Spirit of God, in whom ye were sealed unto the day of redemption.1 Let all bitterness, and wrath, and anger, and clamor, and railing, be put away from you, with all malice: and be ye kind one to another, tenderhearted, forgiving each other, even as God also in Christ forgave you (Eph 4:29-32).

Do you find that fixing broken relationships is difficult? Our self-righteous minds turn discussions into arguments, arguments into anger, and anger into undesirable language, thereby sinning against our loved ones, our neighbors, and God.

All humans, even newlyweds, experience joy and pain, calm and conflict, compassion and animosity, understanding and confusion, peace and quarrels, victories and defeats; and it only takes any two of us sharing the same space. Dear Gary and Emily, and all who are here, married or single, will you allow God's Spirit to renew your mind, to equip you for these times of trouble?"

Following the wedding vows, hugs and kisses were plentiful at the reception line. Then the wedding party and guests made their way to the Crane residence where sumptuous food and good fellowship have become legendary. After all is accomplished and the late hour threatens with sad "Goodbye's," Chris and Pamela have one more surprise. They have seen each other almost every day since their stroll through the garden. Now, Chris raises his hand to get everyone's attention.

"Pamela and I most certainly would never seek to take away any glory and recognition from Gary and Emily's beautiful wedding. Nevertheless, I am happy to announce that moments ago I placed an engagement ring on Pamela's finger."

A hardy and long applause indicates approval. Chris adds that he has sought and received the approval of Pamela's parents. Guests observe that Gordon and Lillian are applauding louder than anyone else is.

So ends the beautiful and meaningful day of July 18, 1970 and begins the married life of Gary and Emily, two people devoted to each other and to Christ and His work.

Also on that day, Christopher Martin Storm used the old tradition of placing an engagement ring on the finger of the woman he believes will in due time become his wife. His love for Pamela is sincere and marked by proper passions. Chris, a devoted man of God, always allows plans for the future to rest in God's hands.

Even though Pamela cannot foresee a future without Chris, she agrees with him in these matters. She accepts his leadership and if it is God's will and direction that they get married, she will always view him as the head of the home.

Visiting the Crane residence often, Chris and Pamela spend much time together. Both are careful not to neglect their responsibilities of their respective jobs, but their favorite moments are those of intimate conversation with one another. More and more Pamela is admiring Chris' devotion to Christ and his desire to live a righteous life pleasing to God. Chris, however, begins to struggle with some of Pamela's ideas and inclinations.

To her mother's disappointment, Pamela attended a secular University in Minnesota instead of a Christian College. This choice shaped some liberal ideas unfit for a Christian woman and especially the wife of someone like Christopher Martin Storm. Lovingly and gently, Chris continues to guide her, but finds that the difference in their convictions is becoming a challenge in their relationship. He is beginning to ponder whether he acted too hastily when he agreed to their engagement.

Recently Chris has accepted preaching invitations in different parts of the country. Some of these keep him away for several days. Pamela's suggestion that she could travel with him on these trips, is Chris' clue to discuss her liberal viewpoints.

"Pam, darling, don't you think people will get the wrong idea if they find us travelling together?"

"Maybe Chris, but after all, we are engaged to be married. We could get separate rooms, if you insist."

"Pamela, I cannot go against the Scriptures that warn us not to allow even the appearance of evil. Would you actually be willing to risk our testimony as Christians?"

Pamela does not answer, but is clearly upset. She walks away. Chris waits a few minutes. Pamela's sulking bothers him a lot. He had said nothing improper. This is the first time since their engagement that Chris has seen her this way. He tries to speak to her, but Pamela again walks away without a word. Before walking out, he simply says,

"I love you, Pammy. I will see you tomorrow."

The next day, Pamela acts as though nothing happened between them. Chris takes her in his arms. Pamela lingers in his arms and with a tender look states that she is sorry for her behavior. This episode forever settles the question of Pamela travelling with Chris when he must be away overnight. Nevertheless, over time other issues come up that introduce these two inexperienced young people to the toughest battle ground on earth, human relationships. They learn much about loving and forgiving, about denying self for the sake of the other, about the sacrifices made in the give-and-take battles of the married life.

At Chris' thoughtful request, Pamela vows not to use pouting any more to show her disappointment. Instead, they agree to calmly discuss differences and allow the Scriptures to guide them to the correct solutions.

Chris' upcoming itinerary includes a week in Chelmsford, Massachusetts to preach. He would use this opportunity to visit friends and family, including the Ragfords and bring them up to date on his activities and plans. He also decides to visit his father, still in prison, and remind him that Christ is waiting for him to repent of his sinful ways.

It seems that all is well and that wedding bells will soon announce Pamela Crane and Christopher Storm's marriage. Would it happen soon after his trip to Massachusetts?

Chapter

18

Virginia Hyatt, a Chelmsford, Massachusetts high school senior, never expected to win the New England Teenage Beauty Contest. Reluctantly, she had given into her school friends' insistence. It changed her life.

Her profile, photo, and victory details in all the local newspapers generated instant fame. The Chelmsford Chamber of Commerce had erected a huge billboard at the edge of town celebrating her victory. Now, five years later, life is back to normal, boring normal.

A regular job with regular pay; compares inadequately with those glamorous modelling and commercial contracts. Robust competition swallowed up those opportunities and other faces replaced hers on that billboard.

Twice a day, Virginia passes this same billboard on the street between her apartment building and work. For the last couple of months the billboard featured a Virginia Slims Cigarette commercial with the slogan 'You've come a long way, Baby.' Virginia does not smoke, but she can relate to that slogan. The Miss Teenage victory had indeed made her feel like she had come a long way. That commercial, using her name and that slogan, has often caused her to reminisce about those busy, but glorious weeks following her teen queen victory.

The Passions & Perils of the Prodigy

This Friday, a pleasant spring evening in 1972, Virginia is in a fantastic mood as she walks home from work. Her boss announced a much needed pay increase. One way or another, she vows to celebrate that increase this weekend. Passing the billboard, Virginia hesitates; it displays a new commercial. One of the largest churches in the neighborhood has placed an ad about upcoming special meetings. Without abandoning her happy mood, Virginia feels a sense of loss. She had formed a type of mental connection with that slim woman in the picture and with the slogan, which fit her own situation.

"I will miss her," she sighs. Minutes later, resuming her stride to get home, Virginia cannot recall any details of the church commercial. Years ago, she had attended church a few times with friends, but found the people different from the exciting life she is looking for.

Virginia spots a handsome stranger crossing the street. The success with the beauty contest has turned her into a bit of a flirt and she never misses a good-looking guy. Hastening her steps, she calculates that their paths will cross by the fire hydrant ahead.

Up close, the man's good looks and overall demeanor catches her off balance. She barely manages to address him. "Hello. I thought I knew everybody in Chelmsford." He smiles genuinely, but does not speak. Nervous and tongue-tied by his silence, Virginia continues." I have never met such a handsome fire hydrant by this man.... I mean ...such a handsome man by this hydrant...." she blushes and both enjoy an icebreaking laugh. Finally, an eternity later, the stranger steps closer, and says. "Thank you," adding a semi-serious warning. "Thou shalt not flatter a stranger in thy streets. By the way, looks come easy. I had nothing to do with that. The rest of life so far has been an assortment of hard lessons in trust and faith. Thankfully, peace comes with every victory."

Virginia, admiring his masculine baritone voice, another link in the chain of this man's charms, has no clue what this handsome hunk has said to her. Hard lessons? Trust and faith? Peace with every victory? She expected an introduction, a name, a comment about his business in town. Eager to make his acquaintance, Virginia stretches out her hand.

110

Chapter: 18

"I am Virginia, but please call me Ginny." As in a slow motion dream, she sees his hand extend and her own hand vanish in his firm grip. Then his lips part again. "I am Christopher Storm from Billerica. I want to see you again next week, Ginny."

Virginia, speechless and giddy with delight, reckons that she had misunderstood him. Her mouth dry and her lips superglued, she doubts that she heard him correctly. Did he really say that he wants to see her again next week? His beguiling smile, exposing a row of snow-white teeth, provides a perfect catalyst for a voice resembling the rumble of distant thunder. He points to a building a couple blocks away and explains. "Lord willing, I will be speaking at that church right over there every evening at 6:00 p.m., all of next week. I will look for you, Ginny." Leaving a befuddled Virginia behind by the fire hydrant, he turns and never looks back. Virginia fights back tears of disappointment. Why would this perfect specimen of a man waste his time with religion? He looks more like the president of a Fortune 500 Company than a preacher.

"What's wrong with you?" inquires Sherry, her good friend and roommate. Virginia, pampering a mood unfit for sharing, buries her frustration inside. How could she tell her friend that she has met the perfect man who turned out to be a stuffy, religious preacher?

"I don't want to talk about it," she says.

"Okay, fine Virginia."

"Don't call me Virginia," Ginny snaps back.

"Then talk to me. Whenever I give you the silent treatment, you lecture me on how friends can share everything with each other. So share."

"Alright; but don't laugh and don't tease me. I met this guy minutes before I got home."

"What guy? What is he like? Is he handsome? Are you going to see him again?" Virginia sends Sherry a disgusted look. "Do you want to listen or do you want to ask stupid questions?"

"Go, go, go Virginia…. I'm all ears."

"Don't call me Virginia." Shaking her head, Virginia stomps off toward her bedroom.

"No, no, no," Sherry begs. "Please, please continue Ginny."

"Okay, I met this guy minutes before I got home. He is crossing the street. He is not from Chelmsford and I really wanted to meet him, I timed my steps so we would arrive at this fire hydrant at the same time. Sherry, when he got closer, I almost fainted. He is the most gorgeous guy I have ever met in person. He is tall and tan, and has a perfect physique. Those blue-green eyes ... I can't even describe him."

"Go on Ginny, did you talk to him? Did you get his name? What happened?"

"You're doing it again, Sherry. You're not letting me tell the story."

"Sorry, Ginny, go on."

"Yes, we talked; and yes, I got his name. And before you ask, yes, he wants to see me again."

"So why the bad mood when you got home? What happened?"

"Well, he wants to see me next week... in church." She pauses, expecting a reaction, but Sherry eagerly draws circles in the air with her right hand, indicating for Ginny to continue.

"He will be preaching there every evening for a whole week. Can you imagine, such a hunk wasting his time with religion?"

"I am sorry, Ginny, but is that so bad? Many people are happy going to church. It may not be for you or me, but if you want, I will go with you so you can see him again. What is his name?"

"I am not sure I remember it right, but I recall that his first name sounds like a last name; something similar to Robinson or Christopher."

"What about his last name, Ginny?"

"Oh, I'll never forget his last name, because he took my heart by storm."

Sherry stares at her friend in disbelief. Excitedly she jumps off the couch and faces Virginia.

"Are you telling me that you met Christopher Storm from Billerica?" Virginia's heart pounding in her chest, yells,

"What do you know about Christopher Storm?"

"Girl," Sherry yells back. "years ago, before you and I ever found this apartment together, this guy dominated the news. Did you not read the papers, listen to the radio, or watch TV... Oh, I forgot, you only read novels, listen to rock radio, and watch sitcoms on TV. You could not care less about the news. I had no choice because my dad always watched the news and read the papers. That's when I learned about this Storm fellow."

"Well, Sherry, don't stop now. Talk to me. What about him?"

"The University recognized him as a child Prodigy who could read and write and memorize long poems and Scriptures by the age of six. Later he drove his teachers crazy with questions and proving their answers wrong. They kept advancing him in school. The boy got special training at the U and never went to a regular high school. He got an MA degree in Theology right here in Boston at age fourteen. Then he went right on to some University in Minnesota for his PhD. Now, as an adult, he is a legendary genius and still makes the news from time to time. You can find his By-line on all kinds of literature. I think most of his writings deal with the Bible and religious stuff, but he has also written many articles on various scientific subjects. Maybe we can find something in the library tomorrow. I want to listen to this man next week. What church….."

"Wait a minute, Sherry. He is my man. I found him." They both laugh and share a friendly hug.

"Ginny, I don't think he is anybody's man; except, maybe God's. So, Ginny girl, are we going to church next week?"

"Well Sherry, just try to keep me out of church next week."

In his hotel room, after meeting Virginia Hyatt, a strange apprehension, is troubling Chris. With the entire Bible in his memory bank, he scans the Scriptures for a justification. Does the remarkable beauty of that girl have something to do with his mood? He rehearses how the Bible deals with beauty. The Bible states that Esther was very beautiful. The Bible does not condemn a woman's physical beauty. How could it? God is responsible for the features of each person. Then the words of Jesus regarding the lustful look at a woman amounting to adultery in the heart register a complaint in his mind.

"But I am not married and neither is she," he disputes aloud.

"But you are engaged to be married to Pamela, remember?" An inner voice argues. Chris, a preacher with a PhD in Theology, shakes his head as he recalls Christ's words to Peter,

"Satan is trying to sift you like wheat." Regaining his peace and confidence, Chris meets Satan's attack by following Christ's example and quotes the Scriptures," Get thee behind me, Satan. Greater is He who is in me than he who is in this world." Not praying often on his knees, Chris makes an exception tonight. He kneels to thank his heavenly Father for a safe trip and for the inspired words of the Scriptures that cover every possible situation, life can offer. He reads a couple of new books he brought with him, then retires peacefully, and satisfied. As he drifts off into welcome sleep, he finds himself mumbling. "I wonder whether she'll show up at church Sunday."

As planned, Sunday evening Virginia and Sherry walk the short distance to the church. As they turn the last corner, they are amazed at the size of the crowd on the church grounds. Police officers are directing traffic and urging drivers of double-parked cars to move on. The eager young women learn that there is no more room in the church and that a truckload of chairs from another church is on its way along with some loud speakers for people left outside. Sherry spots the deep disappointment in Virginia's face and apologizes for failing to predict this scene.

"I should have known this would happen," she laments. "I remember reading that everywhere this guy preaches, he causes traffic jams. Do you want to go home and come back earlier tomorrow night, Ginny?"

"I am not leaving until I get to see this Christopher guy, even if I have to wait all night."

"Wow, Ginny," Sherry retorts, he really got to you. I have never seen you like this. Do you think he will even remember you? Wherever he goes, Christopher Storm attracts women. What are you hoping to accomplish by waiting around here?"

"I don't know, but I do know that I must meet him again. Maybe I am crazy, but I saw something in those blue-green eyes last Friday when we met. He has this penetrating gaze. Do you know what I mean?"

Sherry is amused. Mockingly she says, "no, Ginny, I don't have the slightest idea. Give me a hint, what do you mean?"

"Don't be daft, Sherry. It felt as though he is trying to figure out what I am all about. I must be out of my mind, but I will never forgive myself if I leave now without meeting him again." Sherry stares at her best friend in the way you stare at a stranger. When she sees the truck approaching with the load of chairs, she turns to tell Ginny, only to see her disappear in the crowd.

"Ginny, wait for me. The church is full. You can't get in." Sherry shakes her head. She might as well address the trees. Her best friend is paying no attention to her.

"It's not fair," she laments. "That girl always gets her way. I guess it pays to be gorgeous."

With a sweet smile and a sweeter voice, Virginia squeezes through the crowd. "Excuse me, please." Most women give her a malicious stare, but the men cordially step aside and let her through.

"Aren't you Virginia Hyatt, the beauty queen in the Boston teen contest?" one man inquires.

"Yes, I am. What's your name?"

"I'm Tom Beckman. I was one of the judges."

"Did you vote for me, Tom?" Ginny probes.

"Of course I did. Do you have an appointment with someone in the church? It is completely full, you know?"

"Yes, I know the speaker personally. He asked me to come tonight. I cannot disappoint him."

"I would be honored if you allow me to assist you."

"I would be forever grateful," Virginia chirps with the scheming charm of Delilah and winks at the man.

"Coming through at the request of the speaker," the man announces repeatedly, making room for Virginia who follows him. There are no empty seats and people are lining the aisles. Ginny whispers something into her guide's ear and to the crowd's amazement; she ends up seated in one of the chairs reserved for the clergy, on the stage. Several people recognize her and shout to congratulate her on her reign as a teen beauty queen in the Boston contest. Now Virginia does something the people of Chelmsford will gossip about for years. She walks to the pulpit, turns on the microphone, and makes an announcement. The speakers outside have been set up by now and the crowd of thousands listens in astonishment as Virginia speaks,

"Hello everyone, I am Virginia Hyatt. If you do not recognize the name, you must be a visitor to Chelmsford. Welcome! You are here to meet Christopher Martin Storm and to listen to the amazing message that he is about to share with us. He is a dear friend and I hope you will be blessed by the remarkable way he speaks about God and the Bible. Thank you."

The pastor, some deacons, and Christopher, located in an adjacent room, stare at one another.

"What is that all about, Dr. Storm? Did you know about this?"

Chris, normally quick, is completely baffled. "I met her on the street last Friday and invited her to attend the services. Who is she? Is she well known in town?"

One of the young deacons, Marvin Stern, offers the explanation and some background of this once famous young woman, who had won the Boston teen beauty contest and became the pride of Chelmsford. Chris rises from his chair to take care of this awkward situation, but Pastor Wellington warns him that his early presence on the stage could cause unpredictable behavior of the people who would recognize him. He asks Marvin to fetch Virginia and bring her into the prayer room.

Chapter: 18

Virginia's appearance in the doorway takes Chris back to Friday night. She was beautiful in her business suit; but today, in her yellow silk dress, she is stunning.

Chris remains seated, while Pastor Wellington questions Virginia about her unsolicited commercial over the speaker system. Virginia politely answers the questions. She apologizes, and asks permission to be excused. Pastor Wellington nods and Virginia returns to the platform, where she solicits volunteers to share their seat with her. In a matter of seconds, two men in Air Force uniforms offer her a seat between them.

Hearty applause greets Pastor Wellington as he and Chris appear at the podium. The pastor had planned a thorough introduction for Chris, but he gets no further than, "Allow me to introduce..." when Chris' hand on his shoulder stops him,

"Thank you Pastor Wellington. If you don't mind, introductions are kind of embarrassing." After people hear me preach, they will make up their own minds about who I am."

After his renowned stare at the congregation, he hints to a reason for this 'stare' exercise in a poetic way. "God's work of grace will change your face. Please open your Bibles to Mark, chapter 8, verse 35. I quote,

For whosoever will save his life shall lose it; but whosoever shall lose his life for my sake and the Gospel's, the same shall save it." Chris continues, "Nobody within the range of this microphone is here by chance. God wants you to hear and experience the essential truths found in the Bible. The quoted passage is unclear to some of you. If you do not understand its meaning, you might still accept it as a difficult truth. Let me assure you that living with a difficult truth is far better than living a lie.

Think hard! What drives you? Where do you concentrate your efforts? What is your goal or dream? Are you getting the idea? Most of us live for Number 1, for us. Nothing is more important than our own life. You probably want to ask, 'What is wrong with that?' What is wrong with that is the fact that Christ says, if we live only for ourselves, we are losers."

After Chris expands on these thoughts, in clear, direct terms, he explains the plan of salvation. He gives the invitation for people to come forward, confess their sin, and receive forgiveness. Dozens of people assemble on the platform. Chris bows his head and silently prays that everyone in this congregation would plead the words of David, *'Search me, oh God, and know my heart.'*

He watches people respond to the invitation. It blesses his soul. Pastor Wellington, moved by the response of the audience, shakes Chris' hand.

"What a gift God has bestowed on you, Dr. Storm. I am so looking forward to this week. If you don't mind, may I ask you a question?"

"Please, ask away."

"Why do you peruse the people every time before you speak?"

"I memorize their faces."

"Memorize their faces? You mean you remember how they look?"

"Yes, some are sad, some are proud; some are arrogant, and so on. While I preach, I watch for changes in their countenance. When God's Word impacts a person, their face changes." Pastor Wellington admits,

"Usually when I am introduced to a guest, I can't remember their face an hour later. That you can recall the faces of hundreds is amazing."

An hour later, when most people have left the church, Chris steps outside to see whether anyone there might still need help. He finds Virginia leaning against the building, waiting for him. She appears different to him. That proud look of self-importance has vanished. She greets Chris with genuine thankfulness in her voice,

"Your message has shown me who I really am, a sinner with selfish ideas, attitudes, and imaginations." With triumphant convictions, she adds. "Now I am a forgiven sinner and a child of God."

Chris senses her sincerity and is delighted and grateful to God for her testimony.

"You are also a sister in the Lord," Chris says and explains the meaning of the family of God. Virginia, her face glowing with anticipation, cautiously, asks. "Chris, are you married or attached to someone?"

Chris answers. "Ginny, I am so glad we met and I am grateful to the Lord that you have become part of the family of God. My fiancée, Pamela, is also part of that family."

Friday night, after the final meeting, Virginia finds Chris to say "Goodbye." They shake hands and part. On her way home, surprising herself, Virginia hums one of the tunes she learned this week. She thinks about Chris. How his character has impressed her. How a man so masculine and strong could be so kind and gentle. She sighs,
"I cannot have him…but neither can I let him go.

Chapter

19

When the pilot announces their imminent arrival in Minneapolis, it seems to Chris that they left Boston only minutes ago. The events of the past week in his native New England had expunged awareness of time.

Every incident and every word, smile, frown, laughter and tear shared with friends, family and strangers lingers in his extraordinary mind. There is the gratifying reunion with Rudy and Hilda, who had lovingly accepted the responsibility to raise him and care for his wellbeing and education.

Then there is the visit with his estranged father in prison. For the first time his dad had not interrupted him with abrasive words when he shared the need for repentance and restoration to God. Emphatically he told his father that only God can regenerate a man's mind to change him.

He remembers every struggling Christian, who confessed their failure to gain victory over certain sins and habits. How they embraced the reminder that victory over sin follows total surrender to Christ. It is the function of the Holy Spirit in them.

A proud awareness of accomplishments begins to occupy his thoughts. He is probably the youngest successful preacher and theologian in the world. Immediately Chris senses the Lord's rebuke.

"If you begin to seek your own glory, Chris, you will become useless to me." This inner, spiritual voice of warning also indicts Chris of improper reactions to Virginia Hyatt's physical beauty and charm. It is a betrayal of Pamela's faithfulness in their relationship.

The pilot's landing announcement offensively interrupts Chris' reflections. The feeling that something remains undone irritates him. Unsuccessfully he tries to put these thoughts to rest and turn his attention to Pamela and others who have come to welcome him back home. He has never been an effective pretender. He cannot hide his emotions from people and certainly not from Pamela.

Graciously enduring the well-meaning sentiments from the welcome committee, Chris settles back in the leather cushions of the University limousine with Pamela by his side. They exchange loving words and an occasional kiss. Pamela moves closer and practically sits on his lap when Chris whispers a reminder that they are not alone in the car. Her face red with displeasure, Pamela moves to the far end of the bench seat and wipes a couple of tears from her eyes. After a week of separation, she expected a pleasurable reunion. Why is her fiancé bothered by her tender attention?

This incident marks the beginning of many soul-searching moments about their relationship. Earnestly and frequently, Chris lingers in prayer, seeking solutions for his confusion about Pamela. The answer in his heart is always the same,

"You have allowed the physical beauty of a woman you hardly know to disturb the proper relationship with your fiancé, who has always been faithful to you."

In the end, his intimate knowledge of the Scriptures and the Spirit within him provide the conviction to accept God's faithful forgiveness and completely restore his relationship with Pamela.

He takes Pamela to one of her favorite restaurants and vows his complete devotion to her. He has never mentioned Virginia to Pamela. He prefers to keep that Chelmsford experience a matter of the past.

The ambiance of the restaurant, including a single red rose in a vase and a candle in the center of the private table seemed to Chris the perfect setting for his intentions to patch everything up between them. However, when Pamela gently reaches for his hands across the table, looks into his eyes, and asks a feared question, she crushes Chris' plans.

"Tell me the truth, Chris; did you meet another woman in New England?"

The brain of the young genius proposes dozens of evasive answers. Yet, convicted to do the right thing, he answers the question truthfully.

"Yes, I met the former Boston teenage beauty queen, Virginia Hyatt. I was attracted to Virginia, but I love you, Pamela. We are here tonight to renew our engagement vows to one another. Are you willing to forgive me for my behavior in the past few days?"

Pamela remains stone-faced. She does not flinch. She does not smile. She shows no reaction to Chris' confession and his resolve to renew their vows to one another. At this worst possible moment, the waiter appears to inquire if everything is okay. Receiving no answer, he tiptoes out of this embarrassing situation. Finally, Pamela tenders a determined smile and makes a request,

"For the rest of our lives, Chris, not another word about Virginia Hyatt, okay?"

Ignoring the other customers, Chris gets up, gestures for Pamela to rise, and answers her request with a hug and kiss. The cheerful applause of the other guests seals the successful rekindling of their relationship.

For several weeks, all remains well between them. Frequently they discuss wedding plans and their ideas about raising children. Would Pamela be a stay-at-home mom or would she assist with the financial support of the family? That question had a short life. Chris firmly states that mother and father, not strangers, will raise their children.

Near the end of April 1972, the loving couple faces a nightmare. Chris and Pamela would hereafter refer to that day as 'The day of the letter.' Like a Halloween scare, the large, white envelope occupies the center portion of Chris' office desk. It is not in the basket with the rest of the mail. Its presence in the middle of his desk seems to demand immediate attention. Chris glances at the return address: 'Virginia Hyatt.' "Oh no," he moans." This means trouble. What will this do to the promise to avoid her name forever? Keeping the letter secret would be equal to a lie. I must share it with Pamela." Chris stares at the letter as one would stare at a poisonous serpent.

"I could trash it," he reasons and throws the letter into the wastebasket unopened. In vain, he attempts to concentrate on the rest of the mail. He cannot put the letter out of his mind. Moments later, Tammy, his secretary, enters to deliver a few phone call memos. She spots the letter in the wastebasket and replaces it on Chris' desk.

"This must have fallen off your desk, Chris," she says in a tone, which celebrates her keen eye and the notion that Chris is lucky she came along when she did.

"Thank you, Tammy," Chris whispers, too late for Tammy to acknowledge. He decides that the best strategy would be to take the letter to Pamela so they can open it together. Yes, he reassures himself that is the right way to proceed. One noisy exhale later, he is back in full command of his senses. He calls Pamela and invites her to dinner.

"I want to share something with you, sweetheart."

"What is it, Chris? Share it now. You know I hate waiting."

"Well, consider this a great opportunity to practice patience. I will pick you up at 6:30."

Because it is her favorite restaurant, Chris takes Pamela to the same place where they had restored the failing joy of their engagement. Seated at a corner table, Chris introduces the purpose for the meeting by stating that he received a letter addressed to him, but that he decided that they must open it together. He places the letter on the table in front of Pamela. The moment Chris interprets Pamela's face he realizes his enormous misjudgment of the expected outcome. Her face turns red. Uninhibited by the presence of other diners, she yells at Chris and accuses him of breaking a promise. She never wanted to hear that woman's name again.

Before Chris can prevent it, Pamela storms out of the restaurant. They had not even ordered. Chris tosses a $5 bill on the table and runs after her when the waiter yells,

"Sir, your letter."

"Take it and burn it," Chris yells back.

"Sir, I cannot do that. It is an unopened piece of mail. It could be a Federal offense to handle it. Please take the letter with you."

"Okay." Chris grabs the letter, folds it twice so it will fit in his back pocket, and goes looking for his betrothed Pamela. He finds her, crying, on a park bench near his car. They exchange a long look, but neither of them speaks. Finally, Pamela, still choking on tears, reaches for Chris' hand.

"I am sorry, Chris. I embarrassed both of us in there. I never want to go back to that place." Chris nods, but says nothing. Pamela continues, "Do you still have the letter?"

"Yes, I do. I asked the waiter to burn it, but he refused, fearing that it may be a Federal offense."

"I'm glad he refused. I think to get Virginia out of our system I need to know what is in that letter."

"Are you sure, Pammy? We could destroy it and forget about it."

"Don't be silly. She will bother us again. I think we need to open the letter and if it requires a response, you must respond."

"Okay, if you feel up to it now, you open it." Chris pulls the crumpled letter from his back pocket and hands it to Pamela. She manages a phony grin.

"I can't open the letter; it may be a Federal offense."

"I love you Pamela, no matter what Virginia has to share; I am all yours and will be all yours forever."

"Turn away, Chris. If it is okay with you, I want to read it first. Then I will give it to you."

"Okay, Pammy. Go for it."

Chapter: 19

The next sound out of Pamela is hilarious laughter, followed by a strange statement. "Congratulations, Virginia. And by the way, you are very beautiful."

Chris rips the letter from Pamela's hand and joins Pamela in laughter and relief. An 8 x10 photograph shows Virginia, next to a man. The caption reads, 'Virginia Hyatt and Marvin Stern announce their engagement.' A personal note to Chris thanks him for the sermons, which led her to the Lord.

Her fiancé is the young deacon who ushered her from the podium into the prayer room after her unsolicited performance at the church microphone.

"There is a lesson here, Pammy. We didn't look before we leaped and we paid for it dearly."

"Well, Chris, but it turned out alright, didn't it?"

"No, it didn't. I am hungry, and we cannot show our faces again at our favorite restaurant."

"Are you saying you need fast food?"

"Yes, I am"

"Look over there. See the Golden Arches?"

"Pamela, are you willing to eat at McDonald's?"

"Of course, I will eat anywhere with my beloved."

"Big Mac, French fries, and side salad, here we come!"

The next day Pamela surprises Chris with the beautiful card she purchased for Virginia and Marvin. 'Congratulations on your Engagement. May the Lord bless your betrothal as He has blessed ours. Signed, Chris and Pamela Storm.'

"You are wonderful, Pammy. I think it's time we stop talking about getting married and pick the day so we can announce it to your parents, our friends, and the world."

"Do you mean it, Chris? Are we getting married this year?"

"Well, it takes two. I am ready. What do you say, Pammy?"

"Chris, I was ready the first time I met you. Can we make it soon? What do you think about around the end of July? I love July weddings."

"Pammy, I will leave all those details up to you and your parents. However, I have a suggestion for our honeymoon. After spending years in Minnesota, I have never visited Duluth. I recall reading a magazine article about the Great Lakes when I was a youngster. The waves of those five lakes touch the shores of seven States, plus Ontario, Canada. The largest one of the five, Lake Superior, is in fact the largest freshwater lake in the world. Do you agree that Duluth on the shores of Superior would be a great honeymoon destination?"

"O Chris, you will love Duluth with its alpine streets. We can reserve a hotel with great views of the lake. I will find us one of the best. I love your idea for our honeymoon."

Chapter

20

Gordon and Lillian Crane are enjoying a leisurely Saturday afternoon at home. Lillian is proud of her husband, a handsome, self-assured man, but sometimes likes to tease him and probe his reaction to outlandish statements.

"Gordon, I am more excited about Pamela's upcoming wedding than I was about our own."

"Well, you should be, darling. Pamela is marrying an internationally famous genius while you ended up with an Archeologist, playing in the dirt all over Egypt. And that reminds me, where would you like to have dinner on our upcoming anniversary?"

"Oh, Gordon, I love you. Nothing seems to shake your confidence. I thought you might want to wash my mouth out with soap after such a ridiculous statement. As far as our anniversary dinner, we have a couple of weeks to decide."

"I love you too, Lilli. When Pamela was born, things were tough for a while. Parenting did not come easy. Nevertheless, her arrival made us a family. Together, we built some wonderful memories. Now that she is about to leave the nest I know we will miss her. However, I am as excited as you are about their wedding plans. I do not fear that the two of us will suffer from the proverbial empty nest syndrome. Do you?"

"How do you feel about their rather sudden decision to get married so soon, Gordon? You don't suppose she is pregnant?"

"Lilli, did you forget who her fiancé is? That boy is so straight; he blushes at an off-color joke. I hate to admit it, but I trust him more than our sweet Pamela."

"I guess you're right. Pamela confided in me that he would not allow her to travel with him because it gives the wrong impression of their convictions and would stain their testimonies."

Chris and Pamela walk in and interrupt their cozy conversation. Gordon and Lillian greet them with a hug. It is late. They chat for a while and then Gordon and Lillian retire. Chris leaves a few minutes later. Gordon scratches his head.

"Did those two look different to you tonight?"

"Different? How?"

"They must have really enjoyed their date, because their faces seemed to glow like the full moon."

"They always look like that, Gordon. They are in love."

"Okay, if you say so. However, I think they did something special tonight and they want to keep it secret. I know my mischievous daughter. Her face betrayed some mystery; some secret."

"You are imagining things, Mr. Crane. Goodnight."

The next morning, Lillian answers an early phone call, "Crane residence." A man's voice asks for Pamela Crane. "I am Pamela's mother. May I ask who is calling?"

"I am sorry, I will call later." The man hangs up.

"Who was that, Lilli," Gordon wants to know.

"I don't know. He asked for Pamela, but would not give his name."

"Aha. Does that sound as though our little Pammy has a secret?"

"Why do you always have to be right about our daughter?"

"It's a Father-Daughter thing, my dear. Mothers get to shine in many other areas." Lillian tries to recall the man's voice. He has a slight accent, but she did not recognize him.

Chapter: 20

Later, at the breakfast table, Gordon and Lillian study their daughter's face. Lillian cannot hold back any longer.

"What are you so happy about, Pammy?"

"Well, what do I have to be sad about? I have wonderful parents, a great home, and a fantastic fiancé."

"And who is the man who called for you before the rooster crowed this morning?"

"Why didn't you tell me, mom? I was waiting for that call?"

"I just did. He said he would call back. Who is that guy?"

"Can't a girl about to get married have a couple of secrets? You will know soon enough." Gordon, smiling, answers that question.

"Of course, Lilli. Pamela will soon be on her own, making many important decisions. Let her practice now; before Chris can get on her back about the wrong ones."

"I'll have you know that Chris and I made this decision together. He can't get on my back about it."

"What decision is that, Pammy?"

"Oh you think you are so clever, Dad. Remember, every trick I know I learned from you and mom. My secret remains my secret."

The phone has not a chance to ring twice before Pamela answers, "This is Pamela. Okay, let me call you right back on another phone, Sir." With that Pamela, taking two steps at once, is off to her upstairs bedroom. Gordon and Lillian confide in one another that they have no clue what their daughter may be up to.

Chris stops by to fetch Pamela for a lunch date. Gordon recognizes the same sheepish smirk on Pamela's face that he saw two weeks ago.

"They are not just going to lunch," he says matter-of-factly. "They are up to something."

"There you go again," Lillian, teases. I did not notice anything. Only that they seem to have forgotten our anniversary. At least you did not forget. Thank you for that beautiful card you left on the nightstand.

Here is the one I bought for you. I could not find the right words on those commercial cards, so I added my own to complete it."

> A man, named Gordon, became my spouse.
> He shares my life and shares my house.
> When he goes to the Holy Land,
> He digs for treasures in the sand.
> But with him home it's sure to be
> A Happy Anniversary.

Gordon pulls his wife of thirty-two years close.

"Happy anniversary, Darling. I thank the Lord for bringing you into my life. We are good together."

Pamela and Chris are back two hours later.

"Mom and Dad," Pamela declares cheerfully, "Chris and I have a surprise for you. It is a gift from the two us. Well, I guess Chris financed most of it, but it was my idea. This gift comes with a condition. With strings attached, so to speak."

"Pammy, spill it already. I can't stand the suspense," Lillian begs.

"Okay, both of you come to the kitchen window." Gordon and Lillian gladly obey, but could not believe their eyes when they spot a brand new 1972 Mercedes 300 SL with a giant red ribbon around it. They owned a similar vehicle for many years, but after 250,000 miles, the car is due for replacement.

"Happy anniversary Mom and Dad," Pamela and Chris say at the same time. Gordon and Lillian are speechless.

"We can't accept that from you kids." Gordon finally utters. "You will have a lot of expenses of your own when you get married."

"With the University paying most of the expenses, I have been able to put away a few dollars," Chris explains. "That brings us to the condition attached to this gift," he continues. "Pamela and I would like to use the car for our honeymoon trip, if that is alright with you."

Chapter: 20

Gordon and Lillian exchange one glance and both shake their heads. "No way, kids, you are not driving our car anywhere. Where are the keys, Chris?" Not wishing his future father-in-law to outshine him, Chris answers,

"The keys are in my pocket and nobody's hands except mine and Pamela's will ever touch my pockets."

After hugs and hearty laughs, the foursome hurry to the shiny vehicle and with Gordon at the wheel, end up at one of the finest restaurants in Stillwater.

"Food and drinks are on us," he announces proudly. "Now don't be shy; make your order fit the celebration of this grand occasion."

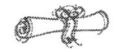

Chapter

21

Triggered by the generous anniversary gift, Gordon and Lillian Crane reciprocate by planning their daughter's wedding to be the most lavish event this area has ever witnessed. Two hundred twenty invitations go out to relatives and friends. In addition, the main bulletin board at the University includes a wedding invitation addressed to all faculty members and students who have attended any of Christopher's classes.

With the positive RSVP count at six hundred fifty, it became clear that Chris' students adored him and almost all of them will be attending the wedding.

The ballroom of a large hotel in south Minneapolis turns out to be ideal choice for this event. Minneapolis weather on Saturday, July 22, 1972 also cooperated with a median temperature of seventy-nine degrees. The festivities, covered by reporters from several newspapers and television stations, proceed perfectly until the sirens from emergency vehicles overshadow the dance music and grow louder until they stop at the hotel. Chris learns from a hotel employee that a man jumped from the third story balcony in a suicide attempt. He whispers something to Gary and the two hastily exit the room, leaving an alarmed Pamela and wedding party behind.

Chapter: 21

"Where are we going?" Gary asks on the way to his car. Chris' answer did not register with Gary right away.

"They probably took him to Fairview Hospital, a few blocks from here."

"Took whom?"

"The man who jumped from the balcony, Gary. We must find out what made his life so miserable that he would ignore Christ's offer for an abundant life and instead try to end his."

"Do you know him, Chris?"

"Of course not, but I know he is a lost soul. I need to talk to him."

"On your wedding day, Chris?"

"Gary, this man, if he is not dead already, could die any moment. Is any wedding more important than the Gospel truth we can share with him?"

The man is not hard to identify among the other victims in the emergency room. Apparently, he landed on his feet. His feet and legs were twisted and contorted into odd shapes. He is conscious, but moaning in pain. A doctor and a nurse are administering pain medication.

"Are you family?" the doctor inquires. Chris' reply produces a dumbfounded look on the doctor's face.

"Not yet. We will not be relatives until he becomes a member of God's family. I am here to share some facts with him, which can change him into a brother in Christ."

At that moment, a woman in the waiting room, waving a copy of a local Saturday newspaper above her head, points to Chris and shocks everyone with an announcement.

"That man is Dr. Christopher Storm. He is getting married today."

Like the name Billy Graham, 'Christopher Storm' has become a household word. People within earshot of that woman's announcement are now congregating around the area. Chris is about to demonstrate how to administer the truth in love. He speaks harsh words in a gentle and loving tone of voice, "Sir, you are a fool who has made a lot of mistakes in his life. Today you committed the most foolish act of them all. Did you not know that a leap from the third story balcony could turn out to be quite detrimental to your health?"

As some of the people giggle, the man's face remains sad and serious. Chris, turning to the crowd, continues.

"Can anyone here figure out why a person would choose eternal torment over an abundant life in Heaven? I have read, studied, and meditated on that subject and never found the answer. Please, anyone, can you help?"

A young man occupying an adjacent bed because a log splitter has severed three fingers from his left hand, speaks up.

"I don't believe in God." Chris turns toward him.

"Maybe not, Son. However, your philosophies are temporary. You will be face to face with God on Judgement day. Then you will believe. Can anyone quote John 3:16?" Gary, eager to do his part, jumps at the opportunity,

"For God so loved the world that he gave his only begotten Son, that whosoever believeth in him should not perish, but have everlasting life."

"Did you all catch that? Did you figure out your part? *'Whosoever believeth in Him."* Turning to the man crippled by the fall from the balcony, he adds, "My job is done here. We told you divine truth based on the authority of the Holy Scriptures. God is never willing that anyone should perish. The rest is up to you."

Chris and Gary hope to rush back to the wedding party, but first answer questions from reporters who followed them from the hotel. A small crowd from the waiting room surrounds them. Everyone wants to know more about his world famous memory gift. Chris is patient and kind, but states that this is his wedding day and he needs to get back to his bride.

"However," he adds. "Let me leave you with this: "Anything I know about God and his salvation through Christ is in the Bible. If you do not believe that the Bible is the Word of God, you are wasting my time. If you do believe the Bible is the Word of God, find one and read it. All the answers dealing with sin and salvation are in that book."

Chapter: 21

Ignoring any further advances by reporters and onlookers, Chris and Gary escape the flood of camera flashes and questions.

"There they are," someone yells as Chris and Gary rejoin the wedding party. Pamela's face is one big question mark. Chris' passionate hug returns her lovely smile. His promise that they will talk later is good enough for her.

The wedding guests continue to celebrate late into the night, but Chris and Pamela sneak away to their honeymoon suite. Pamela had the foresight of making reservations for the first night of their wedding in this hotel and reservations in Duluth for the next five days.

As Chris places the key into the lock of the honeymoon suite, Pamela notices that his hand is trembling.

"Are you nervous, sweetheart?"

"I have to admit it, Pammy. Yes, I am nervous. I am not sure exactly what will happen behind this door. We are totally inexperienced and I am nervous about being able to please you, darling."

"Oh, Chris, please do not worry about that. If Adam and Eve knew what to do, I think we will be able to figure it out as well."

"I love that about you. Words of encouragement seem to flow so naturally from your lips. I have always admired your thoughtfulness. I love you so much."

The heart-shaped bed with red and gold décor dominates the overall splendor of the room. White marble columns, each topped with a bouquet of red roses, are located on each side of the large picture window, and at the entrance to the stylish sitting room. Chris asks, "How much did we pay for this room, Pammy?"

"Are we going to discuss finances tonight, Chris?"

"No, I am sorry. Forgive me. Tonight we will enjoy one another."

The next morning, waking in the marriage bed, Pamela communicates the serenity of the moment with a sleepy yawn.

"I love you Chris," she says warmly. A sumptuous breakfast in the hotel dining room starts their first day as husband and wife. Neither can fully comprehend that they are now married. The waiter addresses Pamela as Mrs. Storm. Pamela gasps, "I am Mrs. Storm now," she whispers to Chris' delight.

"Yes, you are, and I am Mr. Storm."

Heading to Duluth, the new Mercedes performs magnificently. So smooth is the ride that Interstate 35W appears to be paved with velvet. To avoid reporters from invading their privacy, Pamela made hotel reservations under her maiden name. Nevertheless, reporter cameras and a crowd of spectators greet them at the hotel. The lighted billboard leaves no doubt where the famous couple is spending their honeymoon:

Welcome Dr. and Mrs. Storm
Congratulations Christopher and Pamela.

A Duluth newspaper had covered the wedding. Hotel management did not miss the opportunity to cash in on this advertising opportunity. Encouraged by the crowd, reporters urge the couple to schedule an evening at the hotel when the Duluth community could enjoy a demonstration of Christopher Storms world-renowned memory gift. Allen Larsen, the hotel manager, adds fuel to the excitement by offering free hotel accommodations and meals for the couple for the duration of their stay. Chris reasons that this decision needs Pamela's endorsement and when Pamela nods her head in approval, he shakes the manager's hand and suggests Tuesday Evening, 7:00 p.m., leaving all the details to the reporters and Allen Larsen.

To Mr. Larsen's delight, Tuesday Evening finds the hotel restaurant crammed. The largest conference room, furnished with 120 chairs, is filling up quickly. A small orchestra provides soothing dance music. However, perhaps for fear of forfeiting a seat, nobody is dancing. By 6:30 a.m. only a few, seats remain. At 7:00 a.m. sharp, Allen Larsen gets things started by welcoming his guests and introducing Chris and Pamela.

"Ladies and gentlemen, welcome to our fine establishment. We count ourselves fortunate to have Dr. and Mrs. Christopher Storm as our guests and are proud to present Dr. Storm's celebrated memory demonstration. Please welcome to our stage Dr. Christopher Storm."

Accompanied by wild applause and whistles, Chris makes his way to the stage and unsuccessfully gestures for silence. Finally, the applause subsides and Chris begins.

"I do not know what you have heard or read about my memory gift. I want to set things straight right from the start. All the credit for this gift goes to God. Therefore, my favorite memory demonstrations deal with the Bible. However, tonight I want to get to know all of you. I will attempt to learn all of your names and a few other facts about each of you. As you came in, our assistant, the lovely Jennifer, instructed you to print your name in a book. In fact, I see that a few laggards are signing the book as we speak.

Jennifer will now bring the guest book and take roll call. As she reads your name, please raise your hand, and then briefly stand up. I will attempt to remember your name, your face, and the location of your seat. When Jennifer has finished, I will give further instructions. Are there any questions?"

The only response is soft murmur; but then someone shouts,

"Are you really attempting to remember more than a hundred names after hearing them one time?"

"Yes, I will attempt to do that, if you promise not to lynch me if I get one or two names wrong." The laughter and hardy applause is encouraging and Chris is ready.

"Okay Jennifer, you're on." Jennifer steps to the microphone and begins reading names. In a few minutes, she completes her task and Chris continues his instructions.

"I recorded your names, faces, and seat locations in my memory. Now, if our paths ever cross again, I should be able to recognize you. In a few minutes, I will ask you to rise from your seats and congregate around this area. However, before you go, I have a couple of questions. "Ronald Anderson, are you left handed?"

The reply comes from the third row.

"Yes, I am, Sir, how did you know?" Chris ignores the question. "How about Linda Scott, Fred Donner, and Sandy Cruise, are you also left handed?" All three reply affirmatively from the audience. Sandy is stunned.

"Sir, how could you know that we are left handed?" Chris is enjoying himself as he replies,

"That is so simple. You all raised your left hand when Jennifer called your name."

"I have a couple more questions. Angela Fields, do you suffer from back pain or leg pain?'

"Yes, I have sciatica pains in my left leg and thigh. Please tell us how you do this stuff."

"Angela, when your name was called, you hesitated, and labored to rise. This is typically a sign of pain in the back or legs.

Now, the next demonstration is by far the easiest one. In my spare time, between these other observations, I have watched Denise Caldwell, here in the front row. This is my question for Denise. "Why do you think your company failed to show up, as they promised?" A perplexed Denise blushes, then answers.

"Dr. Storm, my boyfriend promised he would come. He is in big trouble. Will you tell us your secret?" Chris is happy to answer.

"I have no secret, Denise. You made it so easy. Since you took this seat, you have turned to check the entrance door seven times. You also placed your oversized purse on the chair next to you to discourage anyone from sitting there. I am sorry your boyfriend did not show. Please tell him that we missed him. Now, please everyone gather in the immediate vicinity."

The audience is having a good time. The lively chatting while people make their way to the floor is mostly about their doubt that any man could remember more than a hundred names and faces after a single exposure. Some remind others that Christopher Storm has demonstrated his abilities throughout the country and even in Europe. Yet many insist that it is impossible and seem willing to bet that Chris will fail in his attempt.

Chris taps the mike to gain attention. Holding up a handful of envelopes, he says,

"Jennifer has written your names on these envelopes. I put a card with a seat number into each one. I will find you in the audience, call you by name, and hand you an envelope. If I get your name wrong, please correct me right away, so I do not hand you someone else's packet. Please do not open your envelope until everyone has returned to their seat."

The multitude of surprise expressions heard as Chris addresses everyone by name and shakes their hand, indicates the absolute success of his demonstration. With an envelope in their hand, everyone returns to their seat. A few scuffles over seats, indicates that some people were not quite sure about their seat number. Chris teases as he addresses the people who failed to remember their seat numbers.

"You could have cheated by opening your envelopes to find the correct seat number. Of course, now we need to discover how many of you were involved in the short scuffles and may have ended up in the wrong seat. I watched closely. Four of you attempted to occupy the wrong seat. Before you open your envelopes, I have written the four names on a piece of paper and am now handing it to Jennifer. Please open your envelopes."

Prolonged applause once again indicates the success of the memory demonstration. Chris continues,

"This is all in fun, so I am asking three gentlemen and one lady to rise and indicate that they attempted to or actually occupied the wrong seat."

Encouraged by applause, four people stand up. As the applause dies down, Chris asks Jennifer to read the four names.

"Andrew White, Carl Taylor, Herald Fields, and Marjory Nyman"

"Andrew, Carl, Herald, and Marjory did we call out the correct names?" All give an affirmative answer. Chris pauses at the mike and looks over the audience,

"Ladies and Gentlemen, it is my custom at every opportunity to share a few words of good news. After reading and studying thousands of books, journals and magazines, I have concluded that the most important news for you and for me is found in the pages of the book called The Holy Bible. No matter who you are, I am confident that you have heard the name of Jesus Christ before. A couple thousand years ago, He was brutally crucified. God Almighty required the blood of a sinless human being to pay for the sins of all humankind. As Christ shed His blood on that cross, He exclaimed *'It is Finished'*. What did He finish on that cross? The salvation of everyone who sees the need of forgiveness for his or her sins and in faith accepts these facts.

You will find a stack of Bibles on the front table. If you do not own a Bible, please take one. I am done. The rest is up to you. I want to thank you for a fun evening and hope to see all of you again in God's kingdom, often called Heaven."

To Chris' delight, the applause is lively and seems sincere.

Pamela's schedule for this honeymoon trip includes leisure and rest for Sunday, Monday, and Tuesday. For Wednesday and the rest of the week, Pamela planned some of Duluth's historic attractions, such as the Leif Erikson Park and Rose Garden. Historians credit this Norwegian, Icelandic explorer with being the first European to land in North America, around 1000AD, before Christopher Columbus.

Also on Pamela's list for Wednesday is a dinner cruise on Lake Superior. Chris praised Pamela for her choices. He studies the statue of Leif Erikson at the Garden entrance long enough for Pamela to remind him that Leif's statue can be seen many other places, including St. Paul, near the capitol of Minnesota.

Chris and Pamela return to the hotel for a light lunch and relaxation before preparing for the dinner cruise tonight.

The tour boat is luxurious, completely enclosed, with large windows and climate control. Attractions along the Western shore of Lake Superior include the Glen Sheen Estate with the 39-room Congdon

Mansion. The mansion's only occupants are Elizabeth Congdon, an unmarried woman, age seventy-eight, and her nurse. The University of Minnesota manages the estate. In 1968, the University granted her a life estate. The life estate allows Elizabeth Congdon to live in the mansion until her death.

Chris thrives on the tour guide's historic elucidations. He knows that he will remember this dinner cruise for a long time. Other attractions are the Two Harbors Lighthouse, Gooseberry Falls, Silver Bay, Beaver Bay and many others.

While being seated for dinner, Chris recognizes a woman who was among the hotel guests during his memory demonstration. At that moment, the woman locates him and approaches.

"Dr. Storm, could I have a few private moments with you?" Pamela's look signals a warning, but Chris senses that this woman has a spiritual restlessness. He tells Pamela that he will return soon. Chris leads the woman to a quiet corner of the main deck and encourages her to share her concern.

"Dr. Storm,"

"Please, call me Chris,"

"Chris, I am dying of a dreadful disease, a result of my sinful lifestyle. I need clarification about the salvation process you mentioned at the hotel demonstration."

"Mrs. Wilder,"

"It's Miss Wilder, Chris, I never married."

"May I call you Greta?"

"Of course. I am impressed. You remember my name."

"Whether or not your disease is caused by your lifestyle is not important. The important issue is that you do realize the need for forgiveness of all your sins. The fact that you are contemplating salvation provides the starting point of your new life in Christ. God forgives all past, present and future sin. God demanded a sacrifice. Jesus Christ paid that sacrifice, when he spilled his blood on the cross."

"But you don't know what I've done and how I caused many people to betray their spouses throughout my adult life. I feel so dirty."

"Greta, Allow me to share a verse that I believe will be meaningful to you. It is found in the Old Testament book of Isaiah, chapter I, verse 18, *Come now, and let us reason together, saith the Lord: though your sins be as scarlet, they shall be as white as snow; though they be red like crimson, they shall be as wool.*"

"Chris, I have never read the Bible."

"Greta, before you can believe, you must know *what* you believe. I have told you how to claim salvation, simply by believing that Christ died for your sins. The Bible is your guidebook. I always carry a pocket addition. Please accept this and read it faithfully. Begin with the New Testament."

"Chris, thank you so very much. For the first time in my life, I sense hope. I do believe. I believe that I am forgiven, based on what we talked about."

When Chris and Greta return to the dining room, Pamela reads in their faces that something significant has taken place. Greta's face, sad and burdened earlier, seems to reflect a sense of freedom.

"What happened to her?" she asks.

"She learned about hope and salvation. She is a new person."

"I am so proud of you, Christopher Storm. And you know what?"

"What?"

"I love you,"

"Oh yeah? Prove it,"

"Prove it? I thought you were a man of faith.

Chapter

22

The honeymoon is over. Sunday, July 30, 1972 the newlyweds arrive in the home they purchased two months before the wedding. Located in Stillwater, close to the Crane residence, it is a lovely split-level with a walkout basement on the Minnesota side of the Hudson River. The home is only partially furnished and is without curtains or drapes. Pamela is not happy. Accustomed to luxurious furnishings in her childhood home and equally luxurious hotel rooms, she feels that marriage has handed her a demotion.

"Next week it's back to work," she laments. "When do *you* plan to get the rest of the furniture, Chris? I don't like living this way."

"Pammy, I hope you meant to ask when will *we* get the rest of the furniture."

"Yeah, okay. I guess I am in a grouchy mood today. I do not know why. Forgive me."

"We do not have much experience in furnishing a home. Do you think your mother could help?"

"My mother? You know how Mother does things. She hires an interior decorator and leaves it all up to him. I am going to do exactly the same thing. Problem solved"

"Won't that be quite expensive, Pammy?"

"Well, as you said, we have no experience so the interior decorator is the solution."

Chris sighs. His active mind visualizes dollar bills dashing across the threshold filling the pockets of designers and storeowners. He realizes that the financial management of this new family is bound to encounter conflict. He had a glimpse of Pamela's spending tendencies when she suggested the gift of the expensive Mercedes for her parents. He reluctantly agreed because Gordon and Lillian had insisted on paying 100% for the wedding. However, that expensive gift seriously depleted his account balance.

Unreasonable spending now could mean serious financial trouble. Would the matter of money become their first serious disagreement and result in their first fight as a married couple?

"Pammy, I think we need to think about this. I do not want to purchase furniture on credit. Right now, other than this home, we have no debt. I want to keep it that way."

"Who said anything about credit? Don't we have the money?"

"I think we can pay cash if we don't rush into anything and purchase things gradually as we can afford them. An interior decorator would push to furnish the entire home right now because they probably collect a commission on the products purchased. I think we should try our own ideas with the help of friends who have furnished their homes. What do you think?"

"Chris, look around. The kitchen table and the two chairs Dad found in his garden shed are now adorning our dining room. This furniture, if you have sufficient imagination to call it that, is eager to make the acquaintance of a dump truck. The tattered love seat would do dishonor to any thrift store. Do you really expect me to live this way? I would be ashamed to receive any visitors.

Fortunately, we do have a decent bed, but it sits in an indecent bedroom with no curtains or drapes, a paradise for window peepers."

"Pamela, we can hang a sheet, towels, or something over the window. We just got home from our honeymoon. Can we revisit this subject tomorrow, please? Why don't you come over here where two empty arms are waiting to squeeze you?"

"Okay Casanova, here I am."

Chris rises early Monday morning to fix a continental breakfast, which he delivers to the bedroom. Pamela is awake, stretching, and yawning.

The door chime interrupts Christopher's embellished speech intended to impress his wife on the first morning in their own home,

"It's breakfast in bed for my gorgeous wife…who on this blue planet has the nerve to disturb our peace this early?"

"Dr. Storm?" Chris nods.

"I am Francois Arquette, your interior designer at your service." The man speaks fluent English; but Chris detects a French accent. Briefly, Chris considers the man to be at the wrong address, but remembers that he addressed him by name.

"Monsieur Arquette, I did not call you. How do you happen to come to this house?"

"Dr. Storm, it was your mother-in-law who called me. For many years, I have designed and re-designed The Crane residence. Dr. Crane has placed an order with our firm. The order states that I am to work with you to recommend furniture and decorations for your home."

"Monsieur Arquette, there is some kind of misunderstanding. We are not ready to finance such an undertaking."

"You will be happy to know that Dr. Crane has requested that all the invoices be mailed to her. So may I come in?"

"I am sorry, but not today. Please leave your card. I need to discuss this with my wife and her parents before we can proceed."

Pamela is thrilled, but does not sense the same emotion in Chris."

"We can't accept such an enormous gift from your folks. It wouldn't be right."

"Chris, there is something you don't know about Mom and Dad. They are a lot better at giving than receiving. This decision to pay for our furniture makes them feel less guilty for accepting the Mercedes.

The day we showed up with the gift-wrapped car, I saw the same look in their eyes I have seen a few times before. When Grandpa paid for all the tools and equipment Dad needed for his job as an archeologist, Mom and I heard about it for days. He was wondering how he could secretly repay him. Grandpa had inadequate insurance when he ended up in the hospital with a heart attack. Dad made an arrangement with the hospital to send all the uncovered bills to him, insisting that Grandpa would never find out."

"Your parents have unquestionably learned the biblical principle of holding all their possessions God has provided in an open hand, ready to give where there is a need. Let's invite ourselves to their house tomorrow night and discuss this whole matter."

Chapter

23

Winter in Minnesota holds many challenges. Driving on ice-covered roads is not the least of these. Pamela's job as a legal secretary at a St. Paul Law Firm requires a daily commute on busy Highway 94. There are records of frequent multi-car pile-ups during the winter months on major Minnesota Highways such as Interstate 35W and Hwy 94. In January Pamela becomes a victim of such a car pileup, involving fifty-three vehicles. She witnesses major injuries and the death of a young man. Her car, only slightly bumped by another vehicle, has caused her no physical harm, but emotionally she suffers a serious setback.

Since Pamela is physically unhurt, when Chris arrives at the scene he ministers to several victims before returning to her. He finds her crying hysterically and is unable to comfort her. An ambulance driver stops near them and insists that Pamela needs professional care. Chris agrees and follows the ambulance in his car.

This is the second time in a matter of months that Chris sees the predicament of accident victims. Some were in shock and seem to feel no pain while others whimper and still others cry aloud. Pamela is in the same emergency room with many of these victims until she pleads for a different room. The scene is too much for her. Chris sits by her bedside, holding her hand; he speaks gently and assuredly to her, pledging that all will be okay. The medication works swiftly, calming Pamela. As she dozes off, Chris takes the opportunity to share the saving message of the cross of Christ with many of the victims. He fetches a few Bibles from the car and hands them out to several patients.

Pamela is discharged the next day and eager to go home with her loving husband. His gentle manner in caring for her and the love and sincerity in his eyes revealed a side of Chris she had not known before. He is the kindest and most gifted man in the world to her. This incident raises her respect for this world famous genius and she considers herself fortunate to be his wife.

The memory of the tragedy she witnessed on Hwy 94 leaves Pamela less than eager to return to work. She also needs to determine why she missed her monthly cycle again this month. Pamela has kept that fact secret, but now decides to share it with her mother before returning to work. Lillian Crane is all smiles.

"Are you going to make me a Grandma, sweetie?" Pamela seems surprised.

"You mean I could be pregnant, Mom?" Lillian kisses her daughter's forehead and says,

"That is normally the reason a woman misses her period, Pammy."

The aged family doctor settles that question with that famous prophetic announcement, "You are going to have a baby, my dear. I would say around the middle of July. Years ago your mom and I worked together to deliver you. I never thought I might live long enough to deliver the second generation baby." Both women thank Dr. Saarlander and add a friendly hug for the man who has served the Crane family for so many years.

That evening at the supper table, Pamela is unaware that Chris has studied her face for several minutes.

"Okay Pammy, out with it."

"Out with what?" she teases.

"You've got something to tell me."

"How do you know, Chris?" She asks with genuine surprise.

"Remember, I got an A-plus in Psychology. Your face gives you away. You are harboring a secret."

"Well, it's not much. It's just that we have to go shopping."

"Shopping?"

"Yes, shopping for baby furniture."

"Come here, you, you wonderful creature." Chris exclaims, ignoring the fact that in his excitement, he upset the bowl of tomato soup, spilling it all over the table. After discussing this and that about this new phase in their marriage, Chris announces some news of his own by asking a question.

"How would you like to spend part of the winter in Arizona?"

"Arizona? How? We have jobs here."

"Dr. Lovett, the senior pastor of a large Sun City Bible Church in Arizona, called today. He is the spokesperson for three other churches in that area. I am expected to accept their invitation to spend a week at each church, speaking every evening from Sunday to Friday. That means a whole month in sunny Arizona. I told him that I would miss the snow, the cold days, and the icy roads in Minnesota. He accused me of lying, so I quickly recanted and said I will come, but only if I could bring my wife."

"When, darling, when are we going?'

"The meetings are scheduled for February 11th through March 4th. Will this interfere with any doctor appointments or any issues as far as the baby is concerned?"

"No, it won't. The baby is due the middle of July; there is no conflict. I love it, I love it, I have never been to Arizona. This will be so much fun. Finally, I can be part of your speaking ministry where you meet these beautiful young women."

Chris, not amused by that remark, nevertheless answers with a fitting retort.

"This time the most beautiful woman is traveling with me. I am convinced that she and God will watch me and assure proper behavior."

In preparation for the trip, Chris finds substitutes for his classes at the University. Because Pam and Chris have decided that she will not work outside the home while raising their children, Pamela terminates her position at the law office.

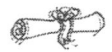

Chapter

24

The temperature on Friday, February 9, 1973 at the Minneapolis airport reaches a low of twelve degrees, cold enough to turn water into ice and rain into snow. In Phoenix, a sunny blue sky has driven thermostats at the airport into the seventies. By the time Chris and Pamela retrieve their luggage and climb into the waiting limousine, they have removed long sleeved clothing. This is their first encounter with summer temperatures in February. They love it.

Relaxing in their comfortable hotel room, they recall some of the nasty Minnesota snowstorms in March, April and even occasionally in early May. They learn that Arizonians call temporary residents from the colder states 'snowbirds' and Pamela remarks that they can call her anything they wish, as long as she can spend the winters in a place such as this. Chris agrees.

"I have read about winter temperatures in Arizona, but I much prefer feeling sunshine on my skin to reading about it."

Saturday morning Dr. Lovett, pastor of Sun City Bible Church invites them for dinner at his home. They learn that residents in Sun City enjoy memberships in several county clubs featuring swimming pools, golf courses, parks, a manmade lake, hobby workshops and much more. However, there is a catch. Sun City is a retirement community. Residents must be fifty-five or older. Nevertheless, as their guests, they can share all these benefits for the duration of their stay.

The advertisement for the meetings, with a photograph of Chris, allows people to recognize him even before his first sermon. People stop them as he and Pamela enjoy a stroll in the park by the lake. Phoenix newspapers sent reporters to Massachusetts when his fame as a Boy Prodigy spread across the nation. Some older folks remember the stories. They are eager to meet that man in person and treat him as a celebrity. Chris answers many questions and patiently signs autographs, always adding a Bible verse.

Pamela is proud of her famous husband and exuberant when a young woman asks her to autograph an article Chris had published. Even when that woman requests that she should sign the autograph as, 'The lucky wife of Christopher Storm,' she beams and wittingly signs it, 'Pamela, the lucky woman who carries Christopher Storm's baby.'

Later that evening, when people ask Chris whether the woman claiming to carry his baby, is his wife, he is baffled. He has told no one that Pamela is expecting. Back at the hotel, Pamela admits to spreading a bad joke, which could throw doubt on Chris' reputation. She apologizes. Chris never holds a grudge and the thing is quickly forgiven and forgotten.

Sun City Bible Church prepared for an overflow crowd. Flagmen direct all vehicles to the parking lot of the church across the street. Their own parking lot is equipped with chairs and benches, large TV screens and speakers. This arrangement can seat 7000 people. Police officers and volunteer fire departments are on duty to direct traffic and maintain order.

With all the seats occupied long before the scheduled start time, several young people sit on the brick wall surrounding the parking lot. Police officers consider the wall, about six feet high, and eight inches thick, unsafe and order the youngsters down. However, no sooner do they drive kids from one area that they pop up in another. The authorities are not to blame when a fourteen-year old boy falls from the wall backwards sustaining severe head injuries.

Pamela and the pastor's wife, Mrs. Lovett, plus several other women in the group are crossing the parking lot when emergency personnel place the boy into the ambulance. Pamela, seeing the boy's cracked skull begins sobbing uncontrollably. The women try to comfort her, but Pamela turns pale, becomes lightheaded, and loses consciousness. Mrs. Lovett, walking next to her grabs her in time to ease her onto one of the benches. Addressing the other women, she suggests that Chris should not learn of this incident until he finishes his sermon.

Several emergency vehicles are on site. The ambulance with Pamela, accompanied by Mrs. Lovett, leaves minutes later.

Inside, Chris addresses his powerful message to Christians, with this opening line,

"Some Christians are so full of themselves that there is no room for God's Spirit to work in their minds and hearts." He continues by quoting many of Christ's profound statements, often lost in the bottomless pit of the fleshly human mind. He reminds the congregation that if they are not for Christ they are against Christ. No one can serve two masters and whosoever shall seek his life shall lose it. He observes a sea of serious faces when he states that in the average church congregation there are less than 10% of Christians determined to live a righteous life. Many greedily pursue worldly possessions, ignoring the fact that riches have wings. He states that less than 1% of Christians actually manifest the fruit of the Holy Spirit, who is within every born-again person. In closing he says,

"Tomorrow night, God willing, we will discover the tremendous change that takes place in every completely surrendered Christian."

Not finding Pamela in the audience, Chris is eager to learn what happened to her. Mrs. Lovett cautiously informs him that Pamela fainted, but is now peacefully resting in room 302 at the hospital. She escorts Chris to hasten the reunion with his frail wife. Pamela is still pale and shaky, fighting tears. Sorrowfully, Chris realizes that Pamela is a weak and vulnerable woman, who may experience emotional setbacks with every unpleasant situation in life. Deep in thought about this fact, he reasons that is why God chose him for her. I am supposed to supply the strong shoulder to cry on and lean on. Silently he prays," I need your help, Lord"

All six services at the Sun City Church go well. Chris cherishes the comments from many members who have determined to leave their lukewarm Christianity behind and live a life totally surrendered to God's leading.

The following Sunday, Chris ministers in nearby Peoria and is blessed with the results there as well. Pam feels better and attends every service. She finds strength and determination in her husband's authoritative preaching. Pamela once told a friend that when Chris preaches, she feels the way Mary must have felt, sitting at the feet of Jesus and hanging on every word. "I am no Martha, messing around with the dishes while Jesus is in her house proclaiming one truth after another."

Thursday evening after the service, Chris and Pamela are enjoying a Prime Rib dinner at Coco's Restaurant when Pamela abruptly places both hands on her stomach and hurries to the Ladies' room. Sensing that Pamela may need help Chris askes Belinda, their server, to check on her. Belinda reappears at the table in a minute.

"Dr. Storm, you must go to your wife now. I think she had a miscarriage."

Belinda calls an ambulance, which arrives within minutes. This is the second time within a few days that Pamela needs emergency health care. Chris sits on the edge of Pamela's hospital bed. It is difficult for him to see his wife so defeated, fearful, and depressed. Will Pamela recover emotionally from the tragic loss of her baby? Will her disposition affect their ministry? Will it be an impediment to his preaching? Never before did Chris entertain such questions about his call to the ministry.

Chapter: 24

Friday evening, Chris reluctantly ends his visit with Pamela in the hospital. Driven by his sense of duty, he returns to the hotel to dress for the final meeting at the Peoria assembly. Pamela perceives his hesitancy. She has never seen him so uneasy. Concerned, she asks,

"Is something the matter, Chris?"

"There isn't time to explain, Pammy. Tonight I go with a heavy heart." On the way to the church, Chris tries to make sense of his reluctance to preach tonight. Since he was seven years old, with child-like faith he had accepted all the memorized promises and deeds of God. Love, joy, peace, and patience were constant realities that carried him through even the most trying phases of life. Why did Pamela's depression over the lost baby and the gloomy view of their future strike him so hard?

His adversary, the devil, seemed to use the Scriptures to assail his mind with accusations. Did he make the best choices in life? Why did he marry when the 7th chapter of 1st Corinthians clearly warns that marriage could be a detriment to the ministry of a preacher?

'He that is unmarried careth for the things that belong to the Lord, how he may please the Lord: But he that is married careth for the things that are of the world, how he may please his wife (1Cor 7:32-33).

After the meeting, Chris is alone in the rental car in front of the hotel. He knows that doubts and fears have caused a shift in his tone at tonight's service. He cries out,

"Lord, you ordained marriage. Why are these Scripture passages turning into torture? Is my love for Pamela wrong? Lord, I am weak. Powerful sermons have turned into hollow idioms. Tonight, doubts and fears have replaced the power and confidence your faithful Spirit desires to lay on the heart of every preacher and disciple. Father, what causes this weakness and mental persecution? Lord, guide me to recollect the fitting Scriptures for this moment. Once again, the inspired words of the Apostle Paul come to his rescue. *Therefore, I take pleasure in infirmities, in reproaches, in necessities, in persecutions, in distresses for Christ's sake: for when I am weak, then am I strong (2 Cor 12:10).*

With new strength and a fresh conviction of his calling, Chris gets out of the car. Somehow, he senses that this experience of weakness will help to fashion the sermons scheduled for the church in Youngtown next week and the final one in Glendale.

The hospital discharges Pamela Saturday morning. Chris arrives to take her to their temporary home in the hotel. Pamela greets him with a tender embrace and a confident smile.

"Did you settle things between you and the Lord, sweetheart?"

"We had words and I told him that where He leads me I will follow. It seems that is what He wanted to hear. I have peace again."

Sunday morning, Chris is happy to meet the challenge of preaching at the Youngtown Church. Pamela is by his side as the leadership greets them. The congregation is a rather young group compared to the folks in Sun City.

Pamela is astonished how her husband can preach unique sermons every single time. There is not a hint of a 'canned sermon' in his preaching tonight.

During the customary 'Storm Stare', as people have nicknamed his short silence before each sermon, Chris notices four well-dressed older men, sitting together. They seem out of place among this young, mostly casually attired, congregation.

Chris begins his sermon with an opening passage, he never used before.

"He that hath an ear, let him hear what the Spirit saith unto the churches; To him that overcometh will I give to eat of the tree of life, which is in the midst of the paradise of God." Chris continues, "I see a number of young people here tonight. The Bible has a special message for you. This is the advice of the Apostle Paul to his young coworker, Timothy, *Let no man despise thy youth; but be thou an example of the believers, in word, in conversation, in charity, in spirit, in faith, in purity.*"

Then Chris addresses the problem of unspiritual preaching.

"A man who seeks to minister to others, must be a man completely surrendered to God. A preacher promoting his own agenda and labeling it the 'Word of God,' is guilty of blasphemy. Only the true Spirit of God can minister to your spirit. The rest is idol worship. This is a harsh message of truth. Receive it in the Spirit of love."

Before closing in prayer, Chris studies the faces of the four older men. He guesses that they are scouts sent out from the church in Glendale, where he is to minister next week. They seem to be pleased.

Every evening, in Youngtown and the following week in Glendale, hurting people come forward to confess their doubts and depression. Many leave with their faces shining with new hope, confidence, and assurance of eternal life.

Reporters were present at every sermon and their newspapers columns claim to have witnessed the most powerful preaching anywhere during the 1970's. One Christian magazine listed the history of failing churches since the 1950's, but added that the number of church buildings have not declined to the same degree as the memberships. The author of the article added that a serious lack of true, Spirit-filled Christians in the modern church renders the church powerless to influence the world for Christ.

Chapter

25

Back home in Minnesota, Chris and Pamela, although neither verbalized it, become aware that something has changed in their relationship. At first, it is not anything so specific that either can list it on a piece of paper. General everyday conversations seem mechanical, less intimate. At times, both struggle for a meaningful subject to discuss. Nevertheless, soon the issues surface when Chris addresses them.

"You are visiting your parents more often than ever before, Pamela. Some evenings when I get home from work, you are not here. May I ask why?" Pamela is ready with her response.

"Chris, you may not realize it, but when you come home from work, you are not the cordial, happy person you used to be. May I ask why?"

"Touché; you are right." Both manage an awkward smile betraying the fact that they are grateful for this honest, overdue exchange.

"I guess I go to my folk's house often because I can talk to Mom about anything and she is always helpful."

"Are you saying that you cannot talk to me about those things?"

"You often seem busy and in deep thought. About what exactly, I cannot guess. Maybe you blame me for the miscarriage and the fact that I failed to give you a child." Pamela bows her head and quietly sobs. Chris moves next to her on the couch and puts his arms around her.

Chapter: 25

"Pammy, I never blamed you. In fact, I blame myself. Maybe I should not have taken you on that trip to Arizona. Maybe you needed more rest."

"Chris, what is it then? You are not the contented, happy person I knew before that Arizona trip. We got back in March. Now it's June. Something happened in Arizona that changed you."

"Pammy, I feel now that teaching at the University is the wrong profession for me. I used to enjoy teaching, but after the successful ministry in Arizona, where God changed the lives of so many people, I feel called to do more preaching. With God's gift of this supernatural memory, it would not be difficult to learn a foreign language. Maybe God wants me to serve in another country." Pamela's next question takes Chris by surprise. It did not seem appropriate for the current discussion.

"Do you still want children, Chris?"

"I do, but I wondered whether you were afraid to try again. Recently you haven't cuddled up to me the way I remember."

"Isn't cuddling a two-way street?"

"Yes, but a guy needs a little encouragement. Those long flannel nightgowns you have been wearing to bed lately send the wrong message."

"Well, the nights have been cold, Chris."

"Exactly. Your thick flannel nightgowns make the nights cold. Have the moths eaten the negligées I used to bring home?"

"You 'used to' bring home, with the emphasis on 'used to'. If you bring home a new one tomorrow, let us see what happens. Anyway, we need to discuss how your hopes for traveling throughout the world harmonize with plans for raising children."

"It's getting late. Let us save that heavy subject for another day. God will work it out for us, as long as we are together on this."

The next evening, Pamela emerging from the bathroom, in a slinky negligée, becomes the spark that ignites the passions held hostage by recent moods.

"Pammy, darling, you are the beloved described in the Song of Solomon; so soft, so warm, so tender, so loving, so perfect." Chris is holding her in a tight embrace when Pamela adds,

"And so destitute for air to breathe."

Chris apologizes,

"I am sorry, Pammy; did I squeeze you a little too hard? I think I am trying to make up for lost time. Tomorrow, before I rush off to work, let us meditate on the love chapter. Maybe we can resolve to love the way God loves us."

"I assume you are talking about 1st Corinthians, chapter 13. I feel so limited, so deficient, every time I read that part of the Bible. Can anyone here on earth love another with that kind of love?"

"Maybe not, but everyone can determine the most urgent need for improvement. Let's approach it that way tomorrow, okay?"

"Okay, Professor Storm. See you in class."

The next morning, after much meditation about the qualities of true love, the discussion turns to present and future events. Verbal exchanges about raising children, changing jobs and future endeavors remain in the jungle of uncertainty. If Chris were to accept speaking invitations from around the globe, would Pamela travel with him? Would the whole family travel when children are born? Would royalties from his writings be sufficient to sustain them? Chris never seems to worry about such things, but Pamela is uneasy.

"Chris, our friends and family are here in Minnesota. Could we stop talking about moving anywhere else?" As is typical for Chris, he does not answer right away. Instead, he takes Pamela into his arms and studies her face.

"I don't want to do anything to hurt you, Pammy. I think you agree that we must both trust God to guide us in all these important decisions. It will be a test of trust for both of us. Would it not be wrong and foolish to worry about something that might never happen?"

"You are my rock, Chris. I will trust God and I will trust you."

Chapter: 25

The test comes at once. On his desk at the University, Chris finds two letters with foreign stamps. One is from a large church in Winnipeg, Canada with a regular attendance of over 5000 people, inviting him to hold evangelistic services for one week. In addition, they wish to consider him as an applicant for the position of senior pastor to replace Dr. Sorenson who passed away suddenly.

The other invitation is from London, England. Chris published many articles on Theology and Science in Europe. His name is familiar throughout the region. This very prodigious London University is offering Chris a position as Dean. The stated salary for this position is noteworthy. However, for Chris, money has never played a significant role in processing a decision.

Pamela's regular greeting,

"How is your day, Honey?" does not seem to carry the same pleasantness Chris has come to esteem. He pulls her close. "Is something wrong, Pammy?"

"No, it's nothing."

"I have not learned to accept the fact that *nothing* clearly means *something*. Please tell me what is bothering you."

"Let's talk about it over dinner, Chris. I do not want to burden you with silly problems the moment you walk into the house. I am sure you have other things to worry about; especially our uncertain future."

"Sweetheart, you know I do not worry about our future. However, it so happens that there is something we must discuss."

"What is it, Chris?"

"Patience, my love; we'll discuss it over dinner." Chris' table prayer includes a plea for guidance in the decisions that lie before them. Pamela does not miss much.

"What decisions, Chris?"

"Please pass the gravy, Pammy."

"Chris, what decisions?"

"Pammy, you dropped a clue earlier when you mentioned an uncertain future. I believe that is the reason you were in a troubled mood tonight. You are wondering whether I will move us out of Minnesota. Is that it?"

"Yes, that is part of it. I keep wondering why God took our baby and whether we will ever have a family settled down in a comfortable home, near our friends and relatives."

"Pammy, I have preached all over the country about true faith and trust in God. Have I failed to encourage you to practice this same faith and trust? Can you not rest in the power of true faith and leave our future totally in the hands of the Lord?"

"You have not failed to preach to me; but please do not preach to me right now. I do not have your kind of trust and I do not know what to do about that." Upset, Pamela flees to the bedroom and slams the door behind her. Chris rests his head in both hands and whispers a prayer for his wife. He understands her. A good wife's center of interest is the home and family. A man spends a great deal of time away from home and finds his life's objective in his work. He has seen other couples struggle with the exact same issues. He decides this is not the time to discuss the invitation from Canada and London. We must spend this evening in tender hugs and gentle conversation about the true love we have for one another and the good times we have shared.

A few days pass. Pamela has prepared one of Chris' favorite meals. Chris carefully picks the moment when the time is right to discuss his invitation to Canada.

"How would you like to take a trip to Canada, Pammy?"

"Why Canada, Chris?"

"Because the deacon board of a large church in Winnipeg has invited me to speak there."

"You mean for a week, like your other speaking engagements?"

"Yes; it is only about 450 miles from here. We could drive. What do you think?"

"You obviously want to go. Otherwise, you would not have brought it up." Chris concedes,

Chapter: 25

"I have never been to Canada. It would be okay with me, but only if you come along."

"I guess I don't have any reason not to accompany my famous husband as he adds yet another country to his list of worldwide travels."

Chapter

26

Chris and Pamela leave Minnesota for Winnipeg around 9:00 a.m. on Thursday, July 12. They plan to stay in Grand Forks, North Dakota, leaving about 150 miles for the second day. The car performs well and the trip turns out to be an excellent opportunity for discussing many overdue subjects.

In Grand Forks, they check into a five star hotel. The restaurant features a prime rib special, one of Pamela's favorite dishes. For desert, a slice of strawberry cheesecake and a tasty cup of coffee provide a perfect finish of a good day.

The Winnipeg Hotel reserved for them is within walking distance of the enormous church property. Various buildings spread over eight acres of prime land with four acres reserved for parking. Chris and Pamela have never visited a church of this size. Such magnitude is overwhelming. Chris, ignoring the fact that Pamela is not aware of the senior pastor's position offer, makes an untimely remark,

"Just think, Pammy, this could be our new home. I could be preaching to thousands every week." That comment strikes Pamela as odd.

"What are you talking about, Chris?"

Chapter: 26

"Well, their senior pastor, Dr. Sorenson, passed away suddenly a short while ago and they are interviewing pastors to replace him. They encouraged me to consider the position."

"Christopher Storm, if you withheld that bit of information on purpose, I should think there is good reason for me to be very angry with you. Chris, just say that you do not consider applying for that position, and I'll be okay."

"Can't we even discuss the matter, Pammy?"

"Really, Chris, if you want to play such games with the future, you should have remained single. I am not a ping-pong ball; I am a wife and an expecting mother."

"Pammy, darling, are you pregnant?"

"No; but I expect to get pregnant; and for that I need you to live where I live and I certainly don't live in Canada."

"But Pammy, you see that lady over there getting out of that red car? She is pregnant and I assume that she got pregnant in Canada. I have all the confidence that we could get pregnant in Canada as well."

"You are joking, but I am really angry with you for keeping this job offer a secret. I am not moving to Canada and that is final."

"I am sorry, Pammy. There was never a good time to share this important piece of news. Although you have often stated that I must be the main decision maker in the home, I do not want to act on such an important move without your consent. I will not accept this position unless we agree to take this giant step in our career together."

"Come here, you handsome hunk of a husband. As you said a few days ago, our future is in God's hands. Let's hope He shares His decision with both of us so I do not have to set you straight."

Wherever Chis speaks, the churches run elaborate advertisement campaigns. Chris pays no attention to them. Saturday night Darrel Greenwood, the chair of the deacon board, calls,

"Dr. Storm, you may have been wondering about the details of the announcements in our bulletin. We also sent out 5000 flyers, and placed ads in several newspapers and on several radio stations. They read as follows:

'The Legendary American Biblicist, Dr. Christopher Storm, will be the speaker in the main auditorium every evening at 6:00 p.m., beginning Sunday, July 15 through Friday, July 19. We will introduce Dr. Storm to the congregation in our 10:00 a.m. Sunday Morning Service. Please come and meet him.'

"Are you ready for this challenge, Dr. Storm?"

"Mr. Greenwood, I hope the people who want to hear a legendary preacher will stay home to allow room for those who want to learn about the legendary, Almighty God. I will be glad to address the congregation for a few minutes Sunday morning, to let them know what to expect from the evening gatherings."

Four acres of parking space did not begin to hold the cars and busses carrying members and visitors to the Sunday morning service. To avoid the crowd, Chris and Pamela leave the hotel at 8:00 a.m., but their plan fails miserably. Many people, who also left early, recognize Chris in the parking area. Some ask for his autograph. Others want information about his gift of memory. Only a few have questions of a spiritual nature. Chris often grieves over the statistic that his gift of memory is more popular than his preaching about Jesus Christ, the Savior of all humanity.

After his introduction, Chris takes the microphone and begins with his now famous gaze at the congregation, which people have nicknamed 'Storm Stare'. For a whole minute, his eyes go back and forth across the huge audience. Knowing that a preacher must never go beyond the written word, he silently prays for the Spirit of Christ to guide his thoughts and his tongue. Then he begins,

"Because you came to church this morning, your unsaved friends and neighbors consider you *religious*. There are masses of people who are religious, but lost. Some of you may be unsure of your salvation. If this statement offends you, perhaps you are hiding behind a facade of religion.

I cannot remain silent about the difference between Christians who offer mere lip service and Christians who are truly regenerated by the Holy Spirit. If you do not want to hear the tremendous message penned by the Apostle Paul, in the book of Romans, then do not come back tonight."

As Chris turns and walks off the platform, an ominous silence turns the air dense. Did he overdo it? The thunderous applause that follows seconds later, relieves his apprehension.

Pamela is always Chris' source of feedback. "Wow, Chris. You scared them for a minute. However, judging by the applause, the place will be crammed tonight."

All afternoon, Chris meditates on the book of Romans from memory. There are moments when he visualizes Christ dictating the letter to the Romans and guiding the hand of this completely transformed persecutor of Christians, Saul of Tarsus. This man totally surrendered and devoted to Christ, authored most of the New Testament. Certainly, the letter to the Romans is one of the most crucial documents ever composed.

Around 4:00 p.m., sirens coming from the direction of the church, alarm Chris and Pamela. Arriving at the scene, they are astonished to find several ambulances and police vehicles. They learn that a woman entering the auditorium in the midst of a large crowd had fallen. Others, stumbling over her, fell and the crowd, unable to stop, severely trampled some of them. One might expect this sort of thing at rock concerts attended by teenagers, but not at a church gathering.

Chris, accustomed to large crowds wherever he speaks, never experienced anything like this. He is irritated that people, who have come to hear him preach, suffered injuries. He decides to leave any mention of the accident to the church staff. He will preach what the Lord has laid on his heart.

Chris begins with his silent gaze, assessing his audience. Sixty seconds is not a long interlude in time, but a preacher in the pulpit, silent for sixty seconds, mesmerizes his congregation to the point where some hold their breath until sounds escape his lips. Finally, his strong, masculine voice arrests the attention of every listener,

"You find it in the book of Romans. The statement uttered by the Apostle Paul, and one that should be on every Christian's lips when God provides the opportunity. *I am not ashamed of the Gospel of Christ: for it is the power of God unto salvation to everyone that believeth; to the Jew first, and also to the Greek* (Rom 1:16). What is the message of this Gospel that has the power to save us? A couple of chapters later, the Apostle Paul answers that question.

Being justified freely by his grace through the redemption that is in Christ Jesus: Whom God hath set forth to be a propitiation through faith in his blood, to declare his righteousness for the remission of sins that are past, through the forbearance of God; To declare, I say, at this time his righteousness: that he might be just, and the justifier of him which believeth in Jesus (Rom 3:24-26).

Can we relate to the passion that drove Paul to serve Christ in spite of imprisonments and beatings? Do any of us sense this same devotion to Jesus who is our Savior? Most likely many of us are too shy or afraid to give an account of our faith."

As always, at the end of his message, Chris encourages people to come forward to share their decisions and have questions answered. He and church ministers remain for several hours to attend to dozens of people coming forward. Some come to gain assurance of their salvation. Others come under the conviction that their Christian life lacks vitality and joy.

The remaining five meetings see no reduction in attendance. By Friday night, the log records a headcount of more than 12,000 attendees, a record for this church.

For a proper farewell, Mr. Darrel Greenwood and his wife Stella, invite Chris and Pamela to have supper with them. As expected, the dinner conversation eventually turns to the senior pastor position.

Chapter: 26

"Chris, have you and Pamela given thought to this opening? It would thrill our membership if you were to accept the position of senior pastor." Chris glances at Pamela and knows he cannot answer in the affirmative. He does not wish to blame her and must take full responsibility for his reply.

"Darrel, I am honored by your invitation. However, this decision is not a lighthearted one. It requires prayer and a clear understanding of God's will for our future as a family. Until God has revealed His will to us in this matter, I encourage you to consider other candidates."

Back in the hotel room, Pamela is first to bring up the subject again, "Chris, I don't feel right holding you back if you want to become their pastor. It would be an opportunity for you to do what you are called to do, to preach to thousands every week."

"Pammy, you need not feel any guilt. You know that we will always make such decisions together, before the Lord. The fact is, I have not brought it before the Lord at all. On impulse, the opening sounded as an opportunity. However, God may select another field altogether. I know that I must preach, but where and when is up to the Spirit's leading. Pammy, there is one more thing I want to mention to you. Every time I see people hurting physically, I want to help. Do you remember that on our wedding night I went to the hospital to meet with the man who jumped from the window of the hotel?"

"Of course I do. Nobody seemed to know where you were. I was the loneliest bride on earth during those moments of your absence."

"Well, I experienced that same urge today when I learned about those people that were trampled. I sensed an urgency to help them physically and spiritually."

"What do you mean, Chris, you are not a medical doctor. How could you help them physically?"

"I know, dear, I am only sharing what occupies my mind at times and whether there is a sound reason for those thoughts. Maybe God wants me to become a medical doctor so I can help people physically and spiritually."

"Talk about changes in our future. I have not even recovered from the possibility of ending up in Canada when the prospect of my husband's medical training is staring me in the face."

"We are not going to solve these issues tonight, Pammy. Let's get some rest. We have a long trip ahead of us."

Before slipping into bed next to Chris, Pamela takes the map from her purse and makes a travel request.

"Speaking of the trip home, I would rather take another road. The freeway is boring. The map shows a border crossing on Highway 75, which will take us to Fargo, North Dakota. We can catch the freeway there; okay Chris?"

"Fine with me, Pammy; if we get an early start."

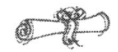

Chapter

27

At the border crossing in Noyes, Minnesota, at Chris' request, they switch drivers. His mind is busy poring over the events of the past week and he has trouble concentrating on his driving. He closes his eyes and is soon deep in thought.

The two-lane Highway 75 is straight and narrow. Opening his eyes occasionally, Chris wonders whether Pamela expected mostly vast fields of grain on both sides of the highway when she changed routes. At one point, when Pamela slows down, Chis notices that they are now passing through the town of Stephen, Minnesota. He remembers reading somewhere that Stephen is nicknamed the 'golden city' because thousands of acres of golden grain surround it.

With his eyes closed, Chris continues his thoughts about options and decisions. How would he and Pamela reach an agreement when his desires contrasted hers? He promised her an equal voice. Would he be able to keep that promise if her discernments differed significantly?

The crash, tremendous noise of screeching tires, twisting metal and shattering glass is the last thing Chris perceives. At the same time, his seat appeared to have turned into a catapult, depositing him against a hard surface. Then everything went dark and ominously silent.

Six hours later Chris slowly becomes aware of overhead lights and the hushed voices of strangers in white attire. He mumbles,

"What is all this? Where am I?" With a burst of realization, he calls out, "Where is Pamela, where is my wife? Is she okay?" A tall man with dark rimmed eyeglasses holds him back.

"You must relax, Dr. Storm. I am Dr. Erickson. Today I have emergency room duty, which I consider a pleasure because it gave me the great opportunity to meet you. I have read many of your articles on modern medicine. It is a surprise to learn that you do not have a medical license."

Chris finds the man's rambling void of true concern. "Where am I and where is my wife?"

"You were airlifted from the accident scene in Stephen, Minnesota to this VA hospital in Fargo, North Dakota. You will fully recover. Your injuries may be painful, but they are not life threatening."

"I don't have any pain. Do I have broken bones? Will I be able to preach again?" The last question puts a smirk on Dr. Erickson's face.
"Judging by what I have read about you, I don't think anybody will be able to stop you from preaching. To answer your comment about having no pain, I am confident that you will change your mind when the medication wears off. You have a nasty cut on the top of your head and severe bruising on your arms and chest from the impact, but there are no broken bones. Don't worry about the pain; our medicine vaults are well stocked."

The word 'worry' restores Chris to the faithful status of a man who trusts God completely.

"Worry is sin, Dr. Erickson."

Dr. Erickson smiles,

"See, you are preaching already."

"Please, tell me about my wife. Is she in this hospital and is she okay?" Chris surveys Dr. Erickson's face and realizes that bad news is imminent.

Chapter: 27

"You will be able to see your wife soon. She is still in surgery. Unfortunately, her injuries are severe. As the driver of the car, she received the full impact of the collision. We cannot provide much detail at this time. After surgery, she will be in recovery for a while. You should be able to visit her tomorrow and park your wheelchair next to her bed for a little while."

"Can you tell me anything about the accident, Sir?"

"Not much. I understand that a vehicle owned by the Overnight Trucking Company crossed the centerline and crashed into your car. We know nothing about the condition of the driver."

"Thank you, doctor, if you learn anything else, please let me know. Now I am tired and would like to rest."

"Of course, Dr. Storm. Would you like something to help you sleep?"

"No, thank you." As Chris processes the news about Pamela's condition, a solemn stare transfigures his expression. Without success, he attempts to recall details of the accident. Oddly, he recalls his last thoughts before everything turned black. He had decided to investigate the possibility of becoming a medical doctor. With his eyes closed, he visualized the initials 'MD' behind his name. Chris is not sure why this idea has dominated his conscious and subconscious mind during the last few weeks. Perhaps it began with the article he read about the group of Christian doctors and dentists, who volunteer time to serve among the poor in third world countries.

An hour later, Chris is still pondering these things and regrets his decision to reject the sleeping aid. His eyelids are heavy. He is very tired, but merciful sleep is not coming to his rescue. When the nurse checks on him, she senses his predicament and administers the sleeping medication.

It is Sunday morning when Chris again asks about Pamela. The nurse carefully states that the doctor will inform him. It seems to Chris that he waited an hour before a doctor comes to his room. He introduces himself as Dr. Hanson, Pamela's physician.

"May I see her, Dr. Hanson?"

173

"You may, but please be aware that your wife is in a coma and we are not sure when she will wake up. A nurse will help you into a wheelchair and take you to her room."

"Dr. Hanson, please tell me more about Pamela's injuries. No matter what the news, do not hold back. I need to know."

"The police officers who were called to the scene of the accident report that your wife was thrown from the vehicle. The semi-truck caught her clothing and dragged her a few feet. She has multiple broken bones and serious head injuries. We do not believe that her injuries are life threatening, but cannot be certain of a full recovery."

The nurse takes Chris to Pamela's room. Dr. Hanson's warnings have not sufficiently prepared Chris for the horrific sight of his once beautiful wife. Bandages cover her head and face. Only her eyes, nose and lips, are visible. Several stitches on her nose and lips imply severe damage to her face. Bandages also cover her arms. Chris dares not lift the sheet to assess injuries on the rest of her body. He cannot remember the last time he cried, but now he sobs aloud, his tears wetting Pamela's pillow. Oh, how he loves this woman! Would God choose not to restore her? Chris has learned never to question the Almighty, but is desperately screening his memory for Bible passages to provide comfort in this tragedy. Numerous Scripture passages begin to comfort him, *'He healeth the broken in heart, and bindeth up their wounds (Psalm 147:3).* The story of God's faithful servant, Job, offers comfort and challenge at the same time. Chris admires Job's faith. Job lost his family and his belongings and suffered with painful blisters and boils. What was his reaction? Chris exhales audibly and whispers,

"Though He slay me; yet will I trust Him (Job 13:15)." He calls the nurse, who returns him to his room. Pamela remains in a coma and on a respirator.

Pamela's parents come Sunday morning and check into a nearby hotel. They visit Chris and Pamela every day. Thursday, Gordon and Lillian Crane, arrange to transfer Pamela by ambulance to the hospital in Minneapolis, where Dr. Tennyson, a family friend, will care for her.

Chapter: 27

Chris is well enough to check out of the VA. He will be staying with his in-laws until he is ready to return to work. Together they follow the ambulance to ensure that they properly relocate Pamela.

Their daily visits become painful when they fail to see any change in her condition. Finally, two weeks later, they find her awake, her head raised slightly. She slowly turns toward them and lifts her right arm to greet them. Chris runs to her bed and kisses her eyes through the bandages. Pamela's arms are still bandaged. However, her hands, resembling embroidered gloves with stitches and scars visible, are now free to touch Chris' face. She had requested a pad and pencil so she could communicate. Pain in her fingers does not stop her from scribbling in big letters.

"Do you still love me?" Chris' tears of joy answer her question before his lips can reinforce it. "Pammy, I love you so very much. I have prayed and waited quite impatiently for this moment to tell you how much I love you and adore you." Chris has his back to his in-laws when Pamela writes on her pad, "You made Mom and Dad cry." He steps back to allow her parents to be closer to their daughter. Both of them are weeping like children. Pamela also produces some tears and there is not a dry eye in the room.

The nurse steps in to shorten their visit. Before leaving the hospital, the three visitors speak with Pamela's doctor to learn more about her condition. Dr. Tennyson is cautious.

"We hope for a full recovery, but a detailed prognosis would be unwise at this time. The health of her mind is encouraging. There appears to be no brain damage. Tests of her sight and hearing produced better than expected results. There is some concern about the damage to the nerves and muscles in her back. She will require therapy before she can walk on her own. For some time she will need strong pain medication. For many patients, narcotics have backfired with addiction. In addition, liver damage is possible with the extended use of medication. This is not to scare you, only to prepare you." After the doctor's comments, Gordon is the first to speak.

"When will you know about the severity of the damage to Pamela's back? In other words, when will you try to have her walk?"

"Pamela has been in the comatose state for four weeks. Even a healthy person would not walk steadily right away. When Pamela is able to sit up without help, we will begin therapy. She will first try to stand up with assistance. Then the therapy will involve standing up and sitting down a few times a minute, eventually without help. This is a slow process, but the ability to stand up from a sitting position will be our signal to provide walking exercises. We should be able to test all this early next week. Do not lose hope if at first we see little success."

Mixed emotions plague the passengers in the homebound vehicle. The exciting news of Pamela's waking from the coma, able to communicate, competes with the uncertainty of her full recovery. Chris says not a word and ponders these things in his heart. Gordon expresses doubt about Pamela's recovery. Chris has great respect for his father-in-law, but cannot remain silent. There has never been an occasion to disagree with him or correct him. Cautiously he states that Pamela's healing is up to God and that God much prefers faith and trust to doubt and fear.

"Lillian, sensing Gordon's frustration after Chris' remark, tries to mellow the atmosphere.

"Well said, preacher man. Don't you think so, Gordon?" Gordon, a solid Christian and mostly kind and agreeable, is nevertheless a bit perturbed by Chris' correction. It takes him two or three minutes, before he reaches into the back seat to shake Chris' hand.

"You are 100% correct, Son. Thank you for setting me straight." Gordon's statement embarrasses Chris. He counters,

"Please Dad, don't put it that way. It is unwise setting your father-in-law straight. My comment was meant to encourage the three of us to trust the Lord." Sunday after church, Chris takes Lillian aside and shares his decision to go back to work. Lillian still heads up the College staff. Chris puts his arm around her shoulders and asks,

"Would it be okay, Boss, if I return to work tomorrow?" Lillian startled at the suddenness of his decision, replies,

"No, it is not okay. There must be a Welcome Party for you and Welcome Signs all over the campus. We cannot bring our VIP Professor back without some fanfare."

"That is exactly why I want to go back to work on short notice. I do not need special attention."

"Okay, Professor Storm. Permission granted." Chris draws Lillian closer and kisses her on the cheek. You are the finest mother-in-law-boss I know." If Chris thought this is the end of it, he does not really know Lillian. Two minutes later, Lillian is on the phone with a few special contacts she can always count on. When Chris arrives on the campus, numerous signs reading 'Welcome Back Professor Storm' greet him. A crowd of students and fellow teachers greet him at the main hall. He shakes his head and says, "Now I believe everything they say about mean 'mothers-in-law'. Wait till I get a hold of her."

Chris finds it difficult to get back into the old routine. Pamela's condition is constantly on his mind. Do the doctors really care enough to do the best for her? He recalls reading articles in medical journals on various surgery procedures. Is this hospital aware of the newest advances in technology? Are they aware of Raoul Palmer's 1950 publication, describing diagnostic laparoscopy. Are they utilizing laparoscopic procedures? He bows his head and gives thanks to God for his supernatural memory. He has always been interested in technical advances. Would the hospital staff allow his input if he can cite the source, complete with publication dates?

Chris shakes his head, I am dreaming. No professional doctor wants to hear about technical advances from a novice. More desperately than ever before, he yearns for the coveted MD behind his name. The list of requirements is long and demanding: A Bachelor of Science Degree in Biology, involving Chemistry, Biological studies, Physics, and Human Genetics. Next, there is Medical school, normally requiring four years of study. A Residence program at a hospital follows. All this before he can hope for a license to practice medicine. Again, he shakes his head. It is a senseless dream. Finally, after what seems the longest day to him, it

The Passions & Perils of the Prodigy

is time to drive Gordon's old Mercedes to the hospital. Chris is pleased that Gordon did not sell the car when he and Pamela surprised him with the shiny new 1972 Mercedes. The accident totaled his own car. Red tape is holding up the insurance money. Perhaps his father-in-law will let him have the old car, still in fine running order.

As he walks into Pamela's room, the frightening change in her appearance startles Chris. Pamela's damaged face, no longer bandaged, red, swollen, bruised, and scarred, resembles a scary Halloween mask. She detects his shock immediately.

"You don't have to pretend with me, Chris. You would have to invent new words of comfort. Everybody else used the old and familiar ones and they made it worse."

"How about a simple and sincere one? Hello Sweetheart. Does that work?"

"You are amazing, Chris. Yes that works; especially the sweetheart part. The doctor refused to produce a mirror. He suggested that I wait until the redness disappears and the swelling goes down. However, the nurse, after some coaxing, brought one. I look scary." She changes the subject.

"Mom said you went back to work today. How did that go?"

"My mind occupied with you all day, I did not do my salary justice today. Are they taking good care of you, Pammy? Pamela does not respond. Chris continues,

"The substitute took half of my classes so I could daydream about you and becoming a doctor."

"Not that again. Why are you suddenly obsessed with that idea?"

"It is not sudden, darling. I have contemplated that option for a long time. You must recall the desk cluttered with more medical articles on technical advances than any other literature."

"Yes, I remember. Nevertheless, you are much more familiar with the Bible and other works concerning the Christian faith. So why not stick with that?"

Chapter: 27

"I applaud missionary organizations, composed of professionals who volunteer their services. They meet a tremendous need in foreign countries."

"Chris, you choose a strange way to encourage me in my condition. Does your wife fit somewhere in your plans? Nobody has shown any confidence that there will be a complete recovery. Who will push my wheelchair while you heal people in the bush of some third world country?"

"Pammy, we are not considering something inclined to happen tomorrow, if it happens at all. Forgive me; this is bad timing indeed."

Chris and Dr. Tennyson shake hands.

"I am glad for this opportunity to talk with you, Dr. Tennyson. How is Pamela doing?"

"Your wife is a fighter, Dr. Storm…"

"Please call me Chris."

"Chris, Pamela is young and basically healthy. We are now hopeful for a full recovery. Did she mention that she stood on her own two feet for a whole forty-five seconds this morning?" Chris directs a delighted grin toward Pamela.

"She did not have a chance, doctor. That is wonderful news. Does that mean she will soon be able to walk?"

"To protect my patients, I do not normally discuss any frightening prognosis in front of them. However, with Pamela I will make an exception. She is very determined and got downright nasty this morning when I refused to give her a mirror. Minor back surgery may be required. Her legs are strong, allowing her to stand briefly this morning, but she experienced back pain immediately afterwards. The initial X-ray did not detect any broken bones. Nevertheless, there may be hairline cracks or damaged cartilage. Additional x-rays, scheduled for tomorrow, will provide a clearer picture."

"Dr. Tennyson, are you familiar with the new X-Ray procedure called Computerized Axial Tomography scans, for short CAT scan?"

"Chris, do you want to join our staff, here at the hospital? Technical advances in the field of medicine appear to be your forte. The only scanning device I am aware of is called an EMI-Scanner, which is installed at the Atkinson Morley Hospital, located in Wimbledon, England."

"That is the one. Sir Godfrey Hounsfield Hanes invented it at the EMI Central Research Laboratories, using X-Rays. The first patient brain scan was performed on October 1, 1971, and publicly announced in 1972." Dr. Tennyson looks at Pamela.

"Why did you keep your husband's genius a secret?" Turning back to Chris, he pounds his forehead with the palm of his hand.

"Forgive me, I never put it together. You are the famous Boy Prodigy from New England; the genius with the supernatural memory. Chris, we must shake hands one more time. I am honored to meet you."

Pamela listens patiently for a while, but eventually interrupts.

"Hello, members of the Mutual Admiration Society, the patient is over here, in bed. Can we please turn our attention back in this direction and make an effort to solve her problems?"

Slightly embarrassed after Pamela's indictment, Chris and Dr. Tennyson manage a half-hearted apology, and Dr. Tennyson leaves the room.

The call comes in the in the early morning hours of the next day.

"Dr. Storm, this is Dr. Tennyson's nurse. Please come to the hospital right away. You wife is in surgery. I have already informed her parents."

"What happened, what is the emergency?"

"Please come right away." The nurse hangs up. In the hospital, Gordon, Lillian, and Chris receive not a clue until Dr. Tennyson comes to the waiting room.

"I am so sorry. The night nurse found Pamela spitting up blood; lots of it. We suspected a ruptured artery near the heart and found exactly that on the operating table. The affected blood vessel had a fragile spot. There were indications that she had suffered minor internal bleeding before. The accident does not appear to be the cause. Does she have a history of weakness or fainting?"

"Gordon and Lillian shake their head, but Chris recalls the first day in Canada, when Pamela witnessed the bleeding young boy in the parking lot, she fainted. He shares this incident with them.

"Lillian asks. "How serious is this, Dr. Tennyson?"

"Any damage this close to the heart is serious. Her system, already weakened by the loss of blood and trauma from the accident, is struggling to fight infections, abating the healing process. We have done what we can. You may as well go home. She will be in recovery for some time."

Chris, struggling with the idea of leaving Pamela, speaks up.

"Mom and Dad, you look bushed. I will stay for a while." Gordon can see that Chris also looks very tired. He winks at Lillian and says,

"You look tired as well, Chris. Why don't you come home with us? That way we can visit her together later." Reluctantly, Chris agrees.

At the Crane residence, everyone heads straight to bed. In the early morning hours, the phone, equipped with a central bell, wakes everyone. Lillian answers it. To Chris' horror, Lillian cries,

"No, no, no!" He finds her in the bedroom, in Gordon's arms. They are both weeping profusely. Chris stands motionless; his face contorted in pain. A sensation in his chest feels as though his heart is breaking in two. His knees begin to quiver forcing him to collapse into the corner chair. He begins to cry aloud.

"No, God. No, no, not my Pamela. I cannot let her go." Gordon and Lillian motion for Chris to sit on the edge of their bed. They embrace and cry together for a long time. At last, Lillian utters,

"She died all alone. We should have stayed. We lost our only child. She never woke up after the surgery. They could not revive her."

Nobody responds to Lillian's account. Tears give way to anger. Everyone's mind processes questions. How could this have happened? Was there a doctor on duty? Do we have to accept that she never woke up? Were the nurses watching the monitors diligently? Do they have sufficient training in revival procedures? Did they call the wrong number? Did another patient die? Is Pamela still alive? Chris jumps up.

"I have to see her." Gordon responds.

"Take the car, Chris. Call us when you get there."

Chapter

28

The death of Pamela Storm, the young wife of Dr. Christopher Storm, and the only daughter of the prominent Crane Family, is international news. Every type of media is carrying the story. Details, published the day before the funeral, result in traffic jams on routes leading to the cemetery. Chris, Gordon, and Lillian have not given any information to the press. They are astonished at the turnout.

At the gravesite, as Chris scans the sea of faces, he is pleased to find many friends from his college days in Massachusetts. He also spots his grandparents, Roger and Doris Coulter and his foster parents, Rudy and Hilda Ragford. He regrets that he left all the funeral plans to his in-laws. In view of their accomplishments, he feels deeply indebted to them. Deep sorrow had paralyzed him.

One more face from the past, one he has not expected to see again, yet is now only feet away, is that of Virginia Hyatt. As their eyes meet, Virginia smiles and begins moving in his direction. Virginia squeezes between Gordon and Chris.

The preacher has finished and they are free to talk. Chris hastens to introduce Virginia to Gordon and Lillian. Without going into details, he says, "Mom and Dad, this is Virginia Hyatt from Massachusetts. We became friends when she attended services at the church where I was speaking."

Lillian's tone of voice is spicy when she replies,

"Virginia Hyatt, I think Pamela spoke of you."

"Oh? I hope it was complimentary, and by the way, it is Virginia Stern now. I am married."

"Is your husband here as well, Virginia?"

"Unfortunately, he is in Florida at a Ministries conference. He regrets the conflict. As a deacon at the church where Chris preached, he became fond of Chris. He credits Chris' message for my decision to trust the Lord."

Her voice, now warm and friendly, Lillian takes Virginia's hand, thanks her for attending the funeral, and invites her to join them for the luncheon at the Crane residence later. Virginia, sincerely pleased, smiles and says,

"Thank you so very much, Dr. Crane, but I have return airline tickets. The plane leaves in two hours. It is so nice meeting you and your husband."

Gordon is happy to let Lillian do the talking. However, to show his support for Lillian's invitation he suggests that Virginia change her tickets and leave later.

"That is very kind, Dr. Crane; but I feel out of place. I don't know anybody here except Chris and am not sure he wants me hanging around." That comment, followed by a prodding gaze at Chris, receives no verbal response. Instead, Chris takes Virginia's hand, thanks her for coming, and wishes her a safe trip home.

For a few seconds Virginia feels the pain of rejection. However, when their eyes meet, without words they communicate to each other the deep understanding only possible between true friends. They part in perfect peace with one another.

Nightmarish memories have plagued Chris since Pamela's last breath. He recalls every moment of their brief marriage. Regrets for failures to show understanding and kindness dominate the scene. If only the delightful times of love and intimacy could have tipped the scales in the right direction. Now it is too late. Would he ever be able to bring all this guilt before the throne of God, and leave it there? Would his sermons now be dull and melancholy? Could the Lord still use him in His plans? Would he, the famous preacher, lecturer, and professor ever find release from this prison of despair?

At the Crane residence, sweet reunions with friends and family ease the burden. Sound assurances from the Scriptures are a balm to his wounded spirit. At bedtime, still at the Crane residence, for the first time in three days, his tired body finds genuine rest. He wakes refreshed and makes some serious decisions before joining Gordon and Lillian in the kitchen.

The change in Chris' mindset becomes obvious to Gordon and Lillian when at the breakfast table he uncovers surprising plans for the future.

"I am considering changes that will affect all of us. Obviously, your thoughts and ideas are welcome. The first move is to sell the house. That means new lodging somewhere. Without beating around the bush, perhaps you could take me in for a while?"

Gordon and Lillian exchange a quick glance. Gordon answers,

"You will always have a home here, Chris. I hope you know that." Lillian nods in agreement and curiously asks,

"Chris, tell us about these changes you are planning."

"Sure, I am going back to school to earn a medical degree." Lillian begins to say something, but stops when Chris motions for silence.

"That means breaking the contract with the University. Do you think you can convince the board, Mom?"

"Refresh my memory, Chris. When does the contract expire?"

"March 1975."

"Would you stay until we find a replacement? Contract breaches are not popular with the board and are generally limited to family emergencies. Perhaps you could continue at the University and study for your medical degree in the evening, but why this change? Are you not happy at the U anymore?"

"As far as a family emergency is concerned, we recently experienced one of those, Mom. Yes, I will stay as long as you need me. Several missionary organizations are begging for professional volunteers, Doctors, Dentist, and Optometrists. I want to help."

It has been a month since Pamela's funeral. Everything in the house reminds Gordon and Lillian that their hopes for the future died with their daughter. There will be no grandchildren, no family get-togethers, no happy times for the four of them. Now, Chris' plans to serve on the mission field loom on the horizon. Lillian counts that as an added adversity befalling their empty nest. She loves Chris. His extended absence would be unbearable. She has enjoyed a special relationship with her son-in-law.

Chris respects his mother-in-law and admires her leadership qualities and business acumen. As never before, he desires to learn her ways of dealing with life. Lillian agrees to assist him in his pursuit for the MD license. To her delight, Chris sells the house quickly and is now living in the Crane home. The three spend quality time together, easing the loss of their beloved Pamela.

Gordon receives another six months assignment in the Holy Land. However, after he arrives there, he learns that a rich archeological find will extend his stay. Lillian and Chris miss him and are disappointed.

The University board approves a replacement for Chris in March 1974, allowing his medical studies to make great progress. He finds the studies helpful in easing the pain of his loss. It is different for Lillian. She has time on her hands; time she used to spend with Gordon. The months of his absence begin to take their toll. She is lonely and grows gloomier each day. One Friday evening, Lillian interrupts Chris' studies,

"Chris, I called Monica Saarlander. We are going out for dinner and then a movie afterward. Do you want to come along?"

"No, Mom. I am buried in these books. Enjoy yourself."

When Lillian returns, she is a different person. The relaxing evening with her friend, Monica is a deserved break and a nice change from the routine. Some people do well alone; Lillian is not one of them.

Chapter: 28

"Chris, come sit with me for a while. You need a break from your books now and then." Chris nods and relaxes on the couch. Lillian settles in the nearby recliner. Chris has learned to read her vibes. Lillian is scheming to chat for a while. He settles back to gratify his mother-in-law.

"Before, when Gordon traveled, Pamela was always here. Now, with Pamela gone and Gordon's frequent trips, I struggle with boredom and loneliness. When I get home from work, I sit alone, night after night. I thank God for your company, Chris."

"Mom, loneliness is a side effect of loving. We miss the people who return our love. Subsequently when they are not with us, we hurt. I miss Pamela every day. Sometimes her memory is so painful that God's comforting words in the Scriptures seem illusive. '*Come unto me, all ye that labour and are heavy laden, and I will give you rest (Math 11:28).*' We have to meditate on some of these marvelous passages to receive the benefits promised." Lillian sighs.

"Of course, you are right; we should not allow self-pity to rob us of joy. It is so much easier to acknowledge the truth than to live it. I guess I will take some time before I fall asleep tonight to meditate on the goodness of our Lord. Goodnight, Chris."

Gordon returns from the Holy Land November 15, 1974. Lillian and Chris have prepared for his arrival with Welcome Posters and with a special meal, one of Gordon's favorite, prepared by a professional Chef, borrowed from a five-star restaurant, owned by one of Gordon's college friends. For Gordon it is one of his most memorable homecomings.

When Chris finishes his studies and passes the final test, he is the first man in history to receive his MD license in two years. In November 1975, when reporters quiz him about the future, Chris answers,

"I hope that one of the fine hospitals in this area will offer me an internship. I am eager to put book learning into practice."

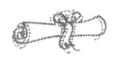

Chapter

29

Several hospitals, eager to add a famous name to their staff, offer Chris an internship. Chris chooses the hospital in Minneapolis that cared for Pamela.

His popularity with the public proves to be a trap. New patients expecting superior medical procedures from a famous Physician, instead encounter the lack of practical experience and skill. Chris is not accustomed to failure and criticism. He accepts it as a spiritual lesson in trust. The result is amazing growth in dependence on the Lord.

On several occasions, Chris notices a nurse in the staff lunchroom, who always sits alone. He asks a fellow intern about her and learns that she is Heather Quincy, nicknamed Heather Quack by her peers. The head nurse caught her using Alternative Medicine on patients, without doctor approval. It is a serious matter. Her dismissal is imminent. Always the friend of the underdog, Chris approaches her, introduces himself, and requests permission to join her.

"I am Christopher Storm."

"My name is Heather Quincy. I know who you are, Dr. Storm. I have read many of your articles. I especially enjoyed your masterpiece about the Congo River and Jungle. My favorite animal in your story is the Silverback 450 pound Gorilla." Her smile immediately engages Chris,

Chapter: 29

"Heather, I could go on and on about life in the Congo. It has mysteries, discovered only recently. The behavior of chimpanzees is well documented, but the odd habits of the Bonobo monkey have scientists scratching their heads." Heather looks around the lunchroom.

"Are you certain you want to be seen with me? I have a reputation in this place."

"That makes two of us, Heather. Being new to the field of medicine, my lack of skill has alienated a few patients. There is a lot to learn. Tell me about your situation."

As Chris and Heather discuss many subjects, he finds her easy to talk with and hopes for additional meetings with her. She is a Christian who enjoys reading and is self-taught in various fields of medicine, including homeopathy. Excitedly, she explains that homeopathy is a complementary disease treatment system in which a patient receives minute doses of natural substances which in larger doses will produce symptoms of the disease itself."

Chris knows all about homeopathy, but intrigued by the excitement with which Heather shares, he listens respectfully. He asks,

"Do you have some at home for your own use?"

"Yes, I maintain a small pharmacy of homeopathic substances in my home and have treated a few patients. It helped them, but I broke hospital rules and will probably lose my job.

Wisely, Chris does not take sides, but says,

"I hope not. It is good meeting you, Heather."

"I am thrilled to meet you face to face, Dr. Storm." Chris extends his hand and says,

"Please call me Chris. We should talk again." He is attracted to her and realizes that Heather is the first woman with that effect on him, since Pamela died, three years ago. During one of their lunchroom meetings, he asks for her phone number, showing his desire to keep in contact.

"In case something gets in the way of our meeting like this."

"That would be sad indeed," Heather admits. She hands Chris a card with her phone number and address. Resolutely she states,

"I live alone."

For the next several days, Heather is absent from the lunchroom. Chris makes some inquiries and learns of her dismissal. This type of unfavorable dismissal will make future employment difficult. He wonders why this news bothers him. Does he care for her that much?

Thursday evening, December 18, after work, he dials her number. Her clear voice delivers a custom message on the answering machine.

"I am not happy about missing your call. Please do not hang up before you leave your name and number."

"Heather, this is Chris Storm. I will call again later." Heather is home; screening calls, but reaches the phone too late.

"Why didn't he leave his number?" she mumbles, "He probably only wants to learn about alternative medicine. He is the famous Dr. Christopher Storm, MD, PhD, and I am Nurse Heather Quack, a Nobody."

Heather has been in a depressed mood. In addition to her dismissal from the hospital, she is struggling with the fear that her father, serving in Cambodia, may be in serious danger. His regular communications and letters have stopped abruptly. Tears come so quickly these days.

The phone rings again. Heather answers it immediately. It is the hospital financial office. They work late every Friday. They want to know whether she wants to pick up her final check or have it mailed to her.

Heather snaps, "Mail it," and hangs up the phone.

She admits that the call from the well-known Professor Storm excited her and wonders aloud,

"Will he call back?" The doorbell interrupts her thoughts.

"Who is it," she shouts into the intercom.

"It's Chris. May I come in?" Never did that door buzzer suffer a more violent punch. A quick appearance check in the mirror shocks her.

"What happened to those eyes? A blind man's white cane could tell that I have been crying. Too late; he is at the door."

Chris shakes her hand,

"Thank you for seeing me, Heather." He notices the redness in her eyes, but wisely ignores it. "I am sorry to show up unannounced. I knew you were home because your phone was busy the second time I called."

"It was the hospital office. I am glad to see you, Dr. Storm."

"Did you already forget my first name, Heather?"

"No, but it doesn't feel right. We just met."

"Hmm, what should I call you then?"

"Of course you call me Heather. It is not the same thing. You are a doctor and you are famous all over the world. In fact, Dr. Storm, why do you bother to come here at all? You can read about alternative medicine in books. You do not need me for that."

"Heather, I am wondering what your plans are now that the hospital dismissed you?"

Heather remains silent and stares at Chris. Finally, she grins and says, "Frankly, Dr. Storm, your interest in me is like a fairy tale."

"Would you like this fairy tale to become real?"

"I am sorry, Dr. Storm. I would prefer to drop the subject."

"Heather, I came because I would like to get to know you better. Will you tell me about your family and your background?"

"Did you come straight from work Dr. Storm?"

"Yes, I did come straight from work. Why do you ask?"

"My life story may take a while. Should we talk over supper?"

"You mean in a restaurant?"

"No, I mean lasagna from the oven; can't you smell it? I think it's ready."

At the table, Chris gives thanks for the food and for the pleasure of their friendship. Heather prays every day, but she considers his prayer odd. He thanked God for the pleasure of their friendship. He would not say that to God unless he meant it, would he? Heather tells her story.

"I was born and grew up in Iowa. There are no other siblings. Mom and Dad did the best they could to keep the hog farm going. They did all right until Mom passed away in 1969 from breast cancer. It took the wind out of Dad. He spent many days alone in his room. I was fifteen. Every time he came out to check on things, I could tell he had been crying. It was sad to see him that way.

One Tuesday morning our pastor came to visit. I do not remember exactly what he said to Dad, but it was something about selling the farm and going into foreign mission work."

"Is your dad a Christian?"

"Oh yes. Mom and Dad were always active in church. Mom taught Sunday school. Dad chaired the Trustee board for several years. He is good with his hands and kept the church facilities in great shape. Before he met Mom, he was a police officer. He was not a Christian then. This is a long and strange story, but one of the inmates he arrested, became a Christian in prison. When he got out, he came to visit Dad and led him to the Lord at our kitchen table."

"What a great testimony to our Lord's availability. Too many people falsely believe that God resides only behind church doors. Go on, Heather. Where is your dad now?" Heather remains quiet and Chris detects her sadness,

"I am sorry. Did that stir bad memories for you?"

"My dad went to Cambodia shortly after Mom died. He left me with his sister's family who treated me as their own. Dad was there in 1970 and survived the Vietnam War when US bombing included parts of Cambodia. Finally, that threat ended in 1973, but Dad is in constant danger from cruel human traffickers."

"Heather, did you say Cambodia? Thousands of people are being tortured and killed in the genocide right now." Heather begins sobbing audibly. Chris tries to comfort her, but she pushes him away, rests her head on the table, and continues to cry bitterly. Eventually she dries her tears with her sleeves and continues,

Chapter: 29

"I know about the genocide. It started in April 1975. The last letter I received from Dad was dated February 27, 1975. He wrote about unrest between the Cambodian and Vietnamese people. He probably tried to protect me, but I read between the lines that he was worried. A couple of months later the tortures and killings in Cambodia began and are continuing to this day. The media may not have complete information, but war stories about Cambodia's attempts to rid themselves of all religions and ethnologically undesirable races continue. There is no end in sight."

"Heather, why did your dad go to Cambodia?"

"After Mom passed away, a deacon from our church took Dad under his wing, so to speak. He saw Dad's depression and approached him about the opportunity in Cambodia. Dad welcomed the means to start over somewhere else. Dad's police background made him well suited for the task. He is working with a missionary group fighting human trafficking." Heather pauses, "Do you know what I am taking about, Dr. Storm?"

"You mean the human trafficking problem? I know that human trafficking is a problem all over the world. I have not researched the specifics about Cambodia trafficking." Heather continues,

"Traffickers in Cambodia kidnap or buy over a million children annually and then sell them to brothels or wealthy private parties who abuse them. Cambodian parents, too poor to support their children, often sell their kids willingly to these slave traders. They may receive up to $400 for a virgin girl. That is an enormous amount of money for a poverty-stricken Cambodian family. Dad said that the traffickers could rent that same girl to rich private parties and collect as much as $2000 per month. These children are victims of repeated abuse. Many young girls die in the process."

"Heather, your dad is a hero, a courageous man."

"I know and I am ashamed. After I turned eighteenth, Dad has repeatedly asked me to join him. They are short on help; but the slave traders are extremely cruel. They beat disobedient children and kill anybody who gets in their way. I am too scared to face that kind of evil."

"Do you know anybody else who is part of that group?"

"The group came together from several different churches. In May 1975, I received a letter from one of the men who worked with Dad.

His name is Ronald Stauffer. The horror had begun. They drive people from their homes. Anyone who resists is shot and often tortured as an example. They evacuated the entire capital city of Phnom Penh.

For a short time, a few Americans, including Ronald and Dad, found shelter at the French Embassy. Eventually they loaded everyone from the Embassy on trucks and drove them to the border of Thailand. Ronald claims that Dad had disappeared from the Embassy. The trucks left without him. Maybe Dad decided to escape on his own. Some of the jungle-smart people chose the woods for their escape. I have never given up hope that Dad may be hiding underground and is still alive."

"Heather, do not give up hope. He may indeed be hiding in a jungle with no way to contact you while the genocide is in full swing." Chris, heading for the door asks, "May I see you again soon? The report of your dad's courage has a profound impact on me; there is a lot to consider. Promise me that you will not look for a new job until I see you again, okay?"

"You are scaring me, Chris. What are you thinking?"

"I'm thinking that I am very happy that you remembered my first name. See you soon."

Continuously, Chris ponders the plight of those Cambodian children and genocide victims. Since his visit with Heather, he has read dozens of articles. The United Nations Children's Fund (UNICEF), headquartered in New York City, is a program established in 1946. UNICEF publications clearly state the needs of children around the world, but they stay away from details about human trafficking or child prostitution.

Chapter: 29

Chris discusses the subject with Gordon and Lillian and learns that they are aware of this problem, but never lost any sleep over it. After all, this is only a big problem in undeveloped countries, far away. He drops a bombshell on his unsuspecting in-laws.

"Eventually, I am going to Cambodia." After a long gaze tinted with unbelief, Gordon speaks. "Cambodia? Why of all places did you pick Cambodia?"

"I have prayed and agonized over this. It is not an easy resolution to prepare for such a trip." Lillian sounds angry.

"Quit joking around, Chris. Are you teasing us?" Chris smiles,

"Yes and no, Mom; I need someone to go with me, preferably a wife. I have someone in mind but she doesn't know it yet." Lillian and Gordon stare at Chris in disbelief. Then Lillian growls,

"Who is this woman?"

"She is the woman who got me started thinking about Cambodia. I think it is only fair that she accompanies me when I go there."

"I ask you again, Chris, are you messing with us, or are you serious. I cannot tell. Are you serious about getting married?"

"I met her in the hospital. She is a nurse. You do not know her. Her name is Heather Quincy. If you wish, I will introduce her to you."

"By all means invite her for Christmas dinner. I want to meet this woman."

Chris calls Heather Saturday morning.

"Heather, this is Chris. May I come over? I have two important questions to ask you."

"What questions?"

"They are not phone questions. They are in-person questions." Arriving at Heather's apartment, Chris senses Heather's anxiety. She is impatient and demands,

"Okay, Chris, ask already."

"Number one; will you join us for Christmas dinner at my in-laws? I will pick you up."

"I guess so; but I am wondering why they would invite me."

"Because I told them that you will go to Cambodia with me."

"What?" Heather screams. Do not tease, Chris. What are you saying?"

"Okay, I won't tease you. Will you go to Cambodia with me when the genocide ends over there?"

"Chris I don't know what to make of your weird question. Could we talk about that another time; maybe after Christmas?"

At the Christmas dinner, Gordon and Lillian find Heather delightful. She is courteous, kind, and sweet. Her education and reading interests mark her as an excellent conversationalist. Chris catches a thumbs-up from Gordon when the women are not looking. Gordon's approval is critical to Chris. He is delighted.

Heather's report about her father's duties in Cambodia has a terrifying effect on Lillian. She voices her opinion about the apparent dangers. Chris is not ignorant about the dangers associated with his plans. He has soaked up mountains of material on the subject. He knows that it would be unwise to rush into things concerning Cambodia and Heather, yet he cannot visualize another plan. Lillian makes a last ditch effort to stop the young couple from going to Cambodia,

"Heather, you must talk sense into your man. I don't want Chris in Cambodia." That comment baffles Chris and Heather. Lillian has just forced the issue of their relationship. He responds quickly, before Heather can say something.

"I am not sure that Heather wants to change her man's mind." He winks at Heather who takes it as a sign not to argue about Lillian's assumption that Chris is 'her man'.

When Chris and Heather are alone, he gets an earful.

"What on earth did you tell them? Are you my man, Chris?" For the time being, Chris wants to postpone any discussion relating to their relationship. He makes an offhanded remark, which puts the blame on people who jump to conclusions. Heather does not know how to take his response but is willing to leave the timing of these things to 'her man'.

Chris requests an appointment with Dr. Turner, the head of the hospital. He entreats Dr. Turner to reinstate Heather Quincy. Dr. Turner is a man of vigilant thought and movement. Nobody on the staff can recall that Dr. Turner has ever been in a hurry. Attentively he asks,

"Dr. Storm, hiring and firing nurses is a little out of my ballpark; what is your relationship with Heather Quincy?"

"Heather and I have become friends. I can vouch for her character. She is a kindhearted woman who deserves a position where she can care for people. She regrets her imprudence, which violated hospital rules. I believe that she will not repeat that error."

"I will discuss this with the head nurse and our employment office. If we decide to reinstate Heather Quincy, we will contact her directly. Thank you for your opinion on this matter, Dr. Storm."

Two weeks later Chris is delighted to find Heather in the lunchroom, seated with other nurses.

Months pass. Chris and Heather meet a few times after work at a nearby restaurant. Whenever the discussion involves Cambodia, Chris expresses his determination to serve God in that needy country. His medical skills have improved over the months and he pictures himself saving abused children, treating their physical wounds and their wounded spirits.

It is during one of these discussions that Heather opens the subject of Chris' unforgettable and unexpected question.

"Chris, we never talk about it, but months ago, whatever impelled you to ask whether I will go to Cambodia with you? Does that question in any way relate to the fact that Lillian thinks that you are my man?" Heather feels as though Chris' penetrating look is probing the very essence of her being. Somehow, she knows that his answer will carry the significance of a lifetime decision. Chris reaches across the table and takes her hands.

"Heather, I would never have asked you to accompany me to Cambodia, unless I hoped that you would be my wife. Heather, will you be my wife?"

Heather is speechless. This is not a joke. Chris really asked her to become his wife. Chris senses her bewilderment and assures her that she need not answer right now.

"Please think about this carefully, Heather. It would be until death us do part."

"Chris, I do not need time to think about this. I have been thinking about it for months. I clearly sense that you care for me; and I know that I love you deeply."

"I am so happy, Heather; I just have to thank the Lord, right now." Chris continues to hold her hands and seals their commitment to each other with a sincere prayer of gratitude.

Chapter

30

Preparations for the wedding are keeping everyone busy. The young couple has decided to invite only a few close friends and relatives. Others will receive announcements, not invitations. Saturday, June 18, 1977, will be here soon and Heather is a singing bundle of joy. In the twenty-two years of her life, she cannot recall a time of such happiness and contentment.

After the wedding, the plan calls for Chris to move into Heather's apartment. He has no need for the items placed in storage when he sold the house. His furniture was a generous gift from Gordon and Lillian. It is of high quality and in excellent condition. Chris suggests an auction before the wedding. Heather welcomes the opportunity to handle the details. She schedules an auctioneer to sell Chris' belongings at the storage facility on Monday, May 23.

Scattered rain showers are in the forecast. The auctioneer supplies tents to shelter bidders. Still, the turnout is poor. Heather looks worried. Chris puts his arm around her and states the obvious,

"It's not over yet, sweetheart." Lillian watches the proceedings and has an idea. She calls the furniture storeowner, a friend, suggests that he repurchase all the furniture for sale it in his pre-owned furniture department. The man shows up and with a substantial bid buys the entire stock.

The Passions & Perils of the Prodigy

Somehow, this act inspires the rest of the bidders and the auction is a complete success. As is typical for Gordon and Lillian Crane, they make a reservation in a fine restaurant to celebrate the accomplishments.

After dinner, relaxing on a sofa at the Crane residence, Chris and Heather scrutinize the list of wedding preparations. Announcements to friends and relatives not located in the Twin Cities area went out a week ago. Invitations to the few local friends and relatives are in the mail. Everything is on schedule.

It is Thursday, June 7. Chris and Heather are enjoying supper at the Crane residence. Of course, the upcoming wedding is the central subject. Heather has ideas for her wedding, but Lillian trivializes her comments. Both, Chris and Heather notice it, but make allowances since the wedding is to take place at the Crane residence. Chris is helping Heather into her coat to drive her home, when Lillian suggests that Chris should find somewhere else to stay tonight.

"In fact,' she adds. "I don't want to see you back here until Saturday, in time for the wedding." Chris and Heather swap befuddled looks that translate into, "what is she up to now?"

During his first two visits, Chris had not paid much attention to details in Heather's apartment. It is located close to the hospital for travel convenience. If location, location, location determines the value of real estate, this building must have ranked near the bottom. Tonight, stepping into the apartment, soon to be the home for the newlyweds, Chris screens it more carefully.

"This is cozy," he comments.

There is a living room with two love seats, a coffee table, TV, and a bookshelf. The dining corner has a round table, four chairs, and a china cabinet. The L-shaped kitchen is tight. It has room for one. Heather's bedroom with the double bed, two nightstands, and fancy drapes outshines the rest. The only other comfortable space is the bathroom. It is large with a separate tub, glass shower, and double sink. Heather's decorator skills, color coordination, and tastefully distributed pictures make the home attractive.

Heather is thrifty and manages her income well. She is willing to live here until she can afford something better. Ten percent right off the top goes to her church. Another ten percent she deposits into a savings account. Her dad taught her that savers do not have to pay interest to lenders when emergencies arise. She pays her credit card balance in full every month.

A shock awaits Chris behind door number two, the spare bedroom. He opens the door and peers at the ugliest orange-and-green-striped couch he has ever laid eyes on. He is confident that furniture superior to this piece can be found at the Stillwater junk yard. Heather perceives his thoughts and coyly asks,

"Is something wrong, Chris?"

"Heather that piece of furniture must have a history. Is there a story behind it?"

"Okay, it does have a history. Mr. Kranz, the property owner in Apartment 2, across the hall, bought that couch brand new when he married Henrietta thirteen years ago. Henrietta was previously married and brought two husky boys with her. They are chubby, like their mother and their new step dad. The family weighs in at about 240 lbs. apiece. That poor couch took a lot of abuse with those substantial derrieres parked for hours in front of the TV. Then one day, the way Helmut Kranz tells it, the couch got revenge. It attacked Henrietta and drove one of its coil springs into a sensitive part of her anatomy. Henrietta's shriek echoed throughout the building.

"You get that, that, that thing out of here this minute," she screamed. When Henrietta screams, Helmut jumps. He jumped right into his friendly neighbor's place and begged for sympathy. Could he please temporarily put that couch in the spare bedroom? So there it is. A piece of wire is now holding back the vindictive spring, restoring the couch to a fine place to sit and rest. This happened three years ago. I reckon that beauty is mine for keeps."

"Heather, we will have to discuss this after I move in. Now I better find a place to stay." Chris calls Dr. Frank Stout, an associate from the hospital.

"Frank this is Chris. I need a place to stay for a couple of nights. Lillian is up to something. She kicked me out of the house. I think she is planning a surprise for our wedding."

"Of course Chris, you are always welcome. I'll tell Trudy to get a bed ready." As the two men get to know one another better, they become friends.

Always the socialite, Lillian proves that even small weddings can be a big occasion. The pastor to marry the young couple will officiate at the Crane residence. Professional decorators turned the Crane mansion into a scene from the glamorous 1920's.

Chris and Heather arrive at the house a couple of hours prior to the scheduled time of the wedding. A man in butler attire directs them to the lower level of the home. He delivers the message that the Lady of the house would like them to remain there until further directions.

Soon, a young woman dressed as a 1920's Lady's Maid and a young man, dressed as a Gentleman's Valet, enter the room. The girl, Katy, addresses Heather as Milady. The man, Norman, addresses Chris as Milord. In an instant, they promote the young couple to Royalty. Even in pretense, it feels good.

Katy and Heather disappear into another room where Heather's wedding dress is waiting to transform her into a beautiful bride. Norman steps out for a few minutes and returns with Chris' tuxedo. At the right moment, Norman furnishes Chris with a blindfold and escorts him to a makeshift room with walls of decorated cardboard. The best man and two grooms' men, hospital employees Chris chose a month ago, greet him as he removes his blindfold.

"I thought I knew this house; where am I?" Norman hints that they are in the vault of Lady Lillian, who holds the key to their freedom. They laugh. The piercing sound of a bugle trumpet is Norman's signal to open the camouflaged exit in the cardboard wall. Chris steps out and repeats the question that puzzled him in the cardboard box.

"Where am I?" The wedding guests, seated in a half circle, facing a stage, applaud as the men join the minister on the stage. All is silent for one minute. Then the bugle sounds the first eight notes of 'The Bridal Chorus from Wagner's Opera 'Lohengrin.' Few wedding attendees realize that this music, first performed in 1850, is now nicknamed 'Here comes the bride.' Today, the majority of American wedding planners still introduce the bridal walk with this enduring piece of music.

Gordon, the beautiful bride on his arm, appears in the doorway. A few years ago, he performed that duty with his daughter Pamela. Those closest to the aisle catch a glimpse of the moisture under his eyes.

In the front row, Heather stops to kiss Lillian, who has been as family to her. Then she kisses Gordon.

The pastor delivers a meaningful message, reminding the young couple that their union in front of these witnesses and Almighty God is a lifetime commitment. He supports his comments with Bible passages that clearly state that divorce is not an option for two Christians.

The beautiful harmony of the duet that follows magnificently finishes this memorable ceremony. Chris and Heather are serious about their vows and pledge to live as though God is watching every moment; because He is!

Professional caterers roll in the evening dinner, a separate service tray for each guest, turning the room into an elegant restaurant. The table for the wedding party with gold and white china, cups, glasses, and other accessories is striking. Dozens of flashes from the camera of the professional photographer promise precious memories in pictures.

Chris and Heather are a picture of contentment. This wedding, these friends, these moments, are memories without equal. After hugs and kisses, when the guests are gone, Gordon, Lillian, Chris, and Heather reflect on recent events. The most sentimental one among them, Lillian, cries tears of happiness.

"No matter where the future may take you two, promise you will never forget us. Heather, God took our Pamela; but now we have you. We love you and Chris."

Hugs, kisses, and tears, all delivered in the true fashion of family love; one more goodbye and the newlyweds are on their way to their honeymoon suite in the plush hotel reserved for them by Lillian.

Chapter

31

It is Monday, June 27, 1977. Chris listens to a radio in his office when the news reports the murder of an old woman in the Congdon Mansion of Duluth. The name of the murder victim arrests his attention. He had learned about her from the guide on the tour boat he and Pamela enjoyed while on their honeymoon. Chris grumbles, "Killers are everywhere, not just in Cambodia."

Two months in Heather's crowded apartment prove sufficient to reconsider housing plans. Tonight they are entertaining guests for dinner. Dr. Frank Stout and his wife Trudy have become good friends after Chris recently spent two nights in their home. Chris walks the couple to their car. Back in the house, he points his head toward the negotiating table in the dining area. Heather loves their discussions at that table. She wonders what Chris is up to now. Chris winks at her and asks,

"Do you know what Frank said when I walked him to the car?"
"Something about my cooking?"
"In a way it is something about your cooking."
"What did he say?"
"He said a cook like you should have a bigger kitchen."
"He did not. You are making things up again."

"In so many words, he did say that. He said this place is way below our means. He said that reporters would sing a different tune if they learned where Dr. Christopher Storm lives. I told him we are frugal with our finances, saving for that trip to Cambodia.

Yesterday I crunched some numbers of our income and outgo. I think we can afford a better place. What do you think?"

"I think this is a perfect time to tell you what I think. I think if you bump into me one more time in that tiny kitchen while I am pouring hot coffee, one of us has to find another place to live. I was here first, so guess who goes." Heather sounds almost serious, but then celebrates Chris' decision.

"Thank you, thank you, thank you Chris. Should we check out some places tomorrow?"

The new apartment in Hudson, on the Wisconsin side of the St. Croix River, which divides Minnesota and Wisconsin, is close to the Crane residence in Stillwater and has many other advantages. They move in on September 1, 1978 and sign a six-month lease. After that, they can leave any time with a 30-day notice.

About a month after the move, on October 2, 1978, Heather visits a local health food store. The store rekindles Heather's love for homeopathy. The manager mentions that she is looking for help. Heather makes an impulsive decision. She terminates her position at the hospital and accepts the job opening at the health food store.

Chris continues his internship at the hospital. He also increases his writing activity. Heather encourages him to write a book about the role of the married man in the family. She feels that feminism has tipped the scale in the wrong direction and upset the balance God put in place. Heather tells Chris,

"Some wives squeeze their husbands into corners where they function mostly like errand boys. Chris, why do men allow it?" Chris did not know that Heather felt that way. He answers,

"God holds men and women responsible for the treatment of each other. If a husband responds in anger and retaliation, no matter how bitter, unforgiving, and disrespectful his wife may be, the husband is directly responsible for his actions to God. God never accepts an excuse that blames another human being. Each person will stand alone some day before the judgement seat of Almighty God. I can visualize a sign over God's throne in big letters, NO EXCUSES ACCEPTED."

"Wow, Chris. Now I know you must write that book. I think people feel too comfortable with excuses, kind of like Adam when he blamed God and Eve for eating the fruit, *The woman whom thou gavest to be with me, she gave me of the tree, and I did eat (Gen 3:12)*."

Chris and Heather's decision to go to Cambodia begins to raise several questions. Should they start a family now? Would it be right to expose young children to the dangerous work they anticipated? If the war in Cambodia continues for several years, would there be time to raise children later? They decide to leave it up to God and use no birth control. After several months, they begin to wonder whether God wants them to remain childless. Heather decides to see a gynecologist. Her diagnosis indicates no reason why she should not be able to have children. The gynecologist suggests that Chris should see a urologist to take this issue to the next level. Chris is not eager to have his manhood tested.

"What if they find that my quiver is empty?" Heather sends him a strange look.

"Your quiver is empty?"

"Heather we must spend more time together in the Bible."

"The Bible talks about quivers?"

"Yes it does and I quote,

Lo, children are an heritage of the LORD: *and the fruit of the womb is his reward. As arrows are in the hand of a mighty man; so are children of the youth. Happy is the man that hath his quiver full of them: they shall not be ashamed, but they shall speak with the enemies in the gate (Psalm 127:3-5)*."

"So, Chris, will you see an urologist?"

"Yes, I will. Preparations for the Cambodia trip include decisions about children. I will make an appointment."

"Dr. Storm, You are healthy. You and your wife should wait patiently. Remember, emotional issues can affect conception. I knew a couple who had tried to have children for seventeen years. Then they decided that she would soon be too old to conceive. They began adoption procedures. In the middle of those procedures, Marilyn became pregnant. Now they have two children and an instant family."

"Thank you, Dr. Payne. We are planning a trip to Cambodia...."

"You don't mean now, when the genocide is in full swing and people are murdered daily?"

"No. We are monitoring that situation carefully. We will leave when it is safe. We would not want to expose children to those dangers."

"You see, Dr. Storm, these thoughts, wondering whether or not to get pregnant now, the hesitancy, worrying about safety, could be impacting your wife. Why not use birth control and plan a family later, when you're sure?"

"Heather and I decided to leave the decision up to God."

"I go to church, Dr. Storm, but I prefer to make my own decisions."

"I don't mind telling you, Dr. Payne, I'd welcome another meeting with you a few years from now, to see how things are working out for you. In the meantime, check out Proverbs 3:5-6. If you are a Christian, these verses will make sense to you. It was nice meeting you. Goodbye."

"Heather, Honey, there is nothing wrong with either of us. Doc says we have to keep trying and be patient about the results."

The subject at lunch is all about the latest news from Cambodia. Newspapers, radio and TV reports tell horror stories with killers and monsters; only these are true stories that drive sorrow deep into the inner man.

Heather is irritated and confused about these reports and asks Chris to explain what started this war and who is behind it. Chris, thoroughly informed on the subject after reading dozens of articles and books, explains the big picture.

"As early as 1973, the Communist Party of Cambodia, known as the Khmer Rouge, began killing as they pleased. Their leader is a tyrant named Pol Pot. His gang guns down anyone who opposes them."

"But Chris, why do they kill their own people? Pictures of human skulls, piled from floor to ceiling in some buildings, are beginning to accompany the news reports. They drive families from their homes and make them slaves who receive one meager meal a day and work seven days a week in rice fields. Starvation, sickness, and death are everywhere. There are stories of children who survived after watching their entire family gunned down, and stories of mothers, shielding their children with their bodies. Nobody seems to know how long this massacre will continue." Heather is close to tears. "Will that country ever be safe for us, Chris? Can we ever make a living in such a backward place? What is behind it?" Chris explains,

"Pol Pot's goal is to kill everyone who has a higher education, or holds to an opposing opinion. Pol Pot and his Communist Party want to achieve equality of status and politics. Remember, Heather, we had our own Civil War fought from 1861 to 1865. It was fought to determine the survival of the Union or independence for the Confederacy, and also addressed slavery."

"But what is the cause of the Cambodian killings, Chris? How did this guy, Pol Pot, gain all that power?"

"Pol Pot is the General Secretary of the Communist Party. As such, he became the official leader of Cambodia last year, in 1975. With him, assuming dictatorial power, the genocide had its official beginning."

Gently, Chris takes his shaken wife into his strong arms, "Darling, where God guides, He provides."

"I wish I had your kind of faith, Chris. It must be nice to be without fear about your future and the troubles in this world."

"Heather, worry turns people into nervous wrecks, not to mention that it proves a lack of faith in God's power to protect and provide. Finish this Bible verse, Honey, *'Without faith it is impossible...'*"

Heather quotes, Hebrews 11:6, *"But without faith it is impossible to please him: for he that cometh to God must believe that he is, and that he is a rewarder of them that diligently seek him."*

Heather likes her job at the health food store. She convinces the owner to market some of her homeopathy products and acquires a few regular clients. Chris is gaining valuable experience at the hospital and thoroughly enjoys helping people with their ailments. He especially enjoys the weekly duty in the emergency room, when people desperately need help. Most cases are routine injuries or painful kidney stone and gall bladder attacks.

Friday, September 15, 1978 is different. The ambulance delivers a young Cambodian woman, Salina Singh, accompanied by her uncle, Toto Chung. Three weeks ago, Salina and her family risked an escape from Cambodia into Thailand. Salina's girlfriend, Lita, had escaped to Thailand in 1976 and had kept in touch. Salina's family hoped to find shelter with Lita for a while.

The Khmer Rouge *(The red army gangs doing the torturing and killing)* caught up with them before the family reached the border. Salina watched as those heartless monsters gunned down her parents and two brothers. Then the men, one by one, raped her, beat her, and left her for dead. Another family traveling by ox cart, escaping via the same route, found her and took her to a hospital in Thailand. When she was able to stand up, the hospital staff forced her to leave. They need the room for other patients. Lita and her husband are poor, but they cared for her until she was well enough to travel to the US.

Her uncle came to Minnesota years before the genocide started. A neighbor once asked Toto Chung why he picked Minnesota. In his broken English, he replied. "Many waters. Many fish. Many woods. Many deers."

Chapter: 31

Toto received Salina's call from Thailand and wired money for her airline ticket to Minneapolis. An airport attendant brought Salina in a wheelchair to meet with her uncle. Toto barely recognized his niece. Pale, thin, and bruised; her face distorted from the blows and kicks to her head, Salina, once beautiful, is now hard to look at. Many of her wounds are infected and demand immediate attention.

Before Chris goes home that evening, his mental address book records Toto's address and phone number. Many times a week, he thanks the Lord for the kind of memory that makes pencil and paper unnecessary.

For several weeks, Chris and Heather have purposely avoided the painful subject of Cambodia. That night, however, when Heather askes,

"How was your day?" Chris tells her all about Salina and Toto. He suggests that they keep in touch with Toto and Salina.

"She will be in and out of the hospital for weeks, as there are several surgeries planned. When she gets better, we should visit them. I reckon they can teach us a lot about their country." Thoughtfully Heather responds,

"Maybe we should invite them to have lunch with us soon. Where does the uncle live?"

"Toto is a woodsman. He lives somewhere on the shores of Lake Mille Lacs, in a cabin he put together with pine logs."

Salina's condition was life threatening, but the medical team restores her to full health. Surgeons replace damaged tissue and bones in her face. After several surgeries, Salina is again beautiful with only small scars remaining. Chris calls Salina shortly after she checks out of the hospital. He tells her that his wife is eager to talk to her. Since then, Heather and Salina have spoken many times. They become phone friends.

Early in November, Heather invites Salina and her uncle to join them for the Thanksgiving meal on November 23. She also suggests that they spend the night in their home. They happily accept. The four friends enjoy great fellowship and conversation.

Salina and her girlfriend, Lita, had taken some English lessons in Phnom Penh, the capital of Cambodia. Her accent is lovely. Chris and Heather enjoy listening to her stories. Salina shares that Lita's parents died instantly when their motorcycle collided with a bus carrying a Khmer Rouge gang. Witnesses insist that the bus purposely veered into the path of the motorcycle; but nobody argues with the Khmer Rouge people. They are untouchable. If you have a question, they are likely to answer it with a bullet to your head.

Lita has no siblings. Alone, she fled to Thailand where she married a Cambodian man. Salina was very ill when she stayed with them in their home, a two-room bamboo hut. She did not notice much. However, she remembers that the couple is happy. They are kind to each other. Salina wishes that she might find that kind of man someday.

Heather studies Salina's face and wonders whether she ever had a boyfriend. As if on cue, Salina tells them that she was once very much in love, but the man married somebody else. She sighs and confesses, "I think of him often. He is not easy to forget. I envy his wife."

Salina and Toto are alarmed when they learn that Chris and Heather are planning a trip to Cambodia.

"Why go there?" Toto wants to know. Chris responds,

"We want to help stop the abuse of children." Toto's face indicates unbelief. His English is still poor since he keeps to himself in rural Isle, Minnesota. He insists,

"Nobody can help. Is okay with everybody. Mother sell daughter to get money for food. Police not care. Police rape too. I in trouble with Police. I come to America." Salina explains that her uncle was always concerned about human trafficking because his sister sold two daughters to the traffickers and received $200 for one and $300 for the other. Chris wants to know why the difference in price. Toto understands the question and answers.

"One very pretty virgin. Virgin more money. Customer pay more. Rich bad guys pay much to seller." Chris is intrigued to learn details.

"Toto, do you know where some of these bad guys do business?"

"What you mean, do business?"

"Where do they take the children they buy?"

"Have many places. Move in Vans. Deliver kids to buyers. Hide in cellars. Keep secret."

"Why keep it secret if nobody tries to stop them?"

"Other bad guys steal pretty girls, like stealing food from market."

Heather has been listening and objects to any further discussion on that subject. She admits,

"I get so angry when I hear these stories. I think I would be able to kill a person who buys and sells and abuses innocent children." A lesson from the Scriptures about vengeance teeter totters on Chris' tongue. He decides to swallow the words. In this case, they may do more harm than good. He has one more important question for Toto and Salina.

"Would you go with us to Cambodia when this war is over?" Salina's recent experience is too fresh and tortures her mind.

"Never, never, never; I never go back to Cambodia." Toto appears to consider the idea, but says nothing.

Chris and Heather are grateful for their beautiful new home. One of the bedrooms serves as Chris' office, and another is the master suite. The other two are available for overnight guests. Neither Toto nor Salina ever experienced such luxury. In Cambodia, most people live in bamboo huts. Only the richer citizens can afford brick or steel buildings.

Used to rough surroundings, Toto is a bit lost. Salina, on the other hand, has always dreamed of visiting America someday. She compliments Heather on her skills to make a home look so appealing. Heather motions for Chris to follow her into the hallway,

"How would you feel if I invited Salina to live with us? She needs to find a job to support herself. That would be easier in the Twin Cities than in Northern Minnesota."

The Passions & Perils of the Prodigy

"What a generous thought, Heather; but what if she cannot find a job, are we willing to support her?" Heather is quick. She uses Chris' own words the one time she was concerned about provisions.

"Where God guides, He provides."

"Okay, sweetheart, if it's alright with God, it's alright with me."

Salina is overjoyed. Even Toto exhibits a grateful smile. The meager income from a small home business would require a serious stretch of every dollar to feed the extra mouth. He decides that if Chris and Heather agree, Salina can stay right now. In a few days, the three should come up to Isle and fetch the few things Salina has acquired since she came from Thailand. That way they will also become familiar with Toto's home and business.

Highway 169 takes them all the way to Minnesota's second largest lake, Lake Mille Lacs. Only Red Lake, if you count both upper and lower, exceeds the 133,000 acres of Mille Lacs. Turning right on Highway 27, they arrive in Isle, population about 600. Altogether, it is a comfortable two-hour drive.

Toto's cabin is located in Isle, on the Southeastern shore of the lake, boasting excellent walleye fishing. The small lean-to attached to the cabin, is Toto's workshop. Chris marvels at the hand-carved handles of the filleting knifes in a glass cage. Toto explains that he buys knifes at thrift stores and garage sales for pennies, removes the old handles, and replaces them with handles carved from hardwood or bone. Anglers pay as much as $65 for his bone-carved knives, featuring the image of a walleye or northern pike. Even the lowest priced fillet knife brings $20.

A neighbor owns a large pontoon boat and the foursome graciously accept his offer to treat them to a cruise on Lake Mille Lacs. At the end of the day all agree that the trip was pleasant and the visit with Toto and his neighbor gratifying.

Salina is a quick learner. She takes an interest in Heather's homeopathy business and becomes her apprentice and assistant. The health food store opens a second location, leaving Heather in charge to manage the first store. The owner allows Heather to hire Salina to assist her. Things are working out well.

Salina has quietly observed the everyday routine of this home and the people in the congregation when she attends church with her hosts. She has questions about the table prayers and Bible readings. Her family and everybody she knew in Cambodia and Thailand practiced Theravada Buddhism with its difficult rules of the 'Seven Stages of Purification'. To Salina, Christianity is too simple. For one man, the man Jesus, to accomplish the salvation of all humankind by dying on a cross, seems unfair to the millions of people who must obey rigorous rules and steps to attain purity. Lovingly and patiently, Chris and Heather answer her questions and stress faith over works. They can only witness, God's Spirit must do the rest.

It is Sunday, August 14, 1978, during lunch, Heather notices Salina's strange behavior. She is picking at her food, but not eating.

"Don't you feel well, Salina?"

"I'm okay. No, I am not okay. I do not understand why the preacher said that one single sin is enough to send us to hell. Is your God that mean and cruel?" Chris winks at Heather and takes over.

"Salina, how many sins do you think it should take to send a person to hell?"

"Well, I don't know, but surely God could forgive one sin."

"Salina, if the police catch two people, one who stole $50, and the other who stole $500, which one is the thief?"

"They are both thieves."

"Of course. You see God is 100% pure, not 99.9%, but 100%. Because of His purity and justice, He cannot overlook a single sin. There must be a payment, a sacrifice, an atonement before God can forgive that sin. He does not accept a bribe, money, gold or any other treasure from this earth. He would only accept the surrendered lifeblood of a pure human being. Jesus was that human being."

That afternoon, in tears, Salina acknowledges her sins before God and accepts His forgiveness. Immediately she becomes a missionary and says,

"We must talk to Uncle Toto about Jesus."

Chapter

32

The carnage in Cambodia continues until finally in December 1978, Vietnam grows tired of Khmer Rouge rebels continually crossing the border. Vietnam invades Cambodia. They remove the Khmer Rouge from power, driving them into the countryside. In January 1979, they take over the capital city of Phnom Penh and Pol Pot flees to the border of Thailand. This is the beginning of the People's Republic of Kampuchea *(Kingdom of Cambodia)*. The Khmer Rouge still harasses the countryside, but Phnom Penh and the surrounding area is safe from those terrorists.

For Chris and Heather, the move to Cambodia, so long in planning, is now a glaring reality. The weight of the decisions concerning the next step is tenacious. Do we need a contact there? Should we learn more about human trafficking before getting involved? Will we need firearms for protection? Will we get along with the few sentences of the Khmer language we learned from Salina? Should we take time to say goodbye to friends and relatives in other States?

Once the decision to go to Cambodia is final, everything falls into place. Chris and Heather are delighted that Salina has agreed to come along. She cautions them that they will arrive during the height of the monsoon season. Toto likes his life by the big lake and stays put.

The trip to Massachusetts to say goodbye to friends and relatives there, turns out to be so timely they could not have planned it better. Upon their arrival, they learn that Roger Colter, Chris' Grandfather, passed away the day before. Chris officiates at the funeral. They stay a few extra days to comfort Doris, Chris' Grandma. Since all the other friends and relatives attend the funeral, Chris is able to say all his goodbyes in one place.

Chris' connections in Massachusetts have followed his career. Those closest to him, consider Chris the kindest man they ever knew. His wish to help the physically impaired comes naturally to a man like him. However, that he would place himself and his wife in harm's way by working against slave traders and child abusers has never entered anybody's mind. All are concerned for their safety.

Before leaving for Massachusetts, Chris had written a letter to the American Embassy in Phnom Penh outlining his plans to help fight human trafficking in Cambodia. Their reply was most helpful. It includes details about visas and a list of personnel he could contact, including phone numbers. Perhaps due to the sensitivity of the subject, no details about human trafficking were included. There is, however, a clear invitation to visit the embassy before 'proceeding with their enterprise'.

Encouraged by the response from the embassy, preparations go full speed ahead. They give the 30-day notice to cancel their lease. Notices go out on a timely basis to hospital administration and Heather's work. Carefully they satisfy passport, visa, and immunization requirements. Because most of the airlines operating between the US and Cambodia are headquartered in New York, it means a stopover in that world-famous city. Salina sees that as good news. She has heard so much about New York. Even Cambodian newspapers have regular coverage of something happening in New York. Altogether, it means roughly twenty-four hours in the air. The confirmed reservations at the Embassy Hotel in Phnom Penh are for Wednesday, August 15, 1979.

Chapter: 32

To please Salina, Chris picks an itinerary that includes an overnight stay in New York. He makes hotel reservations at the Radisson near the JFK Airport. Gordon and Lillian chauffeur them to the Minneapolis International Airport. Reporters record their departure and keep their readers well informed.

From the plane, the night approach into New York City is spectacular. Salina will talk about it for days. Often, Salina reveals a poetic quality in her speech. She comments,

"All the stars fell from heaven and landed on the streets of New York. Many got stuck on the tall buildings." However, as the plane drops lower, she adds, "Now, some of the stars have turned into yellow taxicabs."

They board their connection flight at 3:35 a.m. Wednesday morning. Three exhausted people arrive in Phnom Penh minutes before sunset. At the airport, a man, speaking perfect English, taps Chris on the shoulder.

"Can I help you with something?" Salina looks up and cries, "Khmer Rouge. He is Khmer Rouge." The man shakes his head.

"I am working here at the airport. Why is she saying that?"

Chris probes Salina's face for an explanation, but sees only fear. Then Salina whispers something to Heather, who explains.

"It is the black uniform. The Khmer Rouge always wore black."

The airport employee responds.

"I don't know why airport management chose black, but I think it's temporary. Others have objected as well. I am sorry, Miss."

The man summons a tuk-tuk. (*a covered two-wheel trailer, with room for four, pulled by a motorcycle. In Cambodia, tuk-tuks are the preferred way to travel. They are reasonably safe and cheap.*) For a fee of about 16,000 riel ($4.00), the visitors are on their way to the Embassy Hotel.

The Hotel is well furnished. Nearby restaurants serve healthy Cambodian and American food; but it is clear that the threesome will have to locate more reasonably priced living quarters and food prices soon. With no income and a shrinking pocket book, they would soon be out of money. The schedule for the first couple of days calls for rest and relaxation; sleeping late, three leisurely meals a day, and sightseeing.

Chris and Heather observe the city without a vantage point, but Salina immediately comments that this city is different from the city she left a few years ago.

She sighs deeply. Exhibiting extraordinary insight for a nineteen-year old, her observations are clearly rooted in a hurting heart.

"Everything is different. It is a city populated by people with broken spirits. They are wearing masks of kindness on their faces, but their hearts are filled with sorrow. Their eyes reflect a history of pain and tell a tale of terror, torture, and killings." Salina cries openly and honestly.

"Oh Lord," she asks. "What happened here? All the familiar stores are either gone or managed by different proprietors."

Heather and Salina have become close friends. Salina's pain affects Heather deeply. Silently, both in tears, they hug for several minutes. Their sadness spills over on Chris and the circle of friends soon restores Salina's beautiful smile. In the following weeks, Chris and Heather hear Salina's insights repeated frequently by others who returned after the genocide.

With Salina's translation services, they learn much about the present regime, rental property, house prices, and the best places for shopping. Monday morning at breakfast, Heather, screening an American Newspaper, dives into the subject of housing. They have never discussed this, but Salina's presence is actually a bit awkward. Would she stay with them as part of their family? Would she want to find a companion? She is after all, the right age for marriage. Chris decides to force the issue right now.

"So, Salina, are you staying with us or do you have other plans?"

Salina does not answer, but her body language does. Finally, she utters a single surprise word.

"What?" It is the first time this woman of eloquent speech, stutters. "Ah, ... I... don't... know. I love you both. There is nobody else." It is obvious that she never expected a separation from them. She is close to tears. Chris regrets his sudden and direct approach.

"I wanted to make sure that we are on the same page. Then it is settled. Of course, we will stay together. So, we are looking for a three-bedroom house or apartment."

Heather spots an unusual ad. A retired farmer is selling several buildings. One served as a bunkhouse. It has ten small bedrooms, a large common area, a kitchen, three bathrooms, indoor plumbing, and electric service. The price is lower than even the smallest houses in Phnom Penh.

She mentions the ad and is surprised at Chris' favorable response. Why would he want a building with ten bedrooms?

"Heather, darling, you are a mastermind. You found the building we need when we get children away from the traffickers. Is there an address or phone number?"

"It has only the name of the village. No house number. No phone number; but there are directions." Chris is excited.

"Let's go see it right now." The small village of 'Phnom Chisoris' is about ninety minutes south of Phnom Penh. Chris steps outside and summons the only tuk-tuk driver parked in front of the hotel. Heather and Salina want to be part of the negotiations and join him. The driver looks at the ad and tries to discourage Chris from visiting Phnom Chisoris. Speaking Cambodian Khmer, he tells Salina that only people who like to see a bunch of 10th century AD Angkorian era ruins go there. Chris asks about the farm directions in the ad. The driver, addressing Salina, says,

"I don't know about farms. I think the Khmer Rouge drove all the farmers out of their homes."

"When Chris asks, "do you think you can find this place?" He answers in English. "How much you pay?"

"How much do you want?"

"One hundred American dollars." Chris looks at Salina. "Ask him whether he is a tuk-tuk driver or a thief."

Salina shakes her head. "Cambodians are proud people. If you say that to him, he will consider you unkind and leave." Clearly, the driver has been misrepresenting his skill level with the English language when he grins and says,

"You cheap American. You pay $100 or you go by motodop."

"Motodop, what is that?" Salina explains that it is the backseat of a motorcycle, transportation for one, fast, cheap, and dangerous. Chris makes a decision.

"Girls, tomorrow, I am going alone by motodop to check things." Heather is not happy."

"I want to see the place too, Chris."

"And you will, my love, after I check it out."

Early Tuesday morning, August 21, 1979, Chris looks out the window and finds several shiny Honda motorcycles lined up in front of the hotel. He is puzzled. Are they all waiting for him? Salina grins, "These men are probably friends and relatives of the tuk-tuk driver. They help one another to pick up business."

The minute Chris appears at the door, the drivers go crazy, each claiming to have the best deal for him.

"You take me, I good driver, have best cycle, I drive fast, I give deal, me know Cambodia best." On and on they shout their commercials. Chris picks a driver who looks more mature than the rest. He did not advertise his services, but remained silent. He points to him.

"You." The second Chris makes his choice, the rest of the drivers take off.

"Is that normal?" he asks his driver? The man stares at him.

"Do you speak English?" The man points to his ears and mouth. Chris regrets his choice of drivers and says,

"No wonder you were quiet. Not only do you not speak English, you do not speak at all." The driver pulls a pen and notepad out of his shirt pocket. The pad has a pre-printed message: I was born in America. I can read and write English. Where do you want to go?

Chapter: 32

Chris shows him the newspaper ad. The driver takes a quick look and sticks the ad in the top pocket of his leather jacket. Like most authors, Chris always carries a notepad and pen. He puts a question mark and a dollar sign on the pad. The man shrugs his shoulders, revs the engine, and points to the back seat. To be funny, Chris shrugs his shoulders, and hops on the cycle. The cycle-crazy driver lays a strip of rubber on the pavement, counting on the high backrest to save his passenger's life. Salina yells something in Cambodian. The man slows down a bit until they are out of sight.

The cycle appears to be in excellent condition, purring like a big cat. After a few minutes, they pass through Takhmau on Route 2. Then Route 2 appears to be heading to the end of the world. There are a few minor crossroads, but no towns in sight.

After thirty minutes on the road, a piece of paper flies past Chris' ear; junk from the road, maybe? Finally, a scenery change, they cross a river, swollen with the rain during June, July, and August. The river is the driver's signal to study the ad for an upcoming turn. He stops and fiddles with his coat pocket. The ad with the directions is the piece of paper that flew past Chris' ear. The alarmed driver scribbles his dilemma on the notepad. From memory, Chris pens the directions, word for word on his pad. The man's astonished look is familiar to Chris, catching it every time he demonstrates his memory skills.

The map calls for a left turn onto a gravel road. The driver is concerned about muddy roads ahead. Eventually, a badly maintained bridge crosses the same river and the mud becomes a serious concern. The cycle skids from side to side and for about a mile, the two men push it. Finally, when the road rises it becomes passable again. Two more turns in the road and the cycle stops in front of a narrow, uphill path. There are no buildings in sight. The man studies the directions on Chris' notepad and engages in his favorite activity, shoulder shrugging. After his third shoulder shrug, he proceeds up the narrow path. He runs over an opossum, almost spilling the bike. Chris realizes that the tuk-tuk could not have negotiated this area of the trip and wonders how anybody gets to and from the farm, if there is a farm.

As they reach the top of the hilly path, the farm buildings come into full view. The path joins a much wider road, which leads to the same river they have crossed two times. A locked gate stops them from going any further. The driver motions for Chris to walk around the gate and continue to the buildings, indicating absolutely no desire to go with him.

Chris nervously surveys the area, thinking it would be nice to have anyone, even the deaf and dumb driver by his side. A dog is barking somewhere in the direction of the farm. Chris never completely gained victory over his childhood's fear of dogs and hopes that the barking dog is a confined dog. Nope! A very large hound, a breed he does not recognize, taking giant leaps, is rapidly reducing the distance between them.

"I think this is the day I die," he murmurs. The beast circles Chris, his tail wagging. Then the dog stands on his hind legs and places his front paws on Chris' shoulders. Chris has visions of decapitation; but the animal licks his face and leads the way to the farmhouse. A man with a cane greets him.

"Did'che come about de ad?"

"Yes, how did you guess?"

"Ain't nobody else gonna visit. And iffen they does, they comes by boat on that there yonder river." He lifts his cane and points to the river about a hundred yards away.

"It's a mighty sorrowful trip on this here path, during the green season."

"The green season?"

"Yeah, dats what they calls it here, starten about May."

"Can we discuss your ad? I am interested in the bunkhouse."

"You don't say; the bunkhouse is it? Got a messa kids then?"

"May I please see the building?"

"Come on then. Critters sorta gots the idee dat they own de place; but Annie's gots the answer for dat sorta complication. Ain't never missed with dat twelve-gauge shotgun of hers. Does je mind critters?" Chris grins.

"I'm not too fond of critters, but I suppose one can get used to almost anything if it is unavoidable."

"I reckon one can. Dat thar building with de horseshoe over de door be the bunkhouse. Get'che on in there."

"I wonder, could you send the dog in first to chase out the critters?"

The man with his hand on the door, laughs so hard that the door shakes and the horseshoe falls off.

"You ain't never seen old Hercules in action inside det place. Folks plain doesn't believe my story. Hercules strolls on in there couple a times a day. All dem critters knows his scent by heart. They comes out to play with'm. Hercules lies down and dem critters run all over him. When he has a good mind to play rough, he'll catch a rat or a squirrel, toss'm around a bit and lets'm go. What a fella needs in there is a mean old cat."

Carefully, Chris follows the man inside. Perhaps the farmer exaggerated the critter story. Chris cannot spot any animals. The building is old, but in good shape. Concrete floors and foundation; logs on the outside, rough-cut lumber on the inside. Chris tries a few doors. The hinges squeak a bit, but the doors shut securely.

"You have a price in the paper. Will you take a lower offer?"

"Depends what'je fixin to do with dat building. Iffen je fixin to make money on it, the price stands. If je in some sorta of religious non-profit venture, I can fix de price some."

"Sir, I am wondering about your brogue. Where are you from?"

"I begs yer pardon, never even gives je my name. I am Wilbur Edwards. I growed up in Indiana and talked right good English. Den de folks moves to Missoura, close to de Arkansas border. Dem hillbillies talk mighty strange 'roud der. We picks up some of der dialect, and keeps some of ar own. Can't nobody tell what sorta lingo come outa ar mouth. Anyhow, I was fixin to tell ya about comin to this here place. My younger brother, Dan, found himself in det awful Vietnam War and stayed put at the end of it. Got heself in a mess of trouble with drugs and prostitution and whatall, here in Cambodia. Was caught up with criminals kidnapping youngens.

Me, de wife, and three youngens, all girls, leaves the Ozarks back in 64. Anyway, we come here to set'em straight; but it was too late. Somebody done shot him dead outside Phnom Penh. We found dis here place and made a heap of money with rice." Mr. Edwards stops and stares at Chris.

"Ya looks a bit familiar somehow. Ya ever been to the Ozarks?"

"No Sir."

"So what's your name then, young man?" They shake hands,

"My name is Christopher Storm."

"Ya sure looks familiar," Mr. Edwards repeats.

"So what did ya say ya fixin to do with the building?"

"I didn't say, Mr. Edwards, but my wife and I came to help the authorities fight human trafficking in this country. We want to help put men like your brother behind bars. We waited until the genocide stopped and here we are. I am thinking that your building could house some of the kids after we get them away from the traffickers."

The man becomes quiet, until finally with deep sadness in his voice, he tells about his youngest daughter who went to Phnom Penh with her girlfriend. They never saw either one of them again. The police insisted that this happens every day and they cannot do anything about it.

"We left a photograph of the girls at the police station, but never heard from them," he adds."Mr. Storm, ya know what I's thinkin? If ya is gonna be messin with dem traffickers, I wants to pitch in. Listen up now, got ya an offer. Let me know what ya think. I am an old man what don't need no money. If ye are of a mind to use de buildings, ya can have dem, as long as ya don't mess with Annie and me. We wants to stay in our house and have the deed to that house and twenty acres around it. The rest is yours to mess with, what ya think?"

"Mr. Edwards. I am overwhelmed, but shouldn't you think about this and at least talk to your wife about that decision."

"I talk to Jeannie all the time, but she don't say nottin back. She is quite dead, ya know; died a short spell after settling in this here place, she did. It's me and my two older daughters what worked the place. Then Gracie got herself pregnant and married de fella what got her in dat condition. After dat it is me and my oldest daughter, Annie. She's the one what helped me with the rice farmin. She's a mighty hard worker, that one."

The two men shake hands to settle the deal. Mr. Edwards writes down the terms of the deal and promises to have a lawyer draw up the papers. He also suggests that Chris use his 18-foot fishing boat to get back to Highway 2, and use it to bring his family and belongings down the river. He tells Chris about a shed he built for storing the boat near Highway 2 where it crosses the river. He gives him a key and shows him to the boat in another shed. One more time, Mr. Edwards insists that he has seen Chris before.

"Mr. Storm, where is it that ya growed up?"

"I was born in Massachusetts....."

"Dat's it. I knowed it. My sister, Eleanor, she lives in Boston. Sends a heap of clippings every month, she does. Puts her own words to some. Tells me of dat genius what was born in Massachusetts and preaches, and writes about stuff. One of dem had yar piture on it, it did. Says yar a doctor of some kind with a mess of initials after yar name. How come ya never said nothing about dat? If I gots initials after my name, I'd be spilling the beans to every soul what wants to listen."

"Mr. Edwards, allow me to quote a verse from the Bible"

"Let another man praise thee, and not thine own mouth; a stranger, and not thine own lips (Proverbs 27:2). I try to live by the wisdom of the Scriptures. There is no other wisdom or advice that can match the words of God."

"Dr. Storm....."

"Please, Mr. Edwards, call me Chris."

"Chris, me thinks my Annie and me be lucky folks to meet up with ya. Be in a hurry now to fetch de Missus."

Chris tells his motodop driver to meet him at the river intersection on Highway 2. The man is angry and wants his money now.

"How much?"

"$100." Chris thinks it's too much, but grateful for the gift of the buildings, he pays the driver $50 and promises to pay the other $50 when he meets him on Highway 2.

Heather and Salina are overjoyed. Even before seeing the new premises, they are happy to have a place of their own. The wet months of August and September usher in a moderate October with only a few warm afternoon showers. November promises dry weather replacing the warm rains of the SW monsoon, which have dominated since April. With temperatures and humidity at their lows of the year and the countryside vibrant and green, the newcomers thoroughly enjoy Cambodia.

Chapter

33

It is December. The nice weather is holding. Three months have passed since Chris, Heather and Salina occupied the bunkhouse. By the end of February, the two women turn a drab farm building into a comfortable and pleasant home. They also fix up an additional building to serve as storage. Seven of the ten bedrooms still need furniture and the decorator's touch.

Heather believes that she is pregnant, but does not share it with anyone until she is sure. When she does, everyone celebrates with her. Chris is thankful that they found this bunkhouse. One of the ten rooms can become the baby room.

Mr. Edwards and Annie have been most helpful in locating used furniture at second hand stores and auctions. Now they keep their eyes open for a crib and clothes for the baby. Some of their neighbors, learning of the famous Dr. Storm's new residence stop by and bring useful house warming gifts.

Chris writes an article on Cambodia's struggle to recover after the genocide and manages to get it published by the American newspaper in Phnom Penh. His ability to read and remember dozens of books and articles a week allow him to keep publishing editorials of interest to Cambodian readers. Working with a translator, he writes about proper management of rice fields and the rice harvests. Both, the American and Cambodian newspapers buy his work.

At the end of April 1980, the American paper offers him a regular weekly column entitled ' Storm Stories'. He includes some fictional material on romance, marriage, and family life, and gains a wide readership. The job provides the finances needed. Because the commute by boat and car is less than ideal, Chris rents a studio apartment in Phnom Penh and often stays overnight. Salina, feeling responsible for earning her own living, is talking about finding a job. She is a gifted orator and writer; perhaps she could replace the translator working with Chris. Heather suggests that Chris approach the management at the Cambodian paper about that possibility.

Salina's interview at the paper goes well. Her association with Chris is a positive aspect. However, the interviewer is concerned about the difficult commute and fears that it could result in frequent absences from work. To Salina's surprise, he offers her and Chris helicopter service to and from work for a reasonable fee taken out of their salary. Chris cancels the office lease. The savings will pay for the helicopter fee.

When Salina is not translating for Chris, she submits some of her own work for publication. At first, the editors reject her entries; but eventually, the editors accept an article about her time in America and publish it. The positions at the newspapers allow Chris and Salina to keep their eyes and ears tuned for stories about the underworld of human traffickers.

In a neighboring town, a woman finds a young girl on her doorstep, severely beaten and close to death. She calls the ambulance and then the newspapers. Chris volunteers to follow up and visits the girl in the hospital. The doctors will not discuss the case with Chris until they verify his identity. Through his friendly and encouraging writing style, Chris has earned a favorable reputation. Hospital authorities now grant him permission to visit the girl. However, the girl turns her head toward the wall and does not speak. Chris calls Salina, who immediately wins the young girl's confidence.

Her name is Tanya. She is thirteen years old. She has eight siblings, most of whom have different fathers. Her mother cannot afford food for them, so she sold Tanya and her sister Chantel, to a man for $600. The man put them in a large, blue van. There were four other girls and one boy in the van. Most of them were crying. The boy's head was bleeding from a cut. He did not say how he got the cut. They drove about two hours and then the van stopped. They took Chantel and two other girls out of the van. The van had no windows, but when the door opened, Tanya saw a big white house with a beautiful fenced yard. There were children playing behind the fence. Tanya is able to name people, dates, and places. As Salina translates what Tanya says, Chris commits it all to memory.

This marks the beginning of the work they have planned. All the sacrifices and hardships along the way were a small price to pay for the rescue of innocent children from cruel slave traders. If only they could trust someone on the police force. Chris trusts Wilbur Edwards with information and wonders whether he would know an honest cop. Wilbur recalls a young police offer who worked part time in his rice field.

"A fine fella he is, that one, German accent and all. Annie calls him Santa Claus 'cause his name is Klaus with a K. Never knowed his last name. That were five years back and God knows where he got off to."

"Well, Mr. Edwards, then we'll have to ask God where that fine fella, Klaus, got off to." Chris prays aloud. Wilbur is shaking his head and insists that a man cannot speak to God without a priest present."

"We have a priest present, Mr. Edwards. Listen to this quote from the Bible, *Seeing then that we have a great high priest, that is passed into the heavens, Jesus the Son of God, let us hold fast our profession (Heb 4:14)*."

Jesus speaks for us and we can come boldly to the throne of God with our prayers. God always does what is right and so if He wants us to find that fella, we will. Moreover, if He does not want us to find that fella, then we do not need him."

The Passions & Perils of the Prodigy

"Aint no wonder ya gots famous, ya knows and believes stuff nobody else do."

Friday evening, May 30, 1980, during rush hour traffic, the worst car pile-up Phnom Penh had seen in decades happens right in front of the newspaper building. Police cars, ambulances, and fire trucks rush to the scene. Reporters and journalists talk to victims to obtain details of the accident. Chris watches from the window. One young cop seems extra eager to assist victims. He walks from car to car, helping where he can. On a hunch, Chris decides to talk to him. His heart skips a beat when he catches the name on the police officer's uniform. 'Lt. Klaus Schroeder.'

"Lieutenant Schroeder, my name is Christopher Storm. I am Wilbur Edwards's neighbor."

"How is old Wilbur? I worked part time for him a few years ago."

"I know. We prayed that we would find you. God answered our prayer."

"Now you have my attention. What makes me fortunate enough to have somebody mention my name in prayer?"

"Could I make an appointment to speak with you about a pressing issue in need of honest police work?" In a hushed voice, Schroeder says,

"Sir, you don't want to speak in public about honest police work, making it sound as though there is another kind." Chris is not spooked,

"Isn't there another kind, Lieutenant Schroeder?" Sharply Schroeder says,

"Tuesday, June 3, 7:00 p.m., Embassy Hotel Restaurant." Then he turns, walks away, and continues his work with the accident victims.

Arriving at the restaurant, Schroeder selects a table suited for discreet conversation and safe observation of activities. His police training has served him well for over five years. He lost two companions on the force during a shootout a year ago and has adopted rigid security habits to protect his life and the lives of people in his company. In public places, he always assures that a wall or other solid structure protects his back. His revolver is loaded and unbuckled for swift action.

Chapter: 33

Even though his impression of Christopher Storm is positive, he is cautious. He never met the man before. His reference to Wilbur Edwards may have been a calculated trap. He never mentioned the reason for this meeting. What does this stranger, Christopher Storm, want from him?

Chris, looking for a man in uniform, does not immediately spot Lt. Schroeder, who is in civilian attire. Klaus Schroeder, over six feet tall, excellent physic and blond hair, never remains camouflaged for long. He stands up and motions for Chris to join him. The firm handshake and eye contact build trust between the two men right from the start.

They order a light supper and when Chris offers to say a table prayer, Klaus Schroeder's reluctance about this stranger begins to melt away. Raised in a Baptist home in Germany, he now considers Chris a safe companion.

"So, Mr. Storm, why are we here?" Chris turns to confirm privacy, "Please, call me Chris."

"Okay, Chris. I think we can safely talk, I can spot any unpleasant interference from here." Chris indicates his intention to speak by clearing his throat. Proving his confidence in Klaus, he comes right to the point.

"My wife and I came to Cambodia to assist in any way we can in the battle against human trafficking and the abuse of children. We need help from the authorities and are not sure whom we can trust." A long pause follows. Chris is not sure what Lt. Schroeder is thinking. His face betrays no clue. His lips part for a moment, but he remains silent. Finally, with a look of unbelief, Schroeder speaks.

"Some things that happen in this twisted world seem to belong to another realm. The way we met through Wilbur Edwards; the way I happened to join the troops at the car pileup, which is not my usual responsibility, and the way you happened to notice me, it all seems more like divine guidance than coincidence.

You see, I am working undercover in cracking down on the gangs involved in human trafficking and prostitution. In addition, we have not even addressed the growing problem of pirates attacking refugees in boats. They abduct girls and women for prostitution. Often they capsize the boats and drown the refugees. I don't know your qualifications for this dangerous work, but we are shorthanded and could use help in the office keeping records and doing research." Obviously, Schroeder is not aware of Chris' background and abilities. Chris explains,

"Lieutenant Schroeder, allow me to provide some background about my qualifications. You may not have heard about it here in Cambodia, but much of the rest of the world knows me as Christopher Storm, the man with the miracle memory."

"Of course, I read about you. Just didn't put it together." The two shake hands to mark this momentous introduction.

"Please Chris; call me Klaus, pronounced nearly like 'claws." Chris answers,

"Yes, I know. I speak German and have heard the name before."

"Chris, we have so much to discuss. This is a special moment. I have been losing sleep over the messy and slow progress with the traffickers. You will be an important asset to our group in the office. When do you want to meet the rest of the crew? They will be thrilled. How about tomorrow morning 9:00 a.m. in my office?"

Chapter

34

Chris and the Lieutenant's crew discuss many details at the meeting. The subject of Wilbur Edward's farm and the bunkhouse is exciting to the men. They have been looking for a place suitable to house rescued children. Schroeder contacts the proper channels authorizing Chris to move Tanya from the hospital to the farm. Heather is overjoyed to be involved in this important work by caring for the child.

By the end of July 1980, the crew, nicknamed 'Santa's Champions', remove twelve children from brothels and arrest the operators of the brothels. The success is partially due to Chris' research, which made him a walking encyclopedia on information about communities frequently hit by kidnappers, the gangs involved, hiding places, buyers, and sellers of children.

With hired help, Wilbur finishes the renovation of the bunkhouse, and turns another building into suitable housing. He and Annie consider it a privilege to assist in a project, which promises to bring justice to his missing daughter, Annie's sister.

Lt. Schroeder secures government funds for room and board of the children. To further support the war against human trafficking financially, Chris continues to write articles part time. His royalties along with Salina's employment at the newspaper provide the needed resources to support the family, including the baby, due in early October. Heather moves a bit slower these days.

When Gordon and Lillian Crane receive a letter announcing the expected baby, on impulse, they treat that announcement as an invitation to visit Cambodia. Arriving in early August, Cambodia greets them with very good weather. The reunion with Gordon and Lillian mark the highlight for Chris and Heather since their arrival in Cambodia a year ago.

The celebration of the Crane's visit to Cambodia, all financed by this generous couple, includes visits to the zoo and amusement parks with some of the healthier children. A police escort promises their safety. These children from poverty-stricken families have never experienced such happiness.

When Gordon and Lillian prepare to return to the US, they turn the happy home into a somber place. Saying goodbye is especially painful now. Would they see one another again on this side of Heaven?

The repulsive condition of the two young Cambodian girls, rescued Friday, August 15, 1980, weigh heavily on Chris. Lt. Schroeder's crew, nicknamed 'Champions', located the children, aged thirteen, and fifteen, at the home of a Cambodian Government official, outside of Phnom Penh.

Tinos, a subordinate of the official, is one of several employees invited to enjoy the slave girls. The man purchased the girls from traffickers for the entertainment of his guests. Tinos is an eyewitness to the abuse of these children. Lt. Schroeder is grateful to him, for the tipoff. His testimony will be critical for the outcome of the jury's verdict.

How can the Champions develop their rescue missions, when local government participates in these horrendous crimes?

Undernourished and frail, the girls were raped and beaten repeatedly. The eyes of these abused children disclose unspeakable sadness, which burns a permanent image on Chris' perceptive mind,

Chapter: 34

"Oh Lord; the evil of these people is so painful to me. How can I conquer my repulsion against these abusers of innocent children?"

Tonight, the day after the rescue, while the rest of the house is sound asleep, Chris cannot get any rest. Hercules, Wilbur's dog, barking furiously, interrupts his thoughts. Chris is able to distinguish between the dog's casual bark and the ferocious bark at an intruder. It is obvious that the dog has spotted intruders.

The shot that silences the dog carries the threat of serious trouble. Wilbur had given him a revolver, but Chris never shot it and actually has an aversion to guns. He is not sure he could take another man's life. Nevertheless, he takes the loaded weapon to the window, and peers into the darkness. The yard light casts the shadow of two men standing by the dead dog at Wilbur's front door. He freezes. What will they do next? To his horror, Wilbur appears at the front door. Without hesitation, the men shoot him several times. Then they step over his body, and enter the house. Annie will be next. Chris darts to the house.

When it is finished, one of the men lies dead on the kitchen floor, and the other, seriously wounded, moans miserably. Annie, standing in the doorway of her bedroom, holds her empty twelve-gauge shotgun. She stands motionless, staring at Chris. He walks over to comfort her, but she calmly says,

"I am alright, Chris. They killed my dad and the dog. They got what was coming to them." The wounded man begins to cuss and mumble in his native Khmer. Chris sees Annie reloading her shotgun and takes charge.

"You cannot kill him in cold blood, Annie."

"You don't have to watch if you don't care to," she says calmly, and continues loading the two chambers.

"We need him to identify their gang. Do not kill this man, Annie." Annie lowers her weapon, then gags and hog-ties the screaming criminal.

Chris calls Lt. Schroeder. He and two of the Champions arrive by helicopter an hour later. A look at the two men alarms Lt. Schroeder. He exclaims,

"Oh no; this means serious trouble. These men are the leaders of two separate gangs that recently joined forces. There will be revenge. I cannot figure out why they risked coming here alone." Schroeder removes the gag from the surviving criminal and questions him. The man spits at Schroeder and refuses to respond. The Lieutenant remarks that his interrogation team will be more successful. He guesses that these men were probably checking the place out when the dog surprised them. Once Wilbur appeared in the doorway, they had to silence him.

Lt. Schroeder knows that they are not safe at the farm. When their leaders do not return, the gang will come looking for them.

"We have to get everybody to safety," he declares. Chris asks,

"How? We have fourteen children and a number of adults to transport, including Wilbur and the two gangsters."

"I am calling for additional helicopters. We will need one copter equipped to transport Wilbur. For the time being, the dead gangster can remain on the farm. Let's get him out of the house. My men and I will stay here. There is room for five people in the helicopter. He can take five children. We will temporarily house them at the station."

By this time, everybody in the camp is awake. Some of the kids are crying. Others, so hardened by the experience of evil, show no signs of panic. Heather and Salina pick five of the crying children to leave first. The helicopter takes off.

The other two police officers stay with Heather, Annie, and Salina who have assembled all the remaining children in the bunkhouse. Heather plays guitar and is teaching the children an American song.

Lt. Schroeder and Chris walk to the river to check out the boat the men must have used to reach the farm. They run into a surprise. A young boy sits in the boat, shaking with fear. His name is Stu. Stu is a slave whom the men had brought to run the boat, and guard it while they were gone.

Lt. Schroeder inspects the messy boat. It yields papers and trash, identifying names and locations. He asks the boy why he did not escape with the boat. The boy replies,

Chapter: 34

"They always torture people before they kill them. They did it to my brother."

Finding this boy turns out to be a blessing. Once he is sure of his safety, he spills names and locations like a slot machine. The boy's information and the papers found in the boat lead to the arrest of several gang members and the rescue of thirty-nine children.

Within one hour, three helicopters arrive and airlift everyone to safety. Annie is reluctant to leave her home, but Lt. Schroeder insists that she join the airlift. There is much work ahead. Champion members find homes for the children. They also check out leads that result in the arrest of additional members of the two gangs. Chris, Heather, and Salina stay in town and work side by side with the authorities.

Three days later, Tuesday, August 19, Chris and Heather decide to retrieve needed items from the farm. They hire a helicopter. When they do not return and are still absent Friday morning, Salina is worried. She contacts Lt. Schroeder and begs him to check things out at the farm and take her along. Annie, wondering about Chris and Heather's situation and eager to learn whether all is well at the farm, joins Salina and the Lieutenant.

From the air, they spot the horrible scene. Salina breaks down. She cannot stop crying. Lt. Schroeder buries his head in his hands and repeats,

"No, no, no Lord; please let us find Chris and Heather alive." Annie is in shock and remains silent. Some evil brutes had burned all the buildings to the ground. The helicopter hired by Chris is among the rubble. Angrily Schroeder's pilot lands the copter. They find the pilot of Chris' copter, dead inside the charred machine.

Salina and Annie walk hand in hand, looking for Chris and Heather. There is no sign anywhere of their good friends. Later, when Salina finds Annie sitting on a rock, crying, she puts her arms around her and tries to comfort her.

"Annie, we both lost our home. Maybe you and I can find a place together somewhere." Annie inhales deeply and thanks Salina, who has helped to remove her fear of isolation.

Lt. Schroeder orders arson detectives to determine the time of the fire, and retrieve clues that might identify the arsonists. Fire departments, police, and many volunteers assemble at the farm. Lt. Schroeder divides the search party into four groups and instructs them to spread out in all four directions for a systematic search of the fields and woods. Clues of any kind, tracks, discarded items, pop cans, cigarette stubs, traces of blood; all to be reported immediately to Lt. Schroeder and his team of Champions.

The newspapers solicit the help of their readers in reporting any information they may have about this crime. As the sun sets on this August day, the search party has no useful information to report, other than footprints by the river, which were so plentiful that none could be isolated or individually identified.

The searchers had marked the area they combed to have a starting point for Monday morning. Monday afternoon, the search party finds a piece of clothing, south of the farm, which Salina identifies as Heather's sun hat. They also find a pair of men's sunglasses. Salina cannot say for sure that they belonged to Chris.

After finding Heather's hat and the sunglasses, the search team now concentrates on the area south of the farm.

One team drifts westward during the search and arrives at Highway 2, where they spot tire tracks leaving the grassy area from the woods. The tires carried some of the mud and grass onto the Highway and indicate that the vehicle continued south on Highway 2.

Lt. Schroeder immediately dispenses police cars to concentrate on Highway 2, and search all the way to the border of Vietnam before returning.

One of the police officers on Highway 2 notices tracks north of the town of Takeo, leading west on a gravel road. This road is not

Chapter: 34

normally travelled. His map indicates that the road intersects within a few kilometers with Highway 3, which leads directly to the coastal city of Kampot, about sixty miles south. Located on the Gulf of Thailand, The officer wonders whether the arsonists who kidnapped the two Americans, are planning to escape by boat. He radios his plans to Lt. Schroeder and proceeds west on that gravel road.

He had travelled about six kilometers when he comes across an area where the tracks leave the road, veer off to the right, and stop within a few yards. He finds an extinguished campfire, some discarded food cans, beer bottles, and a pair of Cambodian sandals. Why would a man discard his sandals unless he has another pair of shoes? Footprints of about five people include one, which could belong to a woman, or a small male. Near the campfire, he also finds the tracks of bare feet and footprints produced by shoes with ribbed soles.

The officer bags his finds, snaps some pictures of the area, and continues. The tracks were at times undetectable on the hard gravel, but with only one direction to consider, he continues to Highway 3. Reaching the coast, he observes about a dozen Cambodian and Thai citizens boarding a ferry. One of the men is wearing brown hiking boots. Is this the owner of the sandals discarded at the campfire? There is no sign of Chris or Heather. The officer requests permission to go aboard. However, he has no jurisdiction in Thailand and the captain of the ferry denies his request.

Lt. Schroeder calls his superior, requesting assistance with contacting Thai police to apprehend the man wearing the hiking boots. The Thai police turn it into a joke, stating that in Thailand it is not against the law to wear hiking boots. Hope of finding Chris and Heather is waning, but is not dead. If the arsonists killed them, searchers would have found their bodies or graves.

After a close forensic examination of the items found at the campfire, experts are convinced that the evidence at the campfire points to three kidnappers transporting Chris and Heather, raising hopes that they are both alive. Salina verifies that Chris owns a pair of hiking boots. He usually wore them on the farm. The discarded sandals and the boots are the same size and match the barefoot tracks.

Lt. Schroeder makes the American Embassy aware of the apparent abduction. News of Dr. Christopher Storm's disappearance reaches the American Press and becomes the top story for weeks. The governor of Massachusetts addresses the public via television and requests prayer for the missing couple. Everyone remembers the celebrated Boy Prodigy.

Gordon and Lillian Crane are devastated. They use their influence to send an American team to Cambodia to continue the search for their former son-in-law, his wife, and the unborn child. They have many friends, but none as dear as this couple. Nothing is accomplished. The couple remains missing.

Chapter

35

Natcha Cheng was born on February 29, 1964, in Phang Nga, Thailand. She is the fourth child of hard working rice farmers. Within the next 8 years, five more children are born, placing a serious drain on the family's pitiful income.

Always smiling and singing, Natcha is attractive and playful. She was fourteen when her parents married her off to Jamie Vang, a man twelve years her senior.

Jamie is a hardworking man, and treated Natcha well. However, about two years into the marriage, Jamie's older brother, Nakule, comes to visit; and everything changes. Nakule ridicules Jamie for staying with a woman who has not given him any children.

Natcha learns that Nakule is the leader of a Cambodian trafficking gang and begs her husband to send him away. Instead, Jamie sides with his brother and becomes belligerent toward her. Now, Jamie often leaves home for days without a hint as to his whereabouts. Natcha fears that he is assisting Nakule in some illegal activity, but she does not know for sure.

On August 21, 1980, Jamie returns from one of these trips and brings two other men with him. Natcha notices that one of the men is wearing brown leather shoes, such as she has seen only in the window of an expensive shoe store in Hat Yai.

The men carry a pregnant, American woman into the house. Gagged and fettered, she is obviously their prisoner. All four of them are dirty and smell of smoke.

Natcha asks for an explanation, but the men laugh and say that the woman's belly is full of American dollars; they will wait until the dollars come out, and then kill her. Natcha does not understand. She asks why they all stink of smoke, but does not receive an answer.

The men demand food. After supper, the two strange men leave. Natcha does not know who they are and Jamie does not explain. Jamie had thrown the American woman on the couch, where she immediately fell asleep. Natcha feels sorry for her, but does not dare to defend her.

A few days later, Jamie sits on the couch and motions for Natcha to sit next to him. He is depressed. Natcha sits quietly for a while and holds his hand. He seems to like that, so she decides to talk to him,

"What is the matter, Jamie?"

"My brother is dead," he says, his face sad, but his voice angry. Natcha remains silent for a minute,

"Nakule is dead?" she asks gently. "How? What happened?"

"We found him on the farm. He is dead, two or three days already."

"What farm, Jamie?"

"The farm where they hide the slaves."

Natcha is lost. "What slaves, what farm, what are you talking about, Jamie?" Jamie stares at her with fire in his eyes,"

"If you tell anybody about this, I will kill you."

"What could I tell?" she protests. "You are not involved, are you?" Jamie gets up and walks around for a while. He stops at the couch that has become the American woman's domain. No longer gagged and her feet untied, her movements are restricted by a twelve-foot chain, secured to the couch. It allows her to reach the toilet; nothing else. Jamie strikes the woman's face.

"They killed Nakule," he screams, pointing to the woman.

"Jamie, you think that woman killed your brother?"

"She was there," he yells, and strikes the woman again.

"Jamie, who else was with the woman; does she have a husband?"

"Yes, he is a famous doctor in America."

"Where is her husband?" Jamie laughs and slaps his thighs,

"He went fishing. We sold him to the seafood boys."

"Jamie, tell me everything. Where is this farm, how do you know about it?" Jamie repeats his earlier warning,

"Natcha, if you talk about this to anybody, I will kill you and your brothers and sisters." Natcha is terrified. Never before has he threatened her family. She assures him that she would never betray her own husband. Jamie reads her face. Then he continues,

"When the police raid a brothel; they take the kids to this farm in Cambodia. Nakule found out about that. The gangs want their people back. Last Saturday, he and another man went to the farm in the middle of the night to check things out. Something went wrong; he never called; I was worried. I went to that farm Tuesday with the two men I brought here. Nobody was there, except Nakule, lying next to a dead dog in front of the house.

We heard a helicopter coming and hid behind some trees. They landed and a man and this pregnant woman got out of the helicopter. The pilot was still in the copter when we shot him dead. Then we tied up the man and the woman. I was so mad about my brother, we soaked everything with gas, oil, and petroleum we found in the barn and set everything on fire. You could see the black smoke a long way, so we did not wait around. We threw the Americans in the truck and got out of there.

Tanawat talked about the slaves who work in the fishing vessels. We got the idea that we should sell the doctor to them for $300. If you ever tell this to anyone, Natcha, I will kill you for sure. We took papers from the American man. Tanawat can read a little English. He said the man is important."

"Who is Tanawat?"

"He is our leader. He is the tall one. Apisit is his brother."

"Jamie, why did you bring the woman here?"

"Tanawat told me what to do with the woman. He said we could get money from America for the woman's baby. He said maybe we can get money for the woman too, but it is too hard. Babies are easy. When the woman has her baby, we will sell it to America. We will be rich, Natcha. Only we have to split the money with Tanawat and Apisit."

"Jamie, the woman looks weak and sick. If she dies, the baby will die too. We have to take care of her."

"Of course, Natcha, you take care of her."

Natcha and Jamie speak only one language, Thai. The woman on the couch has not spoken a word since the men dragged her into the house. Other than catching the names 'Natcha and Jamie', she has no clue as to the subject of their discussions. When the two women are alone, the American woman points to herself, pronouncing her name,

"Heather, Heather, Heather." Natcha mimics her,

"Hatha, Hatha, Hatha."

Natcha has no children. She secretly hopes that Jamie will allow her to keep the American baby. She feeds and bathes the woman faithfully. Eventually Natcha learns some English and Heather picks up some of the Thai language. In English, they are able to communicate secretly. With the exception of Tanawat, Jamie and other family members or guests speak no English.

Having no contact with the outside world, a peculiar friendship develops between the two women. Natcha assures Heather that when the time comes, she will deliver her baby. She has watched her younger siblings being born and has delivered her oldest sister's baby just a few months ago.

Heather goes into labor on October 16, 1980. Natcha is poised and confident. She delivers the baby, a healthy 9-pound boy, with the ease of a skilled midwife. She holds the baby to her chest, and sings a Thai lullaby. Heather is touched. She wants to hold her own baby, but allows Natcha a few minutes.

Chapter: 35

Jamie has been away for several days. Upon his return, when he finds the boy with Natcha, he plucks the baby out of her arms and throws it at Heather. Heather shrieks, but the baby lands in her arms unharmed. Jamie threatens Natcha that he will kill her and the baby if he catches her holding the boy again. Then he demands food and strikes Natcha for being too slow in providing it.

When Jamie leaves, Natcha fixes a long look at Heather, as though she is expecting a ruling from her about Jamie's behavior. Heather knows that the man has the temperament of a killer. She wants to counsel Natcha, but must be cautious.

Unfamiliar with registration procedures in Thailand, Heather makes sure that Natcha has the correct information about the baby. She writes the information on a piece of paper for Natcha.

Name: Christopher Eric Storm
Father: Christopher Martin Storm
Mother: Heather Sylvia Storm
Date of Birth: October 16, 1980
Weight: 8 lbs. 15 oz.

Natcha nods and puts the paper in her day bag.

Chapter

36

It is early in March when Jamie says that he is going into the city to make an important telephone call to America. Natcha feared this day since Jamie told her about the plan to sell the American woman's baby,

"Jamie, you cannot speak American." Jamie yells back,

"Natcha, do not worry about that. Tanawat has put American words on this recorder. I will play it to the telephone. I go now."

"But Jamie…"

"Shut up Natcha. I go now."

Hours later, Jamie returns in an exceptionally bad mood. He frightens the women with his violent behavior. He throws things, kicks furniture, cusses, and teases them with a long knife.

To make things worse, the two brothers from the farm-torching event show up. They are in the same cross mood. Silently, Heather implores God for the protection of the baby, Natcha, and herself. God is faithful. No harm comes to them.

The three men discuss Jamie's failure to extort one million dollars from America. The two brothers coerce Jamie to try again. Tanawat is yelling at Jamie.

"You are stupid. Did you push the 'play' button when the FBI answered the phone?"

"Of course, Tanawat. The recorder was talking to the FBI."

"Next time dial the second number I wrote on the paper. They know the father of the baby. They will pay."

"Okay, Tanawat. Do not be angry with me."

A week later, Jamie makes the second trip to the city and returns, fuming with anger. Tanawat decides to give it a rest for a while. Then he will handle the next call himself.

It is April before Tanawat makes the call. He reasons that Christopher Storm's friends in Minnesota have an interest in the baby. He calls Dr. Lillian Crane at the University office. Tanawat's English is poor, but he carries on a short conversation with Dr. Crane. He gets nowhere. When Dr. Crane askes too many questions, he hangs up.

Tanawat is furious. Jamie failed, now he failed. He returns to Jamie's house where Apisit is waiting. He tells them that it is over. He is done. His new plan is to sell the American woman to the slave dealers at the fish market for $300.

Jamie does not trust Tanawat to share the bounty with him and positions himself in front of Heather, holding his long knife. Tanawat laughs and motions to Apisit. The two brothers overpower Jamie and beat him severely until he stops moving. They assume he is dead. They tape Heather's mouth and tie her wrists. Natcha cries and begs them to release Heather because the baby will die if Heather stops nursing him.

Tanawat thunders a belly laugh. Apisit normally waits for Tanawat's instruction, but this time he speaks up and suggests that they take the baby too. Natcha realizes that her plea for Heather's release may have endangered the baby. She clutches the infant and runs outside. Nobody follows her. Natcha does not know where the energy came from, but she runs six kilometers, all the way to her parents' house. Her oldest sister, Nam, is nursing her five-month old baby and at Natcha's request, she also feeds baby Christopher.

A few days later, Natcha returns to her home accompanied by family members, including a couple of husky cousins. She finds nobody in her house. The spot where Jamie lay bleeding was now clean. Jamie and Heather are gone. She never sees either one of them again.

Natcha's sister, Nam and her husband, Dew, are happy to move in with Natcha. Their parent's house is crowded. This will be a better place to raise their baby. Nam is a healthy woman and nurses both infants.

In the US, the anxiety caused by the disappearance of the American couple, Christopher and Heather Storm, begins to wane. Seven months have passed without any news from Cambodia.

Then, on Monday, March 2, 1981, the FBI receives a call from Thailand. The caller plays a recording of a male voice, speaking broken English. The speaker claims that he has a boy child, about five months old, the son of a famous American couple. He states that he is holding the boy for ransom and will return him to the US if they pay him one million American dollars. The FBI agent, Delmar Downy, responds,

"We do not negotiate with terrorists and kidnappers." The man hangs up before Downy finishes his sentence. The conversation was too short to trace the call, especially since tracing equipment is still in the development stages. To avoid a media circus, the FBI does not contact the press.

Downy knows he is dealing with people of low intelligence. The caller failed to provide critical information. How and where is the exchange of money for the baby to take place?

A week later, March 9, 1981, the FBI receives a second call; this time from Police headquarters in Boston. That morning, Boston had received a call with similar claims, asserting that the State of Massachusetts should be happy to rescue the son of Dr. Christopher Storm, since he is a native of their State, adding that Massachusetts people would admire their Police Department for rescuing the son of their most famous citizen.

There is of course no way to determine whether these are crank calls or not. Heather was seven months pregnant when the criminals abducted her. Certainly, the possibility exists that they did not kill her, allowing

Chapter: 36

her child to be born. Lt. Schroeder had purposely withheld information about her pregnancy from the American Embassy and the press. How does this Thai caller know about it? It seems likely that their claim to have Heather's baby is realistic.

When the Thai caller makes no additional contact for almost a month, it seemed that he has given up. However, Wednesday, April 29, 1981, the FBI switchboard receives the third call regarding this issue. This time the caller is Dr. Lillian Crane. Lillian Crane had accepted a call from Thailand at her office. The caller's English was poor. Nonetheless, he was very familiar with family details. He urged Dr. Crane to get involved in securing one million American dollars for the boy's safe return to the US.

Cleverly, Dr. Crane attempted to gather more information from the caller. Asking why he called her, she learned that the man had forced Christopher Storm to reveal many details. He stated that Dr. Crane should be eager to assure the safe return of Dr. Storm's son. Lillian then asked him to prove that the boy is alive and well. He stated that the Thai woman, who cares for him, would not allow anyone to harm him. When Dr. Crane probed into the whereabouts of Chris and Heather, the man hung up.

The FBI contacts the Thailand US Embassy in Bangkok and the US Consulate General in Chiang Mai. With the limited information available, they are unable to help. Establishing whether the Thai caller in fact has Christopher Storm's son, remains an open case. There is no additional contact from Thailand. Authorities assume that the whole thing is an attempt to procure ransom money from the US and the case goes cold.

Friends and relatives never give up hope. This cannot be the end of it. There must be an active effort to solve the mysterious disappearance of these two extraordinary people in an extraordinary way. They are so young, both under thirty. Their memory must not vanish forever. Only close friends of the Crane family knew about the obscure claims that Heather has given birth to a baby boy. The nagging suspicion that Chris and Heather are dead and that the story about their son is fiction, becomes a painful uncertainty and wears on the health of Christopher's closest relationships.

Hilda, Pastor Ragfords wife, who has raised Chris, loves him dearly and agonizes over his loss. She has written dozens of letters to government agencies, asking not to abort efforts to find the couple. She received only rejection letters. Hilda has spoken of her efforts in one of the prayer meetings and learned that another woman, who has also written letters, received exactly the same rejection forms.

Hilda's health has been poor for some time. On Sunday, May 31, 1981, during the morning church service, Hilda dies suddenly of a massive heart attack.

Chapter

37

Things work out well for Natcha and her sister Nam. Nam loves motherhood and is overjoyed when she realizes that she is pregnant again. Nam's husband is good to them and proudly supports his extended family. However, with the news of another mouth to feed he becomes a bit anxious about finances.

With Nam at home, available to care for the children, Natcha decides to help financially and takes a service position in the home of an American Manufacturer. Their affluent life style is a revelation for her. She loves Christopher and wants that kind of life for him as well.

After working five years for the American family, Natcha has put away enough extra money to start her own business. She moves to Hat Yai, where she opens a profitable fruit stand at the market.

When Christopher turns six, she enrolls him in a children's language school to learn English. Afraid to lose Christopher to authorities someday, she guards him carefully. She gives him strict orders never to speak to strangers, especially Americans.

As the boy grows, he becomes a great help in her business, He delivers customer orders and assists at the fruit stand.

In May 1989, King, a journalist for a St. Paul newspaper is on assignment in Asia, covering Burma, Cambodia, Laos, and Thailand. His weekly column gains a wide readership as he covers the daily routines of people in small villages and coastal regions.

His report on the activities of slave traders and traffickers, who abduct men, women, and children to work in the Thailand fishing industry, results in hundreds of calls to US Government agencies. Eager to see a solution, people would like to see US involvement. The kidnappers hide the slaves in temporary jungle huts and eventually transport them to large fishing vessels where they force them to work in the production of seafood.

Both, the jungle huts and fishing vessels are overcrowded and in deplorable conditions. Eyewitnesses report rapes and beatings of women and children, often with the consent of government people who participate in the brutal treatment of the workers.

Conscious that King's reports could relate closely to Chris and Heather's situation in Cambodia, Gordon and Lillian never miss his column. The alarming accounts of the slave labor issue have their full attention.

Relaxed in his easy chair, Gordon is perusing the Sunday paper of June 18, 1989, describing Mr. King's visit to the market place in Hat Yai, Thailand. Lillian is in the kitchen when Gordon summons her to the living room,

"Come here, Lilli, I am reading King's Column. You have to listen to this." He reads aloud from 'King's Column:

Mystery at the Market
By Victor King

Weary of crowded market places
And narrow dirt paths in small villages,
today I am in Hat Yai. Hat Yai is the fourth
largest city in Thailand, located on
the Southern Gulf Coast. It is an extremely
popular tourist spot for Singaporeans

Chapter: 37

and Malaysians and on holiday, but does not have many Western visitors. That is why the young boy, about nine years old, with light skin and blue-green eyes, is an unexpected sight. He and an Asian woman in her late 20's, operate the fruit stand I chose for the best-looking mangos. Speaking English, I asked his name. He shook his head and pointed to his lips. The assumption that he is deaf and dumb proved incorrect. Moments later, he spoke fluent Thai with a customer. This handsome, white boy, at the fruit stand is more conspicuous than a live elephant in a jewelry store. I addressed him again, using my meager Thai vocabulary. He whispered in Perfect English, "I am not allowed to talk to Americans.' The Asian woman saw him whispering, came over, and slapped him across the head. This boy already had my attention, but this woman's treatment of him placed me on high alert. What is going on here? Who is this boy? How did he get here? What happened to his birth mother?
The owner of a neighboring stand, who speaks a fair, counterfeit sort of English, reluctantly concedes that the boy lives alone with the woman. Nobody seems to know who he is or where he came from. A few American dollars loosened the man's tongue. He starts singing like a cockatoo,

> spilling the name of the woman and her
> home address.
>
> Be sure to catch the column next week for
> an update. The piece will be entitled,
> 'The Trapped Boy in Thailand.'

Lillian, her face aglow with excitement rushes to the phone. Gordon laughs,
"Slow down, Lilli; it's Sunday. Call them tomorrow."

No authentic journalist would ignore the mystery surrounding this boy. When the youngster discards a piece of chewing gum, King cautiously retrieves it. Two years ago, in 1987, he had covered a story involving the first criminal conviction based on DNA evidence. If the DNA of the boy's parents is on file, this piece of chewing gum could solve the mystery of his past.

Supplying all pertinent details of his encounter with the boy, he mails the gum sample to the FBI. The FBI mailroom delivers King's letter to Agent Peter Kurland, in charge of foreign correspondence. Not fond of journalists, Kurland assigns King's letter to the bottom of his IN-Basket. There it remained until two weeks later, when the FBI switchboard routes a call from King to Agent Delmar Downy, who handled the initial contact from Thailand.

Downy has given this case High Priority and circulated memos throughout the department. The mystery of the missing gum sample did not remain a mystery long. Agent Kurland's IN-Basket becomes the object of intense scrutiny. Kurland is currently wearing out shoes, looking for a new job.

The hunt for DNA belonging to Chris and Heather is short and successful. The hospital treating Chris after the car accident has samples of his blood. The clinic processing Heather's fertility tests in Minneapolis provides samples of her DNA. The test results are indisputable the boy in Thailand is their son.

The FBI machine switches into high gear. The FBI's domestic investigative responsibilities intertwine with criminal elements in other countries. Its ability to conduct complex investigations and acquire evidence from abroad for criminal prosecutions in the United States is crucial.

Agent Downy contacts King and reveals the boy's identity. He requests that King keep the fruit-stand woman's house under surveillance until FBI agents arrive.

King is shocked. He is familiar with Dr. Storm's activities and history. He was at every press conference hosted by Dr. Lillian Crane at the University. He was at the airport when Dr. Storm left for Cambodia. Nine years ago, his paper featured a front-page report on the disappearance of Dr. Storm and his wife Heather. Why did it never occur to him that this boy could be Dr. Storm's son? Perhaps, because the couple had gone to Cambodia and this boy is in Thailand, it never registered.

King snaps dozens of pictures and notices something not obvious before. This Thai woman cares about this child. It is now clear to him that the slap across the head he witnessed was simply an act of discipline. Victor King evaluates his involvement in this matter and feels that an injustice is about to befall this innocent Thai caretaker. Certainly, someone other than this kind, hard-working woman, is the perpetrator in the fate of the Storm couple. He makes a decision that could backfire. He will talk to the woman before the FBI arrives.

On August 4, 1989, King knocks on Natcha's door. Natcha is frightened. Before she opens the door, she asks the boy to hide in a bedroom. Then she opens the front door a crack. Immediately she recognizes King from their encounter at the fruit stand. She also recalls his interest in the boy. Alarmed, she tries to close the door, but King easily maintains a hold on the door and assures her that he means her or the boy no harm. Reluctantly, Natcha invites him in.

King explains that the US Government has discovered that the boy in her possession belongs to an American couple who disappeared 9 years ago. She will have to hand the boy over to authorities. Natcha begins to weep, tears streaming down her cheeks. King gently embraces her and tells her that he has an idea that may allow her to remain near the boy. Natcha dries her tears. Her look at King conveys fresh hope.

"How that can happen?" she asks in her faulty English.

"Do you want to go to America with the boy?" he probes.

"How that can happen?" she repeats. King smiles; then shakes his head. In all the years as a journalist, he never had any personal involvement in stories he covered. This is a first. He finds himself willing to finance this Thai woman's trip to the US with personal resources.

"Did you raise the boy since he was a baby?"

"Yes, Hather baby." King does not understand,

"What do you mean, Hather baby?"

"You wait. I get paper." Natcha leaves the room and returns with the note Heather had written the details she wanted on the birth certificate. Proudly she says,

"Hather is mother. She write paper. She gone, I keep baby."

"You know Heather? He asks sharply," What happened to Heather?'

"Bad men takes Hather, sell to fish people, 300 dollars. Sell husband to fish people too, 300 dollars. I keep baby." King gasps. Fish people? Is she talking about the slave trade, the assignment that landed him here in Thailand?

Before this conversation is over, King has most of the missing pieces surrounding the disappearance of the American couple. One issue is still unclear. Natcha spoke about a farm in Cambodia where they keep children rescued from brothels. This requires further investigation. Eventually Victor King connects with Lt. Schroeder who supplies the missing pieces of this puzzle. However, nobody has the means or method to determine whether the missing couple is still alive.

Chapter: 37

King calls agent Downey at the FBI. After detailing his plan to allow Natcha to accompany the boy to America, because she is the only mother the boy knows, Downey thinks that King has lost his mind. The FBI plans to prosecute Natcha as part of the criminal group, responsible for the disappearance of Chris and Heather Storm. King's next statement lands him on the wrong side of the FBI and the law,

"If that is your position, this woman will not be here when your agents arrive."

"Mr. King, if you interfere, I would personally see to it that you are criminally charged with obstruction of justice. Are you willing to risk your own safety and freedom on behalf of this Thai criminal?"

"Stop calling her a criminal. She raised this boy from birth. This woman clearly loves him. She is risking her own life to keep him safe. What kind of justice system would punish her for that?" A long pause indicates that the FBI agent on the phone is considering King's argument." Finally, a milder tone in his voice, he says,

"You are convincing, Mr. King. After all, you are there, close to the action. I am at a disadvantage, sitting at my desk, trying to make the right decisions. We will reassess the issues surrounding this case."

Victor King is visualizing Natcha and young Christopher in Minnesota. Certainly, Mr. and Mrs. Crane would have a great interest in having a part in raising and educating the son of their former son-in-law. Their close relationship with Chris and Heather is common knowledge.

King picks up the phone and calls Lillian Crane. He presents his plan to bring the Thai woman, who raised young Christopher, to Minnesota.

At first, Lillian rejects the idea of allowing the Thai woman to keep the boy. However, after some thought, she admits that she and Gordon at their age, are not in a position to give a nine year old boy the proper attention. Lillian tells King that she will help Natcha to settle in Minnesota. She also promises to assure a proper education of young Christopher.

The Passions & Perils of the Prodigy

Today, Natcha is married to a young man introduced to her by Lillian. Their home is within a few miles of the Crane mansion. They have two more children and are happy. Young Christopher has graduated high school. He is now a top student at the University.

Sadly, Chris and Heather Storm are still missing. The public and many officials think that they are dead.

His true followers think the couple will be back to surprise the world.

What do you think?

The End

CPSIA information can be obtained
at www.ICGtesting.com
Printed in the USA
FSOW01n1442020816
23353FS